THE DINNER PARTY

THE DINNER PARTY

A NOVEL

Viola van de Sandt

LITTLE, BROWN AND COMPANY

New York Boston London

The characters and events in this book are fictitious. Any similarity to real persons, living or dead, is coincidental and not intended by the author.

Copyright © 2025 Viola van de Sandt

Hachette Book Group supports the right to free expression and the value of copyright. The purpose of copyright is to encourage writers and artists to produce the creative works that enrich our culture.

The scanning, uploading, and distribution of this book without permission is a theft of the author's intellectual property. If you would like permission to use material from the book (other than for review purposes), please contact permissions@hbgusa.com. Thank you for your support of the author's rights.

Little, Brown and Company
Hachette Book Group
1290 Avenue of the Americas, New York, NY 10104
littlebrown.com

First Edition: November 2025

Little, Brown and Company is a division of Hachette Book Group, Inc. The Little, Brown name and logo are trademarks of Hachette Book Group, Inc.

The publisher is not responsible for websites (or their content) that are not owned by the publisher.

The Hachette Speakers Bureau provides a wide range of authors for speaking events. To find out more, go to hachettespeakersbureau.com or email hachettespeakers@hbgusa.com.

Little, Brown and Company books may be purchased in bulk for business, educational, or promotional use. For information, please contact your local bookseller or the Hachette Book Group Special Markets Department at special.markets@hbgusa.com.

Book interior design by Marie Mundaca

ISBN 9780316593847
Library of Congress Control Number: 2025939596

Printing 1, 2025

LSC-C

Printed in the United States of America

*For Annie and Peet
And for Jill Dawson*

THE DINNER PARTY

MISE EN PLACE

Stella says I should write a letter. It can be addressed to her, or to no one in particular, or perhaps to a friend. Someone I trust. Do I have anyone like that?

I don't have to post it. I can write this letter to myself. It doesn't have to be read. These words are mine, she says. She says it will help. Acknowledging what happened, describing it in as much detail as I can, trying to remember instead of pushing it all away. Stella thinks it will guide me in my recovery.

I say I have nothing to recover from. She disagrees, and lists the facts as she knows them, written down in the file she brings out every time we meet. Everything that happened that night, in black and white, read out dispassionately, things I remember and things I don't. They're not at all a reflection of how it felt, what went on before it, why I did what I did. Facts don't come into it.

Her request takes me by surprise. I didn't think she'd get into all this after just three weeks. She'd said we'd spend our first few sessions getting to know each other. I still hardly know anything about her.

I don't know how to begin, I admit. She says begin at the beginning, but I tell her that's stupid. There's never any real beginning, unless I'm to go back to my birth, or better yet, the birth of my parents, their lives and families, their jobs and childhood injuries, but that's just so boring. A biography that starts with the lives of the grandparents? Skip the first chapters. Besides, it's facile, seeking explanations in family histories. I was an adult when it happened. My choices, like my words, are mine.

Begin at the climax then, Stella says. I cock an eyebrow. I didn't come. She says that's not what she meant. She means the culmination, the denouement, this thing I did that brought me here. That business with the knife. She says write it down, what happened, to yourself or to a friend. I don't care where you begin.

So, Harry: here goes.

I drop the knife on the counter.

Or at least I think I do. I might drop it on the kitchen table. It's cluttered with the remains of the dinner I made: a dirty knife doesn't look out of place.

Or perhaps I drop it on the floor. Right in the center of the spreading puddle of stickiness that sticks to the knife's blade, the handle, the palm of my left hand.

Alternatively, I wash the knife with Fairy Liquid, rinse the suds, dry it with the rosebud towel, put it back into the block. Like nothing happened. Like I'm destroying the evidence.

I can't remember. It's strange. It's only been a few months. I'm young. Never did drugs. I'm not drinking as much as I did then. I've

The Dinner Party

been talking to people, doctors, therapists: my head works. I've been reliving this moment constantly ever since; I've hardly thought of anything else. So I *should* remember everything.

But I don't. Each time some detail changes, and then that changed detail changes again until I'm left with a hundred different endings for those final moments of that day. I drop the knife on the counter, on the table, on the floor. I wash it and I dry it and I put it back in the drawer. I don't wash it: the knife isn't dirty at all. My hand isn't sticky. There's no puddle on the floor.

But no, there *is* a puddle. I'm sure of it. I make a cake. The recipe says to mix the molten chocolate with the cream and spread it over the top, but the mixture I make is too thin. It pours from the cake onto the table and drips from the table to the floor. From the dining room comes a boozy roar and the crackle of glass and one of them lurches into the kitchen with his hand wrapped in a napkin and a shard of the liquor cabinet's glass door in his palm. Can I have a plaster. And in another moment, earlier in the evening, I myself cut my finger so there's blood on the floor, for sure, and chocolate, and my blood mixed with someone else's — and none of these details I'm drowning in clears up anything. As soon as I touch them, the certainties crumble between my fingers, and time distorts them, and my body remembers different things with many different names.

It begins a week before. Friday night, the living room sofa. I've a notebook on my lap — one of those Moleskine ones, leather-bound — in which I've managed to put down a few half-hearted scribbles that are meant to outline the lackluster short story I'm supposed to be writing. Andrew has surrounded himself with his MacBook and his iPad and his iPhone and is working through his emails. Netflix is on in the background; I'm rewatching *The Crown*. Or, really, I'm gaping at Vanessa Kirby's legs while I pour another glass from the bottle of Merlot.

Without taking his eyes off his computer, Andrew speaks.

"So we're about to finish this thing."

"Oh?" How many meals would I have to skip to be able to wear that kind of dress?

"Evan and I," Andrew says absentmindedly. "We'll be done with it."

"When?" I haven't found a job yet, so this could be my project. Sixteen hours every day: not eating.

"Next week. Friday's the launch."

"Oh." Probably easier to just skip the booze — that'd go a long way. "Great."

"I want to have a party," Andrew goes on. "A dinner party, I mean. To celebrate."

I look away from the TV. Andrew has sunk deep into the sofa, his head against the back, legs spread out on the coffee table. His beautiful face has got a faint blue sheen to it: just last week he bought this 65-inch OLED 4K monstrosity with something called four-sided Ambilight that he keeps gushing about. It casts the entire living room in the colors of whatever we're watching, which in the case of *The Crown* is mostly a cool blue.

"A dinner party next Friday?"

"No." He yawns, scratches his flat belly. "Friday's the launch, I just said. There's a reception after. Godawful drag — introductions, speeches, protestations of grandeur," he mocks with a grin, then groans dramatically. "God, they'll say we're drawing on a level with the Americans."

"Shock horror," I say with a smile. Guilty secret: his mistaking arrogance for confidence is what first attracted me to him. "What could be worse?"

"Knowing they're right." For a moment, Andrew's expression is bleak. Then he brightens. "I just want to make sure we celebrate properly. The day before, the Thursday. Just us."

"You and Evan, you mean."

"And Gerald," he grumbles. "Can't very well leave him out." He glances back at his laptop. The cast of his mouth and the tension in his shoulders betray his irritation.

"Remind me," I try tentatively, "Gerald's the — "

"The fossil we hired to help with the selection — literature — though I can't quite remember why Evan chose him. Royal pain in my arse." He sits straighter and turns to me. "Tell me. If you were an expert in English literature and you'd been asked which of the world's greatest works should be sent into space — no, no, more than that... If you'd been given the *opportunity* to make a new version of the Golden — "

"The Golden Record, yeah."

" — would you just keep moaning about what an impossible task it is?"

"Does he?" I ask, careful not to answer the question.

"At every fucking opportunity. I mean, compare the guys we hired for paintings and sculptures. I spoke to them on the phone like, twice, and they all sent me their lists over email. But *this* guy — "

"Gerald."

"Gerald," Andrew scoffs like the name is testament to his character. "Keeps banging on about how 'to open up the canon is to destroy the canon.' And the annoying thing is Evan and I don't give a shit whether the canon's open or not. He insists on coming round every two days, 'to go over the selections,' and it takes us half an hour to..." Andrew pauses to stare at the TV as Prince Philip takes flying lessons, looking like an ignorant and pampered pillock.

"Well," I say as the scene cuts, "you have to agree with him: it *would* be quite difficult."

"What would?"

"Choosing 'the best books ever written.'"

"Would it?"

"Who can even pick their favorite book?"

"Carl Sagan, *Cosmos*," Andrew says promptly.

"Yes, because that's the only one you've ever read."

"Not true."

"Oh yes, you also read the sequel."

"*Pale Blue Dot*," Andrew confirms.

A warm breeze drifts in through the open window nearby, but to me it feels cold, smelling of frost and wet forest.

"In any case, the dinosaur likes rabbit."

"Sorry, what?"

"Gerald — the dinosaur — likes rabbit. Like, braised or something, whatever that means."

"It's fried and stewed."

"What?"

I mute the television as someone in the scene is about to start another speech. "Braised rabbit. You fry it briefly and then you let it stew."

"So you can make it," Andrew concludes, turning back to his laptop now that the TV sound is off. I stare at him.

"Andrew," I begin, "correct me if I'm wrong — "

"I love correcting you." He grins at me over his screen.

" — but didn't you and Evan, only three years ago, sell your own company?"

"What's that got to do — "

"There are, literally, millions of pounds in your bank account — "

"*Our* bank account."

"So call a bloody caterer."

"I like it when you say 'bloody.' Makes you sound like a proper English lady. Oh, come on," he cajoles when he catches sight of my expression, "calling in a caterer would lack the personal touch."

"I'm a vegetarian."

"You don't have to eat it, do you? And you've got the time. It's just a starter — make whatever you want — then the rabbit, then a chocolate cake: Evan's favorite," he explains. "I just want us to have a good time."

"Matter of good booze, I'd say."

"Well yes," Andrew allows with a smile, "but if wine's all we're serving we're sure to have rather a short evening."

"Fine," I sigh. "All right."

"Really?"

"Yeah."

"Cheers, darling." He leans over to kiss me.

"What time d'you want to start?"

"Seven? We'll come straight from the office."

"Fine."

"Great."

Andrew turns back to his computer and starts some rapid-fire typing.

Up on the windowsill, where the open window brings the summer evening in, an undulating ball of fur unfurls. Nails extend and disappear again into the old pink blanket I'd placed there, and the sleeping cat wakes up. He's an exhibitionist, I think, as he yawns extravagantly, shows off his teeth, stretches to curl his spine into a wave, makes his front paws seem twice as long as they usually are: a display. Of elasticity, of youth, of a body — his, slim and strong — and its contrast with mine: though neither fat nor soft, never slim or strong enough. He stares at me first thing, as if he knows what I'm thinking, then springs from the sill onto the sofa and approaches quietly, perfectly at ease.

Viola van de Sandt

I want to steal the cat's ease, to claim the effortlessness with which he's found tranquility in this house. He's only been here for three weeks, while in the three years I've been living here I've searched in rooms he's never been in and found only a growing sense of apprehension. He meows, and it's a sweet sound but to me it feels like salt sprinkled into raw flesh, and yet Andrew gave me this cat and the cat is a living being so I sit still, don't push him off like I long to when he climbs down my shoulder and across my chest to settle on my lap. To sleep. Imagine that. He nods off within a minute, and I force my body into inactivity, let muscles wither and joints lock, dwindle myself down into a thing, something warm and soft to sleep on. Andrew doesn't look up. I watch him instead of the cat: Andrew, lounging in his shirtsleeves, top buttons open, a gorgeous man.

"Tell me," he begins, and his voice dampens my irritation with the cat, "how many does this make it?"

"How many what?"

Andrew looks up, at me and then at the TV screen. "Times you've watched this?"

"Oh, don't start again."

"You've ribbed me about only ever reading books about space — "

"Out-of-date ones."

" — but when I first met you, you read all the time, and now you only — "

" — watch *The Crown*," I finish. "Or some such."

"Or some such," Andrew agrees. "Why?"

"Don't ask tonight." I sink a little deeper into the sofa. "Please. Another time."

He looks at me while I look at the screen. He puts his arm around my shoulders and pulls me toward him, kisses the top of my head.

The Dinner Party

I never really fell in love *with* Andrew, I think. I didn't realize this until recently. Back when I first met him, four years before the dinner party, I did fall head over heels, felt blushing warmth tingling through my entire body. It just wasn't for Andrew himself. Instead, it was for his slacks, the fold down the length of his legs, his crisp shirt, sleeves rolled up against the elbows, that glimpse of throat and clavicle, hair that's not quite curls but not quite straight, his preppy glasses. The first smile he gave me over the top of his computer screen at the library that day. I felt lonely and abandoned and very sorry for myself and he smiled at me like I was worth smiling at.

He was doing research, he said. After I'd smiled back and we'd both stolen glances, after he finished with his work at the same time I did and we packed our bags simultaneously and together began to walk out of the library. He had a posh voice that sounded a little distant in the beginning, though he told me later that was because he'd been so very nervous, talking to me.

"We're setting up a company, me and a friend," Andrew said when I asked him what he had been working on. "It's going to change the way people work."

"Oh?" I said with a smile, walking on the smooth marble floor like it was water, unable to see anything but the tall, beautiful man walking next to me. Mantovani played in my head, trite and saccharine but delicious in that moment, yes. "How will it do that?"

"We're building this app. It'll allow users to block certain websites or applications that are just designed to take up masses of your time and stop you from focusing on your work. Why are you smiling?"

I couldn't help it. We'd stepped through the revolving doors and out into the street — watery sunlight and hundreds of bikes chained to the railing that skirted the canal — and despite the excitement of having a man like Andrew trying so hard to impress me, and my incredulity at what he'd just revealed about his work, here was a tiny pinprick in this bubble I was floating in: the thought of you, Harry, how we'd met in a place so very near here, on a day so very much like this one.

"You want people to use an app that would help them to stop using apps," I teased. He looked surprised for a moment, embarrassed, but then he laughed out loud and said that yes, that was exactly what they were doing, and it did indeed sound ridiculous when you put it like that.

"Last year," I said, "my mother called and told me she'd bought five books on minimalism. How to declutter your house."

Andrew chuckled.

A clink, cut crystal, Mother's red-rimmed eyes. *We're going out.*

I took the lock from my bike. "Where's yours?" I asked, looking around.

"Oh, I'm here on foot. I'm only in Utrecht for a month or two. We're collaborating with a couple of programmers in the region — you guys make really cool things here."

"Where do you live, then?" I asked as I began to walk toward the city center, bike in hand.

"I'm from the UK." He fell into step beside me.

"Yeah, I figured that."

"Ah, yes, the accent," Andrew confirmed, digging his hands deep into the pockets of his neat navy coat. I wanted to touch it, touch him. Feel how warm he was underneath those layers. "My family lives in London. And Cambridge."

"I have a friend who moved to Cambridge a few days ago," I said, unable to stop myself. "Harry." It hurt a little, saying your name.

"Oh, that's a coincidence. How about you? Where are you from?"

"I'm from here. Well, from the south," I amended.

"Is it far?"

The Dinner Party

"No, it just sounds that way. It's only an hour's drive."

"Really?" He seemed surprised. "It's that small a country?"

"Put it this way," I said, "someone farts down in Maastricht they can smell it up in Groningen."

Andrew guffawed, and I glowed with the pleasure of making him laugh.

"Is your family there?" he asked, still chortling a little. "In the south?"

"No. Not anymore. My dad... Well, my mother's just..." *We're going out.* "She's just moved. Long story."

"Oh, I'm sorry."

"I'm a regular Disney princess," I drawled, "waiting to be saved from a dark past and absentee parents." Andrew laughed again, although it wasn't all that funny, and said that he hoped to see me around sometime.

The next day, I made sure to be at the library early, secured a seat in the same place, kept an eye out and smiled when he came in, early as well, and sat down opposite me. We both pretended to work that day, but I spent more time studying the line of his jaw, and he seemed to like my hair and the shape of my lips. We went into town together at two in the afternoon and he took me to a place I'd never been with you, some tiny café in a basement with open windows. It was so close to the canal that you could smell the water and hear the boats glide through it, those on board faffing about with ice boxes filled with wine and beer. Andrew had rolled up his sleeves, and instead of watching the spectacle of the boats, which I normally loved to do, I sneaked glances at the fine light hairs on his forearms, the knobbly joints in his fingers, his clean fingernails and broad thumbs. He drank tea and so did I, and then cups of coffee, and when the afternoon had nearly ended he asked for a glass of Austrian Grüner Veltliner. The waitress asked if he'd rather like a bottle and Andrew looked at me questioningly, hopeful but not imposing, and I smiled and said okay.

The flutter in my belly, the rush of longing as I looked at him: I realized I was falling in love then. Again, not necessarily with him, or with his looks even, but with the kind of things he told me, the questions he asked, his way of speaking. He had that easy confidence that said circumstances had been good for him, life had worked out the way he wanted, he had a family who supported him. I felt envious, and thought that getting close to him, someone who had things going for him, would be the answer to everything. My mother leaving, you leaving, none of that would matter if I became part of this beautiful, privileged man's life.

"I'm twenty-nine," he told me when I asked. "You?"

"Twenty-three."

"And studying comparative lit," he nodded seriously. I looked to see if he was mocking me, but if anything, his expression carried his own quiet, washed-out brand of envy. "I wanted to study astrophysics."

"Why didn't you?"

"Hadn't the balls."

"I'm not an expert, but I think I can safely say you wouldn't need them."

"No," he laughed. "I mean, I wanted to, but my parents told me it was too academic and that I'd be better off doing something practical. I didn't dare go against them. They'd pay for all of it, had paid all my school fees in the past, so at the last minute I decided to do computer science instead. So you see," he shrugged, "hadn't the balls. Not like you."

"I didn't really need them," I returned. "I don't think my mother even knows what I'm doing here."

"She doesn't care about your education?"

"Not sure. When I got my first BA — "

The Dinner Party

"Oh? What did you — "

"English, as a second language," I explained. "When I got my degree, my mother put ten thousand euros in my bank account, but didn't show up for my graduation." I took a sip of wine. "I didn't have balls. I had money."

"Oh, but so did I," Andrew admitted. "Your parents are rich then?"

"My father was."

"Not anymore?"

"He up and left."

"What, divorce?"

"Even more pedestrian than that," I murmured, picking up a blue Bavaria beer coaster from the table and ripping it apart. "He died."

"Oh. Oh, I'm so sorry." With that, the playful glow in which we'd basked evaporated, and Andrew looked tremendously uncomfortable.

"No matter," I said with a small smile. "A new woman wouldn't have surprised me. The cancer did." When Andrew frowned at me, I went on: "My parents loved each other, but because of their busy jobs they barely spoke. I sometimes think my mother didn't particularly like him. Either of us."

"Why?"

"We used to go out together, my dad and I. Saturday mornings, we'd walk and read together, you know."

"That's nice."

"When we got home, full of stories and theories and big ideas," I said, smiling and rolling my eyes, "I remember the look on her face." My smile faded. "Full of disapproval and...contempt, even."

"Really?"

"She'd been working all morning and there we were, high on fairy tales and things of no consequence, no practical application." I frowned. "That's what it felt like to me, at least. Her silence, I mean. She'd hardly speak to us on Saturdays. She was cold and distant and..." I took a deep breath in. "Well, anyway, that's what I remember. Maybe she has an entirely different take on things."

"So on Saturday afternoons, evenings?"

"Oh, they'd both be hard at work. Sundays, too. Him in the study, she in the living room."

"And you?"

"I had my stories."

"You turned to writing?"

"Not writing, exactly. I pictured stories in my head. I'd lie in bed and have conversations with my characters. I imagined things."

"What kinds of things?"

"Being left in a forest, at night, with my hands tied behind my back. That was one I spent a lot of hours on."

"Right." He scratched his ear, the side of his neck. "Jesus."

"It wasn't sinister or anything."

"Wasn't it?"

"I imagined growing cold and really, really tired. It'd help me fall asleep."

"You couldn't sleep?"

"I had some trouble for a while. When I was too tired to make up my own stories, I usually read. It became like a..." Eggshells cracked, and frozen grass beneath our feet. "There was this silence in the house, in my head, that my dad left behind when he died. Whenever I stopped reading, or imagining, it just followed me around. So I didn't stop."

The waitress — blonde and very, very tall — passed and smiled at Andrew. He didn't smile back. Didn't seem to notice. Sparks of excitement fired in my stomach.

"What age were you when you left home?" he asked.

"Twenty-one. When I came here."

The Dinner Party

"Oh."

"What?"

"I thought you might have left a bit sooner."

"So did I, but then Paul arrived. He wasn't planned," I quickly went on, "I was still very young, but my mother..."

"Oh." Andrew took a sudden breath, shifted his weight. "Oh right," he said again. He clasped his hands together on the tabletop. "You've — you've got a — "

I couldn't contain my smile any longer. "No, I'm messing with you," I admitted, and laughed as Andrew dissolved in confusion. "Paul's my mother's new husband. She remarried."

"Jesus. Okay." Andrew drained his glass and puffed out his cheeks. Mortification looked unreasonably good on him.

"Things at home became better after he came along."

I thought of the dell, bare branches and dark tree trunks and ferns gone white with frost.

"Do you think you would have been happier if you had done astrophysics?" I asked after a moment's pause.

Andrew shrugged. "Impossible to say." His lips were very thin, the upper one ending in a fine upward curve. Something very rare about the lines of his face.

"Is it?"

"The person you'd be if you'd made a different choice ten years ago?" he huffed. "I'd say guessing's pretty impossible." I watched his eyes: they were a different color out of daylight, still somewhere undecided between blue and green but deeper now. His hand was curled around the stem of his wine glass. He'd ordered another bottle, this one a Châteauneuf-du-Pape for fifty euros.

"*You* don't look happy," Andrew said, and colored immediately. "Sorry. I didn't mean — "

"I lost a friend recently," I admitted with a painful smile. "The one I told you about. Harry. Texted me the evening before leaving the country. Just a few days ago."

"Told you by text?"

"And my mother told me she's moving to Berlin. She's there already by now."

"Christ," Andrew murmured. "That's rough."

"Both on the same day."

"Are you close to your mother?"

"Not really. Not anymore. Paul says it's because I remind her of my father, which is..." I shook my head. "Something out of a bad movie."

"Oh is it?" Andrew asked, like he'd never before had to consider the thought.

"A bad movie that keeps getting made," I said. Ballads of the spare children...I started picking apart another beer mat, this one depicting what looked like a tower, a town house, and a church below the words "brouwerij Oudaen."

Andrew must have seen me withdrawing, because he went on: "Do you know what you want to do once you graduate?"

"Try my hand at writing things down for once." I shrugged, feeling uncomfortable about the whole thing. You'd questioned me about it, Harry, but now you'd buggered off and left.

"You've really never put any of your stories down to paper?"

"Snippets, here and there." I hid my hands beneath the table, reached into my sleeve and scratched the inside of my wrist with my left thumb. The skin was sore still. White ferns and bare brown earth.

"Well, if you ever feel there's a snippet I could read...I'm very curious."

I tried to see my surroundings: the dark-brown pub, the brass lights

The Dinner Party

and colored glass, the sliver of canal we could see through the round window, the city it flowed through.

"Writing's a form of bravery, isn't it?" he said.

"What?"

"I've always wanted to be brave," Andrew admitted with a smile that said he thought he was anything but. "Ever since I was a kid. But all I've learned is how to recognize bravery in others."

"If you're not yet the person you'd like to be," I said carefully after some consideration, "doesn't mean you can't grow and become that person."

"You're kind." Andrew seemed touched by what I'd said. Two elderly women, holding hands, shuffled into the pub, sat down at an empty table and ordered two beers with a flick of the hand that said they'd been doing this for years.

My thumbnail pushed through. The skin broke anew.

"Should we get the bill?" I checked my phone for the time. "It's getting late and I have to — "

"Oh don't leave. I don't know that many people here, and you're the first person outside of work I've had an actual conversation with." Andrew carefully pushed my glass a few inches toward me. I looked at it, but saw the room I'd left behind that morning, empty bottles, shards of glass. Pictured your home too, where I'd spent so many hours, empty now, no music, no food, no fire burning in the hearth. What exactly did I have to go back to if I said goodbye to Andrew now? Andrew, whose eyes were glinting with some emotion I wasn't able to name yet, but which made the longing inside my heart beat twice as fast. I wanted to stay with this man, simple as that, and took the glass with my good hand.

"So how long are you here for exactly?" I asked after a moment.

"Six more weeks," he smiled. He seemed relieved.

"And then?"

"Oh, back to London."

"You live there?"

"My parents have a flat there I can — well, borrow."

"You'll live with them?"

"Oh no, they have their own home in South Ken, so I've got the place to myself."

"Great." I didn't know what to say. "Wow."

"And your place?"

"Oh, I've a feeling it doesn't really compare."

"No?"

"Twenty square meters, which is really big, actually — "

"Really?"

" — so I don't think I'll take you there anytime soon," I finished with a grin.

"You're making fun of me, aren't you?"

"Not really. Only a little," I relented.

"It's a shame, though."

"What is?"

"That you won't take me to your room." Andrew touched his nose, very briefly, worried his lip. I felt my face grow hot. "How about I take you to mine?"

I slept with him that night. He was good. Much better than most men I'd shared a bed with — would you have been any better, Harry? It's different, I'm sure. I know I shouldn't write this: it's not something you'd want to read. Maybe it was, once, but I'm sure the moment's passed.

Andrew was gentle, in any case, which counts for a lot. I looked exactly like a girl should then: long, dark hair that fanned out over the pillow. It was wavy because I'd let it dry in a braid, and I'd pinned it up loosely, away from my face. I wore blusher and mascara and lip gloss and

The Dinner Party

had drawn a line along my eyelashes, brown kohl. I must have looked good to him, from above, from behind. He was beautiful, after all. He could have had anyone.

These days, I've cut my hair, my face is unpainted, and if we hadn't spent some years together I don't think you would recognize me now. I look in the mirror and wonder sometimes what I would have looked like if I'd never met Andrew, if I hadn't smiled back, if I'd extracted my bike from the pile and gone home. What if I'd simply left, put my earphones in, finished my degree?

But it all happened as it did. And some of it was better than it would have been if I'd never met him, and some of it was worse. And the worst day of my life would have been an entirely different day, in a different place, with different characters, but who's to say how it would have compared to the dinner party, where everything tipped sideways?

Stella says it doesn't really matter. The past is what it is, and the important thing is what we make of it. How we allow it to influence everything that comes after.

What did I do with the knife at the end of the evening? Why don't I remember? Is it because I can't, or won't? Does it matter, if the result's the same?

I do have a few handholds though. Things I know for sure. I'll write them down for reference:

I know that Andrew and Evan became instant millionaires when they sold the app they'd built. I know they used some of the money to sponsor a space project, Andrew's wet dream, and attached a canon — one "n", mind you — to a spacecraft. The canon's like the Golden Record the NASA people once created, but made anew. Forty years later. They've included no music this time, but pictures of fifty paintings, fifty sculptures, and the digital texts of fifty books. They call it "Version 2.0," which isn't original. I know that, on the morning of the party, I struggle to get out of bed, as I have done for months. That I start the beginning of *The Crown* again, switch to *Hinterland*, sip beer in a coffee mug, buy the groceries that afternoon. I go to the poulterer's for the rabbits, to the supermarket for everything else. I buy the wine Andrew likes, twelve bottles of red — one for the rabbits — twelve of white, two of Prosecco. I heave a crate of beer onto the trolley. I know that when I get home, the silence will have been waiting patiently, so the first thing I do is put one of the beers in the freezer to quickly chill, lug the rest into the cellar. There's a small door in the hall below the stairs, and a stepladder with steep and rickety wooden steps, and then the cellar itself, where it is always cool, and dark, and where blood has a strange color. I know that it is sweltering, the hottest day of the year, and that I sweat a lot. I know that while the sun still shines Andrew's hands struggle to find purchase, that a series of small bruises forms along the waistband of my jeans, that the smell of him disgusts me suddenly, though it never had before. I remember everything that happened in those three minutes at the beginning of the evening, him and me in the kitchen. It's why Stella has me writing this letter. That, and what happened at the end: the knife, and what I did with it. She says the writing might jog my memory.

A vegetarian walks into a poulterer's, asks for two rabbits and is handed two stringy strips of bones and flesh in a thin plastic bag. Teeth still attached.

"I'm — sorry," I stutter, in the best English accent I can muster, holding on to the bag with my fingertips. "The heads, they're — "

"Sorry, darling," the huge man in an apron says. He's standing behind a high old-fashioned counter, glazed brown tiles on the walls, lord of steaks and sausages and the kind of pies you only ever see in Britain. "Can't give them to you without."

"What?"

"They nabbed him selling cats once," an old lady in an even older dress pipes up. She's sitting on the bench at the front of the shop, her back to the window.

"They *said* I sold cats," the poulterer corrects her loudly. "Couldn't prove a thing."

"He leaves the heads on, dear," the lady says to me.

"Yeah, well." I offer the bag back to the butcher, hold it high over the counter. Two happy cartoon chickens on the bag grin at me. "I've seen they're not cats, so — "

"Can't do that," he says, holding up both hands. There's a bright blue plaster wrapped around his finger. A smooth gold wedding band digs into the flesh. "You'll have to remove them yourself, love. If they stop you somewhere along the way — "

"They?"

"The FSA," the lady explains.

"I see."

"Nothing to it," the butcher insists. "Just — " he holds up a large, squarish knife and swishes it down onto the empty chopping board, where it makes a dull thud. "Like that."

"Great. Yeah. Got it." I hand him the cash and walk to the door. "Cheers."

"I always ask Jim from next door," the lady calls after me. "Men don't mind so much, do they?"

"Um." I imagine Andrew with a butcher's knife in his hand, approaching two dead rabbits. "I'll ask a neighbor," I murmur, even though we don't have any.

The door shucks closed behind me. It's two o'clock. The church clock chimes, but the rest of the village square is silent. The owner of the neighboring shoe shop sits on the stoop, nursing a mug of coffee. The little plastic Union Jacks strung between two trees at opposite sides of the square hang limp. There's no wind. Thirty-nine degrees Celsius. There's a film over it all, one that removes me from it, keeps me at a distance. I feel the morning's beer in the back of my head, creating pressure there, and an ache in my throat. From the plastic bag, eight teeth grin up at me.

"Jesus Christ."

I drive home in the BMW 4 Series Coupe Andrew bought me for my twenty-fifth. One of these dark-blue, stylish-but-practical affairs designed for German businessmen with one-point-five children and a wife with her own consultancy business: high heels and juice cartons. The news comes on and I crank up the volume, listen to the lady's voice instead of her words, a burr that drowns out everything else. I get home and the silence is there so I put another bottle of beer in the freezer, the Prosecco and the white wine and the rabbits in Andrew's LG American style fridge that is, for some inexplicable reason, connected to the internet. I sit down on the corrugated iron bench in the patio, take a swig of beer before it's cold: the prospect of having to decapitate dead animals warrants the copious consumption of alcohol, in my opinion.

The sun burns the back of my neck. The branches of the trees behind the pond are still and drooping. I remember a trickle of dust blowing away into the blue-gray air. I wipe my forehead and feel grains of sand shift against my fingertips, the air feeling clogged because it hasn't rained in weeks. The cat appears, suddenly, in the very center of the lawn, stands there and stares with blue eyes too wide for its tiny face, whiskers quivering, ears turning toward sounds I cannot hear, and it tiptoes through the grass, disappears and reappears in short intervals — the

The Dinner Party

grass needs trimming — a moving black spot in a sea of green, then jumps onto my lap and sniffs the bottleneck.

"Want a taste?" I ask. The cat turns away and curls up on my legs, uninterested. "Smart kit," I murmur, and feel a bud of affection burst into bloom somewhere deep in my belly. I brush a finger through his sun-warmed hair, feel his spine, knobbly and thin. He closes his eyes and drops into a doze. His ears move in opposite directions. His tummy expands and contracts with each breath. I can feel the beat of his heart in his chest, and with my index finger I press against the spot, harder and deeper and deeper still until I could hurt him if I went any further.

It startles me. A kernel of emotion channeled into an index finger, pressing down deeper.

The cat doesn't wake up. He's not really a cat, you see. Andrew gave him to me for my twenty-seventh. He's fifteen weeks old, only a kitten. Sleeping now, on my lap again, curbing me, making me sit still. My finger on its underbelly. Once again, I lose all feeling in my arms and legs, bare feet dangling, toes touching the grass, hands falling away from the resting creature, bottle slipping from lifeless fingers.

The rock against my back, that night. The animal sound she let out.

I want to leave, I whisper inside myself. I want to get my car, drive north to... Edinburgh, or Aberdeen, wherever. I never want to see this house again, the red bricks, sagging rooftops two floors up, ivy on the walls adjoining the patio, the garden extending down the house's entire length, and at the far end a pond, three trees, deck chairs under the parasol on the lawn, another tree in the corner where I'm sitting, roots pushing up the paving tiles. I want to leave it all behind, this English house in this patch of very English countryside, too big and too expensive considering how young Andrew is, the house he bought nevertheless because his father told him property's the best investment, so after he and Evan had sold their company, this is the house he chose, an hour's drive from the orbital.

"I want to leave," I whisper, the only thing to make a sound out here. The cat's ears prick up. It needs a checkup soon and Andrew's busy, so I'm the one to do it. I've taken him to the vet three times already. I've left the laundry in the washing machine, and it needs to go into the dryer. The bathroom needs a scrub; there's mold on the grout. Andrew will be back tonight and he'll bring his colleagues with him, and I will serve them food and drinks and listen to their conversation and laugh in the right places, and I'll catch up with Evan, who's not just Andrew's colleague anymore but who's become my friend, and we'll share bottles of wine and the odd cigarette and it will be an evening with friends, and if I won't belong entirely at least I'll belong a little. Which is more than I ever managed in Utrecht, or even back home, where three weeks after moving in Paul took me for a walk one evening to gently ask why I never spoke at dinner time. I couldn't explain it to him. I didn't want him to think I was blaming my mother for mourning my father, and didn't realize yet I didn't blame her for the grieving, but for the way she did it. The silence had already settled in my head and by that time I didn't really mind — I'd grown used to it. *Don't be childish, Franca.*

I find my legs again, my arms, the muscles bunch and strength returns and I get up, dislodge the cat from my lap, go back inside. I put the laundry in the dryer, open the fridge to get another beer, cat dancing round my ankles trying to get into the lower shelves. When I remember I've put the beer in the cellar, I go down the stepladder. The ceiling's low and uneven, and the walls are lined with shelves sagging under the weight of pots of beans and beets and apple sauce, bog roll in jumbo packs, and I stand there for a quarter of an hour, drinking, feeling all of twelve years old again.

The Dinner Party

You'll remark on it later that evening, remember? Not the drinking, but the "bog roll." You'll say I speak differently and I'll ask how, and you'll say that I used to speak like I'd stepped out of a nineteenth-century novel, but that now my English is like a posh person's version of colloquial.

But I don't know any of that yet. I don't know you'll turn up tonight, have no idea you're even anywhere near here. I'm thinking of you less and less — I get along without you well enough. I'm forgetting. All I know as I stand in the cellar is that same nameless dread I felt a week ago with Andrew on the sofa, that feeling expanding into every room of the house, the garden, the village, the country, all the places I have been and will always be alone in. It's a well-worn, mostly harmless feeling: spreads from that tender place behind my stomach and settles into my bones as a dull ache.

I finish my beer and go back upstairs, turn the TV on.

Often when we meet, Stella asks what brought me here. She means that in two ways: here as in her office, where I sit twice a week, and here as in the state I'm in. The first one's easy: I'm in her office because of what I did with the knife, and why I don't remember it. As to the latter, that one's harder to figure out. I worry the hem of my sweater, fraying and inadequate in comparison to Stella's sleek silk blouse, and say something different every time. Not to annoy her or to be contrary; I really believe her when she says that understanding this will be a vital step in my recovery. It's just that every time she asks me, I remember some other snippet of my past and feel it all fresh as if it happened yesterday, and any understanding I might have had previously is upended.

I mention the dinner, of course. Often we return to what happened right before that night, right after. Sometimes I say it's my mother, as I almost feel obliged to: the precedent of history after all, where blame lies solely on the mother and never on the husband, the son, the brother.

Other times I reject that yardstick and say it's my father, the never-ending heart-rending lack of him, Paul and how he took his place, the loneliness at school, university, the cat's sharp claws the fuck against the countertop, and you, Harry, drifting away. All of it is true. These things contain no hierarchy. They're all rather bad, in that they hurt a lot, but Stella likes to point out that they're also not debilitatingly hurtful: it's all happened, and yet I'm breathing. I've got a job, and I'm about to sign a lease on a flat. I'm still here.

"Why do you look so nervous suddenly?" Stella asks.

I stare at the photographs on the cabinet behind her, each one in a simple wooden frame. The cabinet itself is made of wood and looks old, and the photos look old too, washed-out colors and grainy faces, three young men and Stella in her twenties, early thirties? An old man and small children and one of a woman on a beach, facing the sea, her back to the camera. Are these her friends, family? Doesn't she mind people like me looking at them?

"You make it sound lovely," I say. I sit on my hands to stop them from shaking. "I survived, yes, but... Survival's a low bar."

"Is it? Why?" Stella leans forward. For a moment, I think she's going to rebuke me, launch into a speech that proves me wrong, but instead she just takes a sip of tea. Her nails are painted a pale skin color, and there is a ring around her index finger, a thin silver one, very simple, and I think it somehow makes her seem reliable. I don't know why, but the feeling's strong enough to make me open up a little.

"I feel frail," I admit. "Cold." Though the winter's so far been mild. "Yes, I'm to live on my own again." I've looked forward to it ever since I came to Berlin, but now that the first step's been taken... "I don't feel capable. Just scared."

Stella doesn't push back. She just listens.

"Why can't I remember?" I ask. It's a small question, one that doesn't cut close to the bone, and I want to see what she does with it.

The Dinner Party

She tells me about trauma, and stress, and I tell her that what I went through doesn't warrant terms like that.

Stella's silent for a moment, looks at me as if she's thinking of what to say.

"I think," she finally says, keeping her eyes on mine as she speaks very clearly, willing me not to mistake her meaning, "the important thing to remember is that you're the one who's writing this letter."

What about my dad, Stella wants to know. That "formative experience." I tell her it wasn't formative. Rather a nightmare, a disaster the likes of which I, in my young, young life, had never encountered before, never even imagined.

What kind of relationship did I have with him? He was the parent I could talk to, I answer. He liked me for me, not for who I was supposed to be.

"We used to go fishing together," I tell Stella. "Every week. Well, it started out as fishing, and even then it was only my dad with a rod in his hand. We'd go out on a Saturday morning, really early, drive to one of the lakes nearby. My dad would set up shop, fiddle endlessly with his gear, his bait, whatever, and I sat next to him with a book."

"How old were you?"

"I think I was ten when we started. Nine, ten. He was shit at fishing, to be honest."

"Yet he went every week?"

"He had a demanding job, long hours. I think he just wanted some time away from everything. And I wanted to be with him," I shrug. "He'd ask what I was reading, and I'd read him bits and pieces of whatever book I'd brought with me."

"What kind of books did you read?"

29

"Oh," I sigh and look at the ceiling, thinking back. "Oscar Wilde. The Inspector Morse novels. First books I read in English." I smile. "My dad never caught any fish, and I kept reading aloud to him. He'd ask me why did I like this book or that book so much, and he'd tell me about the kinds of books *he* liked. Eventually we were asked to leave by several fellow fishermen — too much noise, too much chatter — and from then on we'd go out for walks in various places, find a nice spot, read together. He loved to read."

"That's nice." Stella smiles politely.

"He hadn't made time for it, not for a long while, but from that point on..."

"What was the last book he read, do you know?"

A tight squeeze in my midriff. The smell of that hospital room. My mother's voice comes back to me, clear as day. "I remember the last time he read *to* me," I hedge. "I don't remember what exactly. We were in this kind of dell, our favorite place, and he read this whole passage about dancing stars and chaos or something. It went way over my head, I know that."

"And he became ill soon after?" Stella asks carefully.

"The next week." I frown. There must have been signs before that, but I'd missed them. Maybe I'd been stupid. Maybe I'd been young. After he died, missing him became the biggest part of my day — not school, or friends, not my mother or even my reading. Just my dad, the lack of him.

Here's how it went.

I was twelve, just. Dad came home from work early. Five o'clock, just after I'd got home from school. I asked him if he was ill. He was never home this early. He smiled and said he just wanted to spend some more time with me, now that I was growing up so quickly.

He went to work next day, came home early again, around four. Went to work, came home early. Three.

The Dinner Party

Dad started working from home after that. My mother did the same. He sat in his study with the door left slightly open, and she brought him tea and coffee. He was always on the phone.

One day when I returned from school, he was sitting in his armchair in the living room. No phone, no laptop, no papers even. Just his hands clasped together against his lips, eyes staring blind. My mother was there, too, wiping her eyes when she thought I couldn't see, fumbling with paper tissues all evening.

Dad didn't leave his chair. He must have, now and then, but in my memory he stayed there, sitting and staring, for days on end. Hands clasped, wrists getting thinner and thinner.

They sat me down one evening, Dad in his armchair, me on the couch, Mother hovering. Dad is ill, they said. No shit (I didn't say this). They didn't say what exactly was wrong with him. Just that he'd have to go into the hospital now and then. There's nothing to worry about, they lied.

Dad sat in a wheelchair. Mother pushed him out the front door, took his arm to help him into the car. It took a while. I went to school.

I came back. Dad was in his dressing gown. Dad only wore pajamas now. Dad slept in a bed in the living room, one with buttons that made it move up and down.

Mother bought me my first mobile phone, and she sent me to school with a note to teachers explaining why I needed to keep it on at all times.

I went to school. Teachers looked at me awkwardly. I came home.

I went to school, the mobile phone didn't ring. I went home and found the house in darkness; I had to use the key. It was winter, but inside it was warm. None of the lights were on. There was a terrible wet, fetid smell. The bed in the living room was empty and the sheets were sticky and there was something slippery on the floor.

I sat in a corner of the kitchen and waited. The fridge was open. The light made the tiles glitter.

The lamps turned on. Mother came home. Dad's in hospital. We'll visit him tomorrow.

I didn't sleep. I went to school. I went to the hospital. Dad's mouth was open. I wanted him to close it. Dad wore thin pajamas that had slipped off one shoulder, white bone through see-through skin. He made strange noises when he breathed.

I didn't go to school. Dad turned plastic. Mother turned to stone. Someone — I forget who — took my hand and led me to the hospital café, put a sandwich onto my tray, soup, orange juice. I chewed and swallowed. I went back to Dad's room. Dad was dead. Dad's eyes were open. For a moment, this confused me. Dad was dead, and I still hadn't turned thirteen.

※

The kitchen smells. It's late in the afternoon, hotter than ever, and I should have finished the cake by now. I haven't even started. The Queen is crowned, survives a scandal, makes a speech, grows into her role. My shirt is soaked and sticks to my chest and the kitchen's drenched in the kind of smell I don't think I've ever smelled before, though I suddenly remember the color on the walls of the room my father died in. It was a bluish-gray, and the sign on the door was a pale gray purple, like aubergine conserved in salt. Out the window he could see nothing but other windows.

Anyway, it smells in the kitchen, terribly. I lift the lid off the rubbish bin, but I remember I put the trash out the night before. The only thing inside the bin is an empty bottle of the protein whey shake Andrew drinks for breakfast, the abiding feature of which is that it smells — and tastes — of nothing at all.

"Did you shit in here somewhere?" I ask the cat. I look under the table, the cabinets. Nothing. The appliances lining the counter all gleam,

The Dinner Party

perfectly clean: presents from Andrew's family, gadgets he bought for me that we never use. I open the lid of the Crock-Pot, careful not to push any of its thousand buttons, but the only smell that greets me is that of new plastic.

So it's the fridge, isn't it. The cat dances around my ankles. I must have forgotten to close the door. It's open, in any case, the door, and inside the light is off, so something is wrong, and the smell... Christ, the smell. It's gone up to forty degrees outside and the rabbits are lying in a pool of liquid of an indeterminate color, dripping through the bag and onto the lower shelves of the fridge.

"Oh Jesus," I gag, and cover my mouth. The bag leaks onto the floor as I carry it toward the bin. I go to close the lid, but the bag is open and the rabbits stare up at me. The flesh glistens, seems to crawl. Their little front paws have been turned into stumps, folded pathetically under their chins. The scent is decay and rotting flesh, and out of the corner of my eye I see the cat jump straight toward the bin.

"Don't!" I cry, and lunge for it. It's already neck-deep in dead things when I grab it by the scruff and fling it out the door onto the patio. "You're like a dog!" I pull the strings of the bin liner and carry it round the side of the house to drop it in the dumpster. "Stay away from here," I warn as the cat peeks around the corner, "or you'll end up the same. Fuck." The bag's dripped onto my toes, left a trail along the kitchen floor. The fridge is dead: the butter is swimming in its dish, and the milk has curdled. The knife lies on the counter.

The clock says five. The poulterer's will have closed an hour ago. Andrew and his colleagues will be here in two hours. The beer's buzzing in my head.

"Shit," I murmur, and grab the car keys.

Winter

THE PLACE IS SMALL. Four by four meters, plus a tiny bathroom, a bedroom that'll just about fit a single bed. The kitchen is a dirty sink and a sliver of a countertop, a cabinet affixed to the wall, one drawer.

I stand in the center of the living room for a few minutes. It's eleven in the morning, a grimy January. Five months since I left the house I shared with Andrew, after an evening I still can't remember the ending of.

The light-blue carpet is stained in a particular way. The glue has come loose, so it's easy to roll up. An old, wooden floor appears underneath. I carry the carpet down the stairs and drop it onto the pavement next to the front door. I've arranged for it to be taken away today.

I clean the sink with bleach. I scrub the toilet, the tiles in the shower stall, the grout in between. I hoover the floors. I wash the windows. I sit down when my arms start trembling, and when I've got my breath back I begin again.

"You see the past as a parade of mistakes," Stella says today. "Everything that went wrong. The people you lost, friends and lovers, your mother, your home."

Viola van de Sandt

I don't know what to say to this. It's been months though, and the little I've told her hasn't been met by mockery yet. Instead, she's listened without judgment, offering interpretations that make sense, so perhaps she's right about this as well.

"Can you tell me about something that worked out all right?" This is Stella's next question. "A decision you made, something you don't regret?"

Today, to avoid looking at Stella, I'm looking at the pen on Stella's desk. It's one of those outrageously expensive ones: Montblanc. Andrew had one, barely ever wrote with it. Stella never writes while we're talking.

But right now, we're not talking at all. Something I don't regret? I can think of sod all. With every passing silent second, I feel more and more ridiculous. How melodramatic, sentimental, to always find myself entirely at fault.

"How about this new flat of yours?" Stella suggests. A notepad lies next to the pen on the desk. Stella's not sitting behind it. We're in armchairs flanked by spindly side tables facing one another, nothing in between. The room itself is small, square, and everything is neat and new except the cabinet and the photos.

"You've organized that all on your own. Chose a home for yourself, arranged the finances. You're planning to fix it up."

"Yes." I rub my face. The desk is behind Stella, and behind that is the cabinet with the pictures on it, the woman on the beach. It's an old photo, colors faded, fashions changed, a hairdo you'd want to fix.

"Franca?"

My eyes meet hers for a moment, then flit away. I place a thumb on the inside of my wrist but I don't move it. The flat I'm renting, yes.

"Well. It'll be a long time before I finish. When I go there too often, I panic."

"That's understandable."

The Dinner Party

"Is it?" I frown.

"It's a big step."

"It's a tiny flat."

"What frightens you about it?"

"I — " I shake my head. Christ, I've no idea. What frightens me? What doesn't, really? I can't even look at Stella for longer than a second for fear of what she might see in me. Stella waits patiently, and in the corridor behind the closed door people are passing — I can hear their footsteps, hear them talking to one another — therapists, patients. Stella clears her throat and my eyes flit toward her again, then away. I look out the window at the park instead. I look at the bare treetops, the smudge of bird shit on the glass, at the children's drawing put in a frame on the windowsill: bare-bones houses and people made of sticks, smoke from the chimneys and strangely some kind of animal in the sky — a goat, maybe? Not a sun.

"I'm like an onion."

"Sorry?" Stella asks.

"You're peeling away my layers," I explain, and try to still my nervous hands, "and you study the young skin underneath."

Stella is silent.

"Do you find it unpleasant, talking to me?" she asks eventually.

"In a way," I admit. "I feel... raw, scrubbed raw, I mean, but also..."

"Yes?"

"It's nice, too." I flash a brief smile. "You taking the time to see what the scales reveal. Your interest, even though I know you get paid for it."

"Good. I'm glad." Stella waits again, then smiles. "It's a novel way of describing what we do here. Peeling away an onion... I haven't heard that one before."

"I'm sorry I'm — " I wave a hand at my chest, my face. "I'm not good at this. Talking about... everything. I just — I remember how I behaved

37

that evening, or didn't behave, really. And the years before, how passive I was. And now I've got this new flat and most days I can't bring myself to go there. I don't dare. So I wait. And wait. That's all I do." Frustration makes my voice bitter.

"These are large strides you are taking. What happened to you," Stella shakes her head, "it's not a small thing people can just shrug off. I know you disagree with me," she goes on, "and we'll keep talking about it, but right now you need to give yourself some time."

"I've done sod all for so long," I cry. "I thought I was improving, that I'd changed, at least a little since that evening, but — you've such a strong sense of purpose and I'm..." I rub my eyes, the courage I felt depleted, my store of words run dry.

"Write about it," Stella advises, as she often does.

I'm trying. It's hard. I wonder if you were better at it, this kind of thing, wonder if you ever went in for it after you had your burnout.

I do a lot of wondering these days. Most of it on my trips to Stella's office. I walk there, thirty minutes, forty if I stop for coffee along the way. I wonder what you'd think if I ever sent this letter and you found it on your doormat. If you'd recognize my handwriting. If you'd open the envelope. If you'd read the letter. If you wouldn't.

And then I get out of my head. I don't want to stay inside there. Stella taught me that. Taught me how, I mean. To take the time to notice things, even on my walks. See, hear, smell. I'm not very good at it, but right now there are crocuses growing in the cracks in the pavement. Little purple ones, peeking out from the sleet. Snowdrops, too, and because they're white, as their name suggests, they wouldn't stand out against the snow if it weren't for these bright green shoots that surround them. I listen to the crunch of my footsteps, the tick tick tick at the pedestrian crossing, people nattering in German. I walk behind couples, colleagues, old friends, and try to make out as much of their conversations as I can. I watch their breaths form little clouds, rise into the gray sky.

It's prettier than I'd thought. Berlin in winter: cold and concrete, but with an orange glow too, through clear glass, the smell of fuel, of sewage and urine now and then, as in any big city, but also that of cinnamon, ladies' perfume, warm food. Conversation filtering out through open doorways, the tinkle of cups and cutlery. Bubbles in beer, cava, champagne. Wine in large glasses.

Stella said something last week that I can't stop thinking about. She said it slowly, as she usually does, in that low, slightly hoarse voice of hers. I'd been telling her, in stops and starts, what happened with Andrew at the beginning of that evening, also how hard it is to talk about it at all, to answer questions I don't have the answers to.

"Your story is your own," she said. "People often ask for details."

"The flesh and blood," I filled in.

"Yes. But you should never feel obliged to share your story with anyone."

This startled me. I couldn't think of a response in time: she'd already moved on and was asking me other questions. I'd come to trust her, I realized, though I couldn't say exactly when this had happened. But everything I'd told her since I first came to her last autumn — it was more than I'd ever told anyone. And I'd never felt obliged.

I've thought of something to say by now. I rehearse it over and over in my mind, resolve to say it aloud every time I'm in her office.

But it's personal, and I lack courage.

※

The wheels of the trolley squeak as I push it through the supermarket aisles. The air conditioning's blowing like crazy. Sweat and wet clothes cool, my stomach feels like it's filled with acid. I rush toward the meat counters, bathed in red light that makes the meat look fresh. There's nothing on the shelves that resembles a rabbit — with or without its head — and the only gamey thing they have is a hundred grams of venison that definitely won't feed three grown men.

You should eat, she'd said. *Mind you turn the stove off.*

"Can I help you dear?" a silvery woman in a flowery apron asks. "You look like — "

" — I'm hosting a dinner party in two hours and the fridge broke down?"

"Oh dear." The woman's smile turns sympathetic. She must be seventy, seventy-five, her long white hair pinned into a neat bun at the back of her head. "I can see why you're stressed. The weather being what it is..."

"I left the refrigerator door open, and the rabbits have melted."

"Oh dear," she says again, and looks at the shelves. "And we don't have any rabbits here, indeed we don't. We only have the venison, I'm afraid."

"And that's not enough."

"How many are you serving, dear?"

"Three men."

"And yourself?"

"Oh, I don't count."

The old lady looks up. "Why, of course you do, dear."

"No, I mean, I don't eat meat."

"But why?" She seems flummoxed.

A misguided school trip and a lifetime's propensity to nausea.

"I've seen how it's made," I summarize, and check my watch. The lady takes the hint.

"Now. What about a stuffed chicken?" she asks.

"A stuffed chicken?"

The Dinner Party

"Yes." She hurries toward another aisle, bends down and unearths a large, fleshy, flabby monstrosity — legs bound, goose-pimpled, wrapped in plastic on a yellow Styrofoam dish. To live your life and end up like this...

"I thought you only stuffed a turkey," I admit.

"There's ever so many programs about American Thanksgiving on the telly these days," the lady agrees. "But a chicken fills just as well. A hole's a hole, isn't it, dear?"

I choke on a laugh. The lady's eyes are twinkling. "So I hear," I say.

"We've only got the one, I'm afraid, so if you've got three healthy men..."

"Only for the evening."

"You might want to add a little something extra, like a chorizo filling?"

"Sure." I follow her down the aisle.

"Pre-cut?" she asks. "For convenience?"

"Sure," I say again. She puts the package in my trolley. "Do you have a recipe I can use?" I ask. "I don't know how to do any of this."

"You've never stuffed anything before?"

"I've always found one hole to be very much *not* like the other."

"Oh, I'm sure you're right, dear," the lady chuckles. "Now, I know there's a very nice recipe online," she continues in a confidential whisper that obliges me to lean in. "Gordon Ramsay, you see. Dreadful man, and too much meat, but if you're feeding three of them... How about some extra cannellini beans?"

"Yeah."

"There." She adds three cans to my trolley and pats the chicken on the back. "That'll fill the bugger up, and no mistake."

"Jesus," I mutter as the old lady retrieves a phone from a pocket in her apron. "Are you for real?"

"See." She briefly turns the screen to me and begins to speak much more quickly. "Just google 'Gordon Ramsay stuffed chicken' and you'll find it, no mistake. Very quick, too. Just add some garlic and onions — "

"I have those."

" — sun-dried tomatoes — "

"I don't."

" — aisle two, and you'll be right as rain. Now, I've got to dash, but I wish you the best of luck, dear."

I watch, dazed, as the lady hurries through the exit and disappears into the street.

"Sorry," I say to a young girl stuffing shelves nearby, "who's — "

"The old bat? She lives in the care home opposite. Runs out on a rainy day, pretends she's working here."

"Oh."

"Don't worry," the girl grins. "They say she used to run a restaurant."

I nod, stare at my trolley, glance at my watch. Five-thirty. I google the lady's recipe.

"Fine," I murmur, "fine," and head to aisle two.

※

I wasn't like this in the beginning. You know me, Harry. You know that this, at least, is true. I didn't come to England to be a housewife, Andrew's fiancée, fussing over dinner, chatting about recipes with old ladies at the supermarket. I'm trying to figure out how it happened. How I got from there to here.

I did look for jobs when I moved to the UK. We lived in London the first year: I figured if I couldn't find a job there, where could I? I thought there would be plenty of opportunities. I did try in the beginning, and then later, near the end.

But I hadn't finished my BA. Andrew had been about to leave

The Dinner Party

Utrecht, and asked me to come with him. I was in love with his beauty, his body, his fancy shirts, the ease with which he negotiated the world; I wanted to spend the rest of my life by his side. He had a family he saw regularly, an occupation in which he was successful, the entire structure of a life. I wanted it, wanted to be close to all of this. So I dropped out. He bought me a ticket. I sat next to him on the plane, and Andrew's parents gave us a beautiful flat to live in. It was crazy. You know my father had left my mother and me a large amount of money and I'd never had to go without, but this, this was something else.

So for the first few months, I sent letters. Not that many. Thirty, perhaps. Never heard back in most cases. I went for a few interviews, for traineeships, first, then internships, but they weren't interested. I never really understood exactly why: if it was because I didn't finish my degree, or because that degree had been in comparative literature, and what use are books when you need to make money? Maybe it was the accent, my foreignness, or maybe it was just because of me, my lack of any practicality?

Then Andrew sold his company, barely a year after we'd arrived, and we — *he* — could buy his own house. Millions to spare, still.

Andrew said I didn't need to look for jobs. That I could do something else. I wanted to be a writer, he pointed out, so I could start a novel. He'd support me. I said it was ridiculous in this day and age for a woman to rely entirely on the income of her partner. So I didn't write. But I also didn't look for jobs anymore.

It was easy. It makes me feel ashamed, but that's what it comes down to. It was hard to apply for jobs and get rejected time after time. Stopping was easy, and I'm a coward. You implied it near the end of the evening. To write would have been to accept my failure, would have required the courage to do something else, imagine a new future for myself. To dare to think that my words, my thoughts could be of interest to anyone else.

Viola van de Sandt

I'd never have thought that when I'd finally get around to it, I'd write not a story or a novel or even a newspaper article, but a letter, and least of all to you.

I don't want to write about this. Stella calls it the tipping point: it's not the only thing that brought me to her — she leaves out the matter of the knife, and what I did with it — but it is the most important. Exploring this further is vital, she says. I say writing about it makes me feel like it's happening again. Makes me want to crawl out of my skin. Nevertheless, she says.

So. Andrew comes home. I'm adding strips of mozzarella to the Vera Wang fine bone china salad bowl his mother gave me when I first moved in with him. It's filled with lettuce, shallots, raw tuna drenched in olive oil. The laptop's on the top of a cabinet, final episode, first series. I keep half an eye on it.

"Christ," Andrew says when he steps into the kitchen, toeing off his shoes. "Jesus."

I crane my neck to look into the hall behind him. "Where's Evan?"

"He'll be here in half an hour. We had a problem with encryption. It's been a fucking nightmare." He opens the fridge and finds it empty. "Where's the beer?"

"In the cellar. Fridge broke down. And I must have left the door open."

"It's brand new." Andrew holds a cut-crystal tumbler — from a set of six by Schott Zwiesel, given to us by his uncle David — under the tap and gulps it down. "What's that?" he asks, nodding at the bowl.

"It's the starter."

"Looks nice," he says. I raise an eyebrow at him. The salad is bland as fuck, and Andrew's just trying to be nice.

The Dinner Party

"Perhaps I should add some tomatoes," I muse, looking at the bowl. "For some color."

"It looks fine," Andrew reassures me. "And you," he goes on, and kisses me with a small smile that says he's sorry it took him so long to say hello to me properly. "You look lovely."

"I think I'll just add some."

Andrew shrugs his suit jacket off and drapes it over the back of a chair. "What's that smell?"

"The damn rabbits," I say over my shoulder as I head into the hallway and open the door to the cellar. "They went off, spectacularly."

"What? But what will you do for the — "

I can't hear the rest. I've filled the cellar with everything perishable, there's hardly any room to walk. I rummage through the crates, find the tomatoes. Their skin's still reasonably smooth.

"What'll you do for the main?" Andrew asks when I return to the kitchen.

"I bought a chicken." I start washing the tomatoes.

Andrew turns to the fridge and slams a hand against the side. "Is it plugged in?"

"Yes."

"All right, all right," he says in response to my tone. "I'll call a bloke in the morning."

I step back from the bowl. "Perhaps some parsley?" I suggest after a moment.

"Ugh, miserable stuff."

"Basil then. There's some in the garden."

Andrew strides out the back door. I watch him through the window. There's a dark patch on his shirt that sticks to the center of his back as he bends down over the pots of herbs. It makes him look vulnerable, I think, and some small muscle near my heart squeezes.

I scan the old lady's recipe. It says to make the stuffing first — that part's easy, then. I open the wrapper of the chorizo, let the slices slide onto the chopping board, take a knife from the block — "Zwilling J. A. Henckels" it proclaims in fine lettering. "Self-sharpening," Andrew's sister Clem had said as she gifted it to us a week after we'd got engaged, "ordered it off Selfridges."

So the knife's sharp, but the meat's sticky, difficult to cut through, covered in some sort of red goo that makes me shudder. As soon as it hits the bottom of the bright blue frying pan, one of those cast-iron Le Creuset affairs, too heavy to lift in one hand, orange fat leaks out and forms a bubbling pool.

"How about this?" Andrew has washed the basil leaves and scattered them over the salad.

"Fine. Could you wrap that and take it downstairs?"

"Sure." He fiddles with the cling film dispenser affixed to the tiles above the worktop, then clatters down the stepladder. "So, Evan's invited a friend," he shouts through the trapdoor.

"What? For dinner?"

"Yeah. Harry something."

"Oh." I stare at the chorizo sizzling in the pan, vaguely try to calculate the odds, and dismiss them. The name's not exactly rare here, is it?

"One of his best friends, apparently, from when he was up," Andrew says as he re-enters the kitchen.

"What, at the University of Cambridge?"

"Yeah. They spent a lot of time together, he said, lost touch when they graduated, then bumped into one another yesterday. At the pub or something."

Evan's ten years older than me. So are you, Harry. The two of you must have studied there at the same time. Can't believe I never thought of it before. Jesus, imagine if you —

The Dinner Party

"I'm starving." Andrew takes a jar of peanut butter from a cupboard, pops two slices of bread into the toaster. It's one of those KitchenAid ones: rounded corners and posh aluminum in a color they call something ludicrous like Candy Apple when it's just plain red. Seven different knobs and dials when you just want a slice of toast. "Some for you?"

"No thanks."

Andrew offers me a bottle of beer instead, which I accept, and opens one for himself. We clink, and drink.

"How was work?" I ask him.

"It's not really work these days, is it?"

I look up, stop chopping onions. There's embarrassment in his eyes, and an apologetic kind of honesty I've only ever seen in them a handful of times before. He colors under my scrutiny and shrugs.

"We're just faffing around, aren't we. I mean, when we were building the app I felt like we were doing something real. But this..." His eyes fill, but he sighs, and then he smiles and knocks the emotion back. "Look, never mind."

"No, tell me."

"I mean, I feel like we're just..." Andrew sighs again. The toaster pops, but he ignores it. "We're just pushing money around, aren't we?"

"You're sponsoring this space — "

"No, I know what we call it." He shakes his head. "What *I* call it. But we don't know anything. About space, or anything at all. I mean, I'm thirty-three and I've read a handful of books and I've no clue — we just pretend to. We buy our way into these projects that we don't have any understanding of."

"You're funding this project. Allowing it to go ahead."

"But it's not real. I mean, we're not creating anything. We're not doing any actual, real *work*."

"Look." I put the knife down. "This — what do they call it again?"

47

"Mission of Interstellar Space Exploration," Andrew says quietly.

"This mission can only go ahead because of the money that you donated. You're helping these people do their research, perform their tests, do, um, readings and... whatever else," I finish, shrugging, and hold up a hand. "That's possible only because of *your* money, that *you* earned."

Andrew gives a watery smile. "Yeah."

"Besides," I add lightly, while I go back to chopping onions, "you're sending a record into space."

"That's only a front. A flashy project to give the donation some extra — "

"It's cool," I interject. "In a dorky, seventies kind of way."

Andrew's grin becomes a bit more genuine. "You know it's not a record, actually. It's a digital — "

"I know," I stop him. "Still." I add the onions to the pan. We both watch them sizzle.

"Thanks," Andrew says at length, and rubs the back of his neck. "I uh... need the loo." He drifts away.

I peel cloves of garlic, but when I begin chopping them the knife cuts into my finger. It bleeds more than it should, from the chopping board onto the tiled floor, and it stings, though less than I'd expect. I hold it under the tap for a moment, rinsing it, and begin to step back to get a plaster when arms wrap themselves around my chest.

"I missed you today," Andrew smiles against the back of my neck as the cat walks in and begins to eat.

"Yeah?" I try to look at him, but his arms tighten and he won't let me turn round.

"Mm." His mouth is open now, warm and wet. His hands press down on my abdomen. "I want you," he breathes into my ear.

The Dinner Party

"Yeah." I'd figured that out already.

"What you just said — " his tongue is on my earlobe now — "you always reassure me. Make me feel better about myself." One of his hands drift down.

"I'm bleeding," I murmur, and try to move away. He presses himself against my back. The cat jumps onto the countertop.

"I don't mind." His teeth graze the side of my neck, and his thumb opens the button of my shorts.

"No, my finger." I try to hold it up for him to see, but he grabs my wrist with his free hand and tugs on my zipper with the other. "I cut myself. I'm bleeding."

"Fuck, Fran." He presses me more firmly against the stove. "It's almost stopped. I want you."

"I need a plaster." The pressure of him against my back makes me bend over above the stove. My hair dangles close to the burner, so I reach down and turn the heat off. The cat comes closer, steps over the chopping board and sits down next to the frying pan.

"I love you." He bites down on my shoulder. His hand slips into my underwear.

"I've got to get going on the chicken," I say, and try to move away. "Stop."

He sinks his fingers in. Groans a little. His smell has changed. He is hot and clammy against me. "You always make me feel good," he whispers wetly in my ear. "Make me feel good about myself."

"Yeah, well, I don't — ah," I wince. "Stop."

He removes his hand, puts it on the small of my back, opens his fly. I make a sound, my breath catches. My abdomen is pressed into the counter's edge, again and again. The skin bruises. The red Marcato pasta maker rattles on the counter. The chorizo's congealing. The onions glaze. The smell is disgusting. The knife lies on the worktop. The cat meows, eyes on mine, ears twitching. I close my eyes. Andrew moans, grabs, bucks. Slimy wetness seeps down the inside of my leg.

"Fuck," Andrew groans. He slumps against me. Delivers an open-mouthed kiss between my shoulder blades. "You're lovely."

I open my eyes. My finger's bleeding into the sink. A trickle of him continues to dribble down. This close, the garlic has a sharp, unpleasant smell. Andrew freezes.

"Shit." He takes his hands off me. "Shit. Sorry."

"It's — "

"Christ." He steps back, allows me to straighten. "You should, um — change. Before they get here."

"Yes." I turn, pull up my shorts. I do not look at him.

"I'll — I'll get the Prosecco." He leaves the kitchen.

I wash my hands. Open the drawer for a plaster, wrap it around my finger. I startle when something soft brushes against my foot. The cat wraps its front paws around my ankle, nails retracted, meowing softly, looking up at me. It licks the toes that peek out of my sandal. My blood curdles, skin prickles, bile rises in my throat, hands tremble, shudders running up my spine and neck and lodging in my head where a great drumming now resounds and the taste of blood in my mouth from where I put my fingers over my lips, and with a jerking movement, I dislodge the cat from my calf and feel the wetness squelch between my legs, knees that turned to mush.

I grip the banister with both hands. I climb the stairs.

※

Well then, there's the tipping point. I describe it to Stella, and throw up on her office floor.

I don't feel better. It's the first time she's been wrong.

The Dinner Party

I don't remember much about my dad. What kind of man he was, what kind of father, what he was like in general. What he smelled like. Whether he laughed a lot or not.

My memories of him, the language I used to describe his death, belong to a girl who lost her dad when she was five, six years old. I was twice that age, actually, and yet the things I can remember are barely there: impressions, smudges on a canvas, smoky tendrils fading in the wind. I close my eyes and I cannot see what his face looked like — his living, breathing, speaking face, I mean. I remember his plastic one perfectly.

A large, warm hand around mine. The smell of old coffee, grown cold in cups left behind all around the house. Suits in blue and gray, ties of all colors, subtle patterns woven with a shiny thread. The back of a head as he sat behind the wheel, gray hair thinning. Holidays when the fine hairs on his arms turned white. The start of an engine. Shifting gears.

He was always going away, coming home, locking and unlocking doors, opening and closing them. He spent such a lot of time at work.

He was CEO of a company that sold life insurance. One of the big ones, ads on national TV. Later, when I went through puberty, I called that irony.

He'd been working since he was seventeen, my mother told me later. He went to university, took evening classes, saved the daylight hours for his first job, something to do with filling forms. He was thirty-five years old when he and my mother — but mostly she — made me. He left for work very early in the mornings. He came home late at night. He worked on Sundays. He was on the phone a lot. He worked hard — many people do — and made a lot of money — most people don't — and he died young. He was unlucky.

We didn't speak much during our weekend walks. He recited, sure, and talked about the books he liked, but in essence he was quiet. He talked a lot with other people, employees, colleagues; he was only an extrovert because he'd learned to be. We walked and spotted birds, rabbits, a deer in the distance. We paused and ate sandwiches and read to each other, quietly. I feel bad about it, this being the extent of my memories of him. Imagine being a parent, and your child had to describe you, and all she'd come up with was this.

The one thing that remains, however, is love: my love for him, and the love he felt, I think, for me. It's a loss, a lack, a pallid dearth that I felt most acutely in the three, four years after his death, and that's stayed with me ever since, but a lack that also slowly morphed into a gift: the gift of the pain that came with missing him. I loved my father, and he loved me. To not have missed him would have been worse, I think.

APERITIF

I put my shorts and underpants into the wash. I use a flannel to clean myself. I brush my hair — shorter now than when I first met Andrew, but not as short as it is when I'm writing this to you. I hurry; downstairs, the doorbell rings. Andrew emerges from the loo and goes to answer it. I dart across the landing, slip into the bedroom just before the front door opens and laughter fills the hall. I pull on a pair of pale linen trousers and a light blouse that I button all the way up.

    I dither. Through the open window, I hear the sliding door in the dining room creak open. Voices drift up: Andrew's, Evan's, Gerald the dinosaur's, I presume. I step as close to the window as I can without being seen and see three men saunter across the lawn. Evan is in sunglasses, light chinos and a black polo, hair slicked back, the smallest of the three. Andrew's wearing his same clothes, handsome as always. With a wave of his hand, he invites the older man who must be Gerald — sixty-something, in a shirt a shade of fuchsia just a bit too bright — to take a deck chair. The three of them sit down under the parasol and watch the fish move slowly in the pond. Evan makes a joke. Andrew laughs. He pops the cork from the Prosecco and watches it fly, follows its trajectory with his eyes. For a moment, his face turns toward the window where I'm standing, but then Gerald asks him something and he turns away.

Sit down. My mother's face barely visible in the dark. The stone I had to sit on damp and very cold. *Go on, we'll be here for a while.*

"Here she is," Evan cheers when I join them outside. He has a glass in one hand and a cigarette in the other, but he puts both on my shoulders and stands on tiptoe to place two kisses on my cheeks. A whiff of cologne: spicy and a little sweet, not at all what men usually wear. "Lovely to see you, darling, as always. Gerald was asking after you. Fran, this is Gerald," he says, releasing me, allowing me to shake Gerald's hand. "Gerald's the man who helped us choose the books. You'll have heard all about him, I expect. Gerald, old man, this is Fran. Andrew's fiancée."

"Franca," I say. Gerald's grip is dry and firm. He smiles at me genially. He's turned the collar of his shirt up, has tucked in a polka-dot scarf. It makes his neck look very short. His skin's unnaturally brown, his thin hair unnaturally dark.

"Franca," he repeats. His bright blue glasses dig into his temple. "As in lingua —"

"Yes," I smile, "like that. Nice to meet you." Gerald inclines his head. I turn to Evan. "I thought you were bringing a friend?"

"Harry should be here in a mo, yeah," Evan confirms as he sits back in his deck chair and takes a drag from his cigarette.

"You were both students at Cambridge?"

"That's right. We've recently reconnected. I think the two of you will get on."

The Dinner Party

"Is Harry a — "

"Want a glass?" Andrew holds out a crystal flute, Spiegelau, doesn't meet my eyes. I take it from him carefully. Our hands don't touch. Rays of sunlight between our fingers.

"Thanks." I turn to Evan again. "Here's to the three of you, then. Your 'Golden Record.'"

"Cheers," they all say, and drink. Nobody says anything for a moment, and the evening presses in. The sun's only just above the treetops, still so hot, but overall it's getting cooler, just a little, and it seems like nature's releasing a very deep breath. The light has lost its brightest edge and has begun to turn golden. The blue of the sky is no longer crisp, but mellow and deeper, showing just a hint of violet. Birds sing, insects chirp, unknown creatures rustle through the undergrowth.

But now the men begin talking again, and the pressure of the day descends, and I swallow a mouthful of Prosecco. I try to listen to their conversation, but it's hard to focus on the words.

"It's a century, in my opinion," Gerald is saying, gesticulating wildly, "and that opinion is shared by many. And I'm not just speaking of literary merit. These books are touchstones that can only be observed through the test of a fixed term."

"So that explains why you've chosen all the old codgers," Evan summarizes from behind his sunglasses, stretched out on the lounger, dropping his fag into the ashtray on the grass. The sun shines on his face, accentuates its angles. He's lost weight, I think. His skin looks paper-thin. "What a relief, indeed, that we haven't publicized — "

"It's a missed opportunity, in my opinion," Gerald interrupts, and one corner of Evan's mouth goes up just incrementally. "Publishing a list like the one we made, it would have inevitably aroused discussion."

"Yes, well, we've all had rather enough of that," Andrew begins. "I mean — "

"Discussion means conversation." Gerald smiles. "And conversation inevitably leads to progress. As soon as we start talking to one another..."

I stop listening. I think about the first time I had sex with Andrew, back in Utrecht. He was very careful then. Very nervous, too, which made me feel brave. I took the lead. Undressed him first, undid the buttons on his shirt, opened his fly like I opened men's flies all the time, put a hand in. For a second, I feel again his skin under my fingertips, smell again the way he smelled then, hear the sounds he made, feel again the rush of being allowed to undress a man who looked like that...

"Excuse me," I say, and get up.

"Where's she from?" I hear Gerald ask as I make my way across the lawn.

"Holland."

"Oh, indeed. I thought I heard something vaguely Scandinavian in her accent."

"Andrew met her in Utrecht," Evan says, "four years ago now, didn't you, mate?" Andrew says something in reply, but I can't hear what exactly as I step back inside.

I hover in the kitchen doorway. There's blood on the floor, not a lot. There's blood on the countertop. The cut in my finger throbs. The garlic lies half-chopped, turning brown. I empty my glass and approach the chopping board. I run a fingertip over the edge of the counter. There are specks of blood on it, but the pasta maker and the stainless steel SMEG kettle look pristine.

The doorbell rings again. I walk toward the door on foal legs and open it.

It's unbelievable even now, months later, when I'm writing this. So many Harrys in this country... I stare, open-mouthed I'm sure, and wonder briefly whether you'd planned this, but you seem just as surprised as

The Dinner Party

I am. It's been four years since I last saw you, and you've changed a little, but not so much that I wouldn't know you anywhere. Your hair is curlier, your skin a little paler, and you look a bit older, yes, but overall you're quite like I remember. You're wearing jeans and a blue shirt tucked in, a strip of old leather tied round your wrist. Your blue eyes are impossibly wide. You're beautiful, as you were, always.

"Fran." You break the silence first. In my memory, your voice was a little lower. "Wow. Look at you."

"Harry. Hey," I say. I can't think of anything else.

"Last place, eh?" you say awkwardly.

"Exactly." I shake my head and step aside. You pass by. You smell the same: soap and something that makes your curls curl — you told me about it when I said I'd kill to have curls like yours. "Did you know I lived here?"

"No." You stop a few feet down the hallway and turn to me. "I had no idea. Why?"

"Evan told me he was bringing a Harry, but..."

"What are the chances, right? I — " You shake your head. "He's an old friend. Bumped into him by chance. Anyway, I thought you were still in Utrecht."

"No, I'm...I'm here." Oh, for the love of god, think of something proper to say. "You and Evan were at Cambridge together?"

"Yeah. How do you know..."

"Evan's a friend."

"Gosh." You take a sharp breath in. "So you're, um..." You need to think about his name for a moment. "Andrew's?"

"Yeah."

"His girlfriend?"

"Mm." Something painful settles in my chest, pushes sideways against my ribs.

"Wow." You look at me. Your eyes are very wide and very, very blue.

"How have you been?" I ask to break the silence.

"I've been okay." You smile, then shrug. "Spot of trouble, but…"

"Oh?" What's happened? "Are you okay?"

"Of course. I mean, wow. This is just… an amazing coincidence."

"It is." I smile at you. "Um, please," I say. "Step on through." I nod at the gift of a bottle in your hand. "The others are in the garden."

"Great."

You walk through the hallway and out the open door onto the lawn. My smile fades. Amazing, sure. Wonderful and awful in equal measure — that too. The men greet you. Evan stands and claps you on the back. He introduces you to Gerald, and to Andrew, who fills a glass for you and accepts the bottle you've brought.

Back in the kitchen, the gas hisses as I turn the stove back on. The fat begins to melt again. I try to cut the garlic, but my hand is shaking around the hilt of the knife, and when nails dig into my trousers I drop it in the sink and the cat climbs up my leg frantically like it's escaping rising water, reaches the waistband of my trousers and struggles for a hold, nails scratching at my pelvis getting tangled in my pants and I can't breathe, can't draw breath the kitchen disappears into a pinprick I can't hear anything except my hummingbird heartbeat can't move an inch until time slows and adrenaline rushes into my arms so I reach down and pull the cat loose from my belt loops and twist its neck until something snaps and the fucking thing stops wriggling. It's warm in my hands, the body, it would have been, I'm sure, would have been warm for a while and its fur still soft and I could have used it as a mitten and warmed my hands with it but it's not a cat anymore it's a thing. I drop the body in the bin.

Spring

I CHOOSE HONEY FOR the walls. The sticker on the can says "Burnt Sienna," but I don't like the image of a town gone up in flames. Honey then, a bit darker than you'd think, older than it sounds. Two walls in the living room. One, I keep white. The last, a dark blue, the kind you see in museums. I use this for a wall in the bedroom, too.

It takes three days, ridiculously long for a room so small. I open the windows despite the cool wind, breathe in the fresh air. I walk out in my splotched old clothes, sunflower and midnight in my hair, in a smudge on my jaw, buy a sandwich at the corner shop. I use my high-school German and apologize, but the woman at the till smiles and tells me I am doing fine.

"How has your week been?" Stella asks.

"Good." I manage a smile. I've been gazing out the window today, the budding leaves, soft breeze rippling — Berlin in spring is a lot greener than I'd expected — but now I turn back to her. "Yeah, it's been okay."

"Any progress on the flat?"

"I've painted the walls."

"Oh great." She waits for me to elucidate.

"Yellow and blue." I take a sip of tea from the mug she's just given me. She's put a lot of milk into it, but I don't mind really. Four years living in the UK, I've grown used to milk in everything.

"How's work?"

"It's a store." I look down at my lap. "People come in and buy salad bowls and cheese graters and chopping boards."

"Are you always in the kitchen department?"

"'Home Accessories,'" I correct. "That's what they call it. And no. They put me in 'Luggage' sometimes. And 'Books.'"

"You must like that."

"Have you ever had a job like that?" It's the first question I've dared to ask her: the first question about herself, that is. I don't want to be inappropriate, don't want her to tell me to back off, for things to become awkward. I've come to like Stella, have begun to trust her a little, bit by bit as the months pass.

"I've never worked in a department store," she answers. She doesn't seem irritated by my question, so I chance another.

"You've always worked as a psychologist?"

"I only got my degree in my mid-thirties." Stella drinks from her own mug. "So I came quite late to the profession."

"Oh." I hadn't expected this. "Here in Berlin?"

"No, back in London. I got a job here. Set up my own practice some years later."

"It's very impressive."

"Thank you."

Conversation falls flat again. Again, Stella lets it. She always does. I want to ask why she left London for Berlin, what she did before that, but I don't dare. I glance at the photographs on the cabinet. Every surface

The Dinner Party

in the room is entirely clean, except for the photos: there's always a thin layer of dust on them.

"How are your colleagues?" Stella asks.

"They're fine. They gossip like...well, whatever. The men as much as the women," I add before she can ask.

"I wasn't going to suggest otherwise," Stella protests with a small smile.

"They either flirt with you or try to make you feel like shit about yourself. And the manager thinks he's discovered innuendo."

"Does it make you uncomfortable?"

"No." I frown, shift my weight on the seat. Then suppress a smile. "It's amusing, sometimes. They think they're being clever, subtle. All the tough talk, the double-talk. Strutting around like cocks, like minor deities. But when you dare make fun of them, they get this startled look in their eyes." My grin grows. "Just for a second, you can see it. They're vulnerable, really."

Stella smiles. Nods as if to say *fair enough*.

"They ask me if I'm seeing anyone," I go on.

"What do you tell them?"

"That I'm not. But then they ask how long it's been, and I say since last summer, and then they ask why it ended, and I — I can't answer."

"Have you made any friends?"

I shake my head. "They don't like me."

"Why do you think that?"

"I'm quiet and priggish and dried-up."

Stella looks at me in surprise. "Do they call you these things?"

"Not to my face. I can hear them thinking it."

"Or the thoughts you hear might not be theirs, but your own."

"*Or,*" I retort, "my thoughts correspond to theirs, because they're right. We all are."

Stella lets it rest. She doesn't argue. She observes. Watches. I'm so tired, suddenly. I've been coming here since last autumn and I still...I want to go home. Drink a glass of wine and then another, put on Netflix and watch *The Crown*.

I get up, walk toward the window. The trees are still waving. Down below, a man jumps out of a DHL van and enters the building carrying a large flat package. I can just about hear the hum of engines, a motorcycle roaring past.

"Do you think Harry showed up that evening for a reason?" I ask, keeping my back to her.

"What reason are you imagining?"

"Not a reason, precisely. Do you think it was...preordained? Fate?" Can't believe I'm using that word. "It was extraordinarily..."

"Serendipitous?" Stella suggests. "Last year, I sat down at a table in a restaurant in Rome, and at the table next to me were my neighbors, whom I thought were staying in Berlin for the summer."

"I understand what you're getting at, but the chances that Harry — "

" — that Harry, who was friends with Evan at Cambridge, should show up at Evan's best friend's house, not an hour's drive away?"

Right. Coincidence, happy or otherwise. I can feel the handle of the knife in my hand, a ghostly kind of pressure against my palm. The window is locked. The windowsill is clear of dust.

"Do you like yourself?" I ask.

"I've come to accept myself. My weaknesses *and* my strengths."

"I hate everything about me," I say against the glass. "Everything I am and everything I do, and didn't do. When I wake up in the morning, first thing I think of is I've woken up wrong."

"'Wrong' in what way?"

"Too late. Woke up too late, didn't go to bed early enough, didn't do enough, work hard enough, am not happy enough. I'm too sad,

The Dinner Party

considering the life I'm living. My... circumstances do not warrant my feelings. Too awkward, too quiet, too passive, too priggish, too reserved, too educated, undereducated, too smart, not smart enough. Not funny," I finish, finally, "not profound, no character or chutzpah. Bland, beige béarnaise."

The tear tastes salty, as of course it does.

"You're doing well, Franca," Stella breaks through.

I turn to her. "You think I'm getting better?" I scoff in an embarrassingly thick voice.

"You've come a very long way since we first met."

I make a face. It doesn't feel like that.

"You have a job," Stella insists. "A flat. A — "

"Yes yes yes." I wave a hand. All of that doesn't mean a thing.

Stella sits back and crosses her legs. "When you first came here, you barely spoke a word, Franca. Hardly dared to look me in the eye. You'd withdrawn completely."

"And now I've become a little less withdrawn," I finish. "Great progress."

"You're quite strong, Franca."

"That's what Andrew said."

"You don't agree?"

"Andrew was a coward who wanted to feel courageous. I'm the same. A *strong* person," I go on, "wouldn't have done what I did. She'd not have given up searching for a job. She'd have done things. She'd not have drunk herself into a stupor just because a friend left."

"How is the drinking?"

"Oh splendid," I drawl, glad to move on to something that's easier to talk about. "It's going very, very well."

"Is it?" Stella asks with an obliging smile. I huff and sit back down. Wipe my eyes.

"I don't drink in the mornings anymore," I say repentantly. It's not a joke, my drinking, I know that. And Stella has better things to do than to listen to sarcasm and deflection. "Just, a few beers late in the afternoon. The evenings. Sometimes wine."

"That's good."

"Not really."

"You're working on it."

I bite my lip. Wonder if I should say this. But Stella already knows a great deal by now.

"Last night," I begin, "I dreamt that I was seven weeks pregnant."

"Oh?"

"Yeah. And it took me by surprise because I hadn't had sex except for this awkward, two-minute affair with a boy who — well, rather like Andrew..."

"Yes."

"So I wasn't very happy, being pregnant."

"That's understandable."

"But the main reason — and this you'll find interesting," I add, and begin to speak more and more quickly, "being a therapist, and dreams, and it's all very Freudian — the main reason I wasn't pleased was not because I didn't want the baby. I thought to myself, in the dream that is, that it might even be rather nice to have some company, that it would be a kind of gift, and I'd make the most of it. But the main reason I wasn't pleased was that I had a really nice glass of bubbly in my hand and I didn't want to put it down."

I sit there. Outside, the treetops sway, much more wildly now, and clouds roll in.

"So yeah," I conclude. "The drinking's going great."

"I see." Stella leans in. Nothing's changed in her gaze. She doesn't judge me. "How many glasses a week?"

The Dinner Party

"I'm very bad at maths," I say.

Stella allows it. "A day, then."

"A few bottles? Sometimes a bit more."

"Bottles of what?"

"Beer. Or when I'm drinking wine…" I think about it. "A few glasses? Three, sometimes four."

"No strong spirits still?"

"No." I can't stand the stuff. Small blessings.

"And your arms?"

"My arms?" I ask after a beat.

"You're wearing long sleeves."

I turn to her. "That's not — " I swallow, shake my head.

"Aren't you warm?" Stella nods at the window. It's only early spring outside, but the day's been unreasonably hot.

"It looked like rain."

"Would you show me?" She nods at my arms. I lean forward in my seat and double over. Oh Jesus. Hide my face in my hands. Do I make this kind of impression on her, still? After talking to her for more than half a year, do I still look like this?

"Go ahead." I close my eyes and hold out my arms.

"Thank you." The chair Stella sits in creaks, soft footsteps on the carpet. Her hands at my wrists, undoing the buttons. Folding the fabric, baring the skin. Her thumbs rubbing the insides of my wrists, just a moment, then retreat.

"Is this why I'm here?" I ask in a whisper as Stella takes her seat again. "With you, I mean?"

"There is the matter of the knife, yes."

"The knife in the kitchen."

"Yes."

"I don't remember."

"That's another reason," Stella says.
"And the thing with Andrew."
"That too."
I nod. Consider this for a minute. "Best get cracking then."

I open two cans of cannellini beans. The recipe says three, but I doubt they'll fit into the chicken. I pour the beans into the colander and rinse them. They look a little like fat maggots: same shape, same color. Something moves, a twitching, wriggling. The beans begin to crawl: up the side of the strainer, out of the sink, onto the countertop.

But no. I take a deep breath, close and open my eyes again. The beans are only beans after all, shiny but still. I add them to the pan. Stir. Through the window, I see the cat settle down on the patio bench, curling up into a very small ball, perfectly whole. I can't see the men but I hear them, laughing, talking about the canon, some guy called Adam, what a slippery sod he is. The beans warm through. I add the tomatoes to the pan, stir, then eye the mixture for a minute. It's supposed to be finished now, the filling.

"A chef would taste it," you say. I look round. You're in the doorway, staring at me. You know I don't eat meat. The cast of your mouth says you're amused, but your eyes are cold. No, not cold — distant. Reserved. I'm a stranger to you now, as you are to me. It throws me off.

"I never pretended to be a chef," I hedge.

"Andrew said you were stuffing a chicken."

"Indeed."

"So I said to myself," you go on with that same remote grin, "I've got to see this. How *on earth* did a girl like you," you gesture with your glass of bubbly, "with your penchant for quick salads and pot noodles, end up not only in the kitchen, but making something as outrageously high-maintenance as a stuffed roast chicken?"

"Your guess is as good as mine." I turn off the heat, move the pan onto another burner.

"Is it?" You look down at your glass. "I gather they've finished some sort of project."

"They're sending a canon into space."

"Oh." Then, after a beat: "Seriously? Do people still make those?"

"Evidently." Our eyes meet. We're both remembering the years we spent in Utrecht, the classes we'd taken, the lectures, how hard it can be to find a place for the things we'd learned in the real world where people were, indeed, still making canons.

"Your old man asked me to tell you they're ready for the starter."

"Great." I wipe my hands and step past you into the hallway. The door to the cellar sticks. My hands feel strangely tingly as I lift the salad bowl from the shelf, collect myself, and carry it up the steps.

"Here, let me." You take the bowl from me. You're very careful not to touch me. "Through there?" you ask, looking back at the dining room behind you.

"Yes."

"I'll call the others." You're about to step through the sliding doors, but stop. "How's the writing going?"

"What?"

You cock your head. "You were going to write a book. It was the only thing you wanted to do, remember?"

I'd told you about my childhood. I'd told you how much my dad and I read together, our one shared thing, and how after his death the silence came. If the house got too quiet, I went ahead and mentally rewrote a book's ending, changed plots, added characters, had conversations with them in my head. When I left home to study literature, I thought the silence would stay there, but instead, it followed me. A fool's hope: my dad was still dead, and I was still alone, and his loss was going to stay with me forever.

So I kept reading, scribbling. He would have approved of that, I remember thinking. I read everything I could get my hands on, much more than any course required. You teased me about it, how other students would go clubbing but I read everything Edith Wharton had ever written over the course of one semester. You'd only found out because you came over unexpectedly one evening and found me crying over the death of Lily Bart. You burst into laughter when I'd explained she was the protagonist in *The House of Mirth*.

"It's nice to see you again, Harry," I smile at you. Enough now.

"Right." You're taken aback, looking at me like I've just talked to you in Farsi. "You, too." You go outside.

꽃

We met six years before the dinner party. I'm sure you remember it, Harry. It was our first class: an introductory seminar on the basic premises of the comparative literature program. What we could expect to learn from texts, what theories had been put forward by which philosophers, how the English department would teach us how to read. The lecturer had tattered clothes and wild hair and an open fly, and he merely smiled beatifically as a titter rippled through the auditorium. Yes, we all thought, we were first-years and we knew shit but surely we'd already gotten the hang of reading. That was why we were here, after all: three dozen people who preferred the company of the written word to that of other people.

Or perhaps that was just me.

In any case, when the noise died down, the lecturer agreed with us

The Dinner Party

whole-heartedly. "Yes," he said, "everyone in this room can read, and similarly we can all use our own two feet and run a hundred meters, but which of us can do so in under ten seconds?"

There were hundreds of tiny flickering lights in the ceiling of the auditorium, twinkling like stars. At night, it doubled as a cinema, I later found out.

"Reading is," the lecturer went on, "a muscle you need to work on. It won't develop if you don't stretch it, overtax it now and then. Reading a story is one thing, but understanding it is another, and that, incidentally, is the vital difference between the humanities and the other sciences."

We only got talking when the lecture was over. I joined the queue to the exit and you let me shuffle down the stairs before you. You wore a black coat with a wide collar that made your red hair seem even redder, your skin seem translucent. These were the first things I noticed about you. I smiled in thanks and then you began to speak.

"First one down," you said, in English, and nodded at the empty lectern, "only seven hundred or so to go."

"Seven hundred?"

"Six lectures a week, forty weeks a year, three years to get our degree. Think he'll remember his fly at the ceremony?"

"Doubt it," I murmured. "Judging by the state of him."

"Fair point." We both grinned. We'd reached the bottom of the steps and turned left to leave the auditorium. I was twenty-one, a few years older than most of the students there, but not enough to show. You, though, stood out: you were very tall and self-assured in a way that made half our classmates stop and take a second look at you — both the girls and the boys — and I guessed you must be in your early thirties, which I later learned you were, of course.

"Harry," you said, and held out your hand. Your grip was strong but careful.

"Franca," I said in turn and squinted in your direction as we emerged into the bright September morning. I couldn't see you properly: the sun crowned your long wild hair, made it gold in places, bright red in others. Your curls were extravagant.

"Franca? As in lingua — "

"Yeah."

"Do people call you Fran?"

I shook my head. "Doesn't really work in Dutch. It's fine in English, though." People around us began smoking. We stepped out of the way and walked toward the center.

"So, where are you from?" I asked after a moment.

"Cambridge. Well, I was born in Leeds, but I studied, and work — worked — in Cambridge."

"Hell, what are you doing here then? Doing literature in Utrecht?"

"Fancied a change," you laughed. "Well. Needed it, really. Wanted to go somewhere entirely different."

"And is it? Different?"

"Not entirely, no. But a change, for sure. Especially now, when I've only just got here."

"When did you arrive?"

"Friday."

"Wow." It was a Monday then, remember? "I guess every small difference must seem big in the beginning."

"It does." We stopped at a bus stop, which was wedged into an alcove in the side of a small church. Bikes and scooters whizzed past, busses trundled in the opposite direction, and you turned to me. You had blue eyes and the shape of your face, now that I could see it properly, struck me as a little strange. It was angular, a broad jaw and a kind of Grecian forehead, but the overall effect had a fine frailty to it.

The Dinner Party

"It helps that everyone speaks English quite well. Yours is *very* good, though."

"Thanks." I blushed. "You um... you don't have a northern accent." I wasn't sure if I could say this, if it wasn't inappropriate to point out that you spoke like the older BBC newsreaders did.

"Oh no," you agreed readily. "It's carefully cultivated, my accent. If it can even be called that anymore."

"Did you change it for work?"

"Yes." You smiled as if you were surprised I'd guessed as much. "I'm afraid to say I never felt quite brave enough to hang on to it down south. I admire those who do. But yours, again, it's very good."

"Cheers."

"See? You're an expert."

"I feel anything but an expert now," I admitted.

"Oh?"

"It's a bit daunting, isn't it?" I looked away at the café across the street. The windows were fogged up on the inside — behind the haze, shadows sat at tables, drank tea and coffee and hot chocolate. Moisture dripped onto the sills.

"Do you mean the lecture?" you asked, calling me back.

"I only knew a handful of all the writers and philosophers he mentioned. I've never read anything they've written. Half of them, I didn't even know how to spell their names."

"We'll need Google, I guess."

"Like, you know, one of these theorists, Poppa or Poppe?"

"No fucking clue," you agreed, and we both laughed.

We watched as a bus arrived, and a dozen chattering students lined up to get on. Neither of us moved, and the bus drove off, tooting as a cyclist crossed the street with inches to spare.

"Do you cycle here?" you asked, as we watched it all happen. "Christ, it's a death sentence."

"Oh, it's not that bad." I shrugged. The bus had already driven off, the cyclist was nowhere to be seen. "So, what happened that you needed a change as big as this? Sorry," I added, regretting it instantly, "it's a very personal — "

"It's fine," you reassured me. "I worked for this big marketing firm in Cambridge. Been there since I was twenty-one. Called me 'the most talented trainee the firm's seen in a century.'"

"Wow."

"I felt like the token — anyway, makes me cringe a little, still, knowing they called me that. They promoted me very quickly, pay rises and bonuses, a house to pay the mortgage on — everything too much, too quickly. I'm sure you can see where this is going."

"You..." I hesitated, hoping to be more considerate than my initial question had suggested, "...ran into difficulty?"

"That's a beautiful way of putting it." You smiled. "Ten years of this, nothing but work, losing friends right and left, hiding in the loo, all that. I collapsed in the office stairwell, they had to call an ambulance. Carted me away like meat on a rack. Mortifying, really. Haven't been back since."

"And you came here?" I asked, for want of anything else to say that wouldn't hurt you. It impressed me, your honesty, felt so disarming in someone I hadn't known ten minutes ago.

"After a while." You took a deep breath, looked at your shoes.

"Are you okay?"

You looked up. You seemed surprised. Your eyes had filled up.

"I know I've only just met you," I went on quickly, my cheeks feeling like they were about to catch fire. "But if I can do something for you — to help you, I mean..."

The Dinner Party

You looked up, and rubbed your nose with the back of your hand. "Thanks. I'm — I'm fine."

"My dad died when I was twelve," I said, recklessly compelled into honesty myself.

"Oh." You were startled. "I'm so — "

"My mother didn't speak for a year after he died. I let that silence fill me up until there was no room for anything, or anybody else. I haven't had a real friend since primary school."

You stared at me with wide eyes. I shrugged, and with the gesture tried to say we're all damaged in some way.

You smiled. You understood. Another bus stopped in front of us, but we both seemed to silently agree that it was too early to say goodbye. "Want to go for a walk?"

"Sure." I smiled too, felt a rush of pleasure, excitement, a sliver of anxiety. I'd told you the most embarrassing thing about myself, right from the very start, and you weren't repelled...

"If we head to the theater, there's a lovely path that follows the river."

"Wherever you want to go," I said, impressed. I'd been here for a week, and yet I hadn't mustered the courage to go anywhere on my own. You'd arrived from the UK three days ago and already you'd been scouring the city. "Lead the way."

We headed down the busy street lined with small shops, brands I'd never heard of, some I had, a gym for students, tables and chairs skirting the pavement, young people everywhere sipping from huge thermos flasks. There was the theater, old-fashioned, white bricks and tiny rectangular windows, but we turned our backs to it and walked down a narrow trail that led to the very edge of the river. The city rose above us, buildings older than we'd ever be, and surrounding us were only trees, large old oaks that had seen more than we ever would, and the water that flowed quietly through the canal.

"Apart from the overlong roll call, what did you think of the lecture?" you asked when we walked onto the Singel properly. I'd seen this path on the map before, remembered that it circled around at least three-quarters of the city center, but I hadn't known it was this beautiful.

"I loved it," I answered in a rush of enthusiasm, throwing caution to the wind, beaming without consciously deciding to do so. "The amount of stuff I don't know, the books I haven't read yet, but will. I'm about to spend three years reading. Talking about it with people who read more than just cookbooks, management self-help? Best thing that ever happened to me."

"Ha," you grinned, "I believe you. You've lit up like a Christmas tree."

I smiled self-consciously. It was new to me, this: you understanding what excited me, and yet not looking down on me for it. What a thing to experience.

"I just didn't really get what he meant in the last part of his introduction, though," I admitted.

"Which part?"

"The bit where he talked about the difference between the humanities and the other sciences."

"Oh, I was very happy with that part."

"You were? Why?"

"It's why I came here," you explained. "I might be wrong, of course — perhaps I just heard what I wanted to. But I thought he meant that science can give us knowledge and facts, while the humanities give us understanding: understanding of the way human beings respond to events. The meanings we give to our experiences, and how they're affected by our time, and our culture, and our history."

I stopped walking, let a group of joggers pass, and goggled at you: "So how does that relate to why you came here?"

The Dinner Party

You considered it for a moment. "Redemption," you then stated bluntly. "From my sins."

"What sins?"

"I spent the first decade of my adult life thinking up ways to get people to buy what they don't need. Profits, revenue — that's all we cared about. We made a lot of money and we didn't think about any of the rest of it."

"And what's the rest of it?"

"What it means for our humanity that the only means through which we measure our prosperity is the economy. Why citizens' well-being is thought of solely in terms of GDP. What degree of stupidity it takes to try and understand love, or curiosity, or creativity, by taking pictures of the brain."

I grinned, and you saw this. "What?" you asked.

"My mother would be so annoyed by what you just said. No, it's a good thing," I added when I saw the uncertainty on your face, "believe me. She'd say that this is all very well, Franca, but people need to earn a living, too, and if marketing is the way to do it..."

"And what do you think?"

"Oh, the opposite," I declared automatically.

"And if you'd never met your mother? Or, let's say," you waved a hand, "she was an artist, not a dime to her name?"

I pressed my lips together, blushed, swallowed shakily. "Good point," I whispered.

"I'm struggling with the same thing," you admitted, touched my elbow to soften the blow. In your expression there was only kindness and understanding. "What do *I* think, versus what I feel I'm supposed to think."

"Yeah," I chuckled. Before us, the path sloped up again, curved, led back onto the street. "You put your finger on the sore spot, there."

"Takes one to know one," you agreed, and we walked down cobbled streets, past medieval courtyards crowned with trees and statues in weathered sandstone.

I remember thinking then, in the early days when every street had an unknown name and I needed a map to get to a shop in the center, that in Utrecht history peeked out from behind every corner, that the light that shone out through stained-glass windows had a special kind of depth that I hadn't seen anywhere else. Utrecht was a fairy tale. Things seemed possible here in a way they never had before. And you: you'd blithely attested to your fears and failings, had recognized mine in twenty minutes when I hadn't myself after twenty years. You knew who you were, seemed so confident despite the troubles you'd had. I admired you so much for that: I didn't know myself, and felt like a stranger, always.

STARTER

Evan insists I join the four of you at the dinner table. The chicken's not even in the oven yet but Evan says he doesn't care one whit about that. I do. I don't want to sit here, at this table, Andrew acting normal like always.

"Come and eat, Fran," he entreats despite my protests, and pulls back the remaining chair. "You're looking peaky. Are you all right, darling?"

"Fine," I murmur. "It's — nothing. I'm fine."

"You've set the table for four," Evan observes, looking round. "Andrew, mate, get another plate for your girl here, would you?"

"She's not — of course," Andrew stammers. "Sorry." He pushes his chair back and leaves the room. There's something off in the way he walks, and the backs of his ears are red. He's confused too, I think, and I'm relieved to see something that's familiar in him. He'll be rude when he comes back — rude to Harry, probably. He's wary of strangers, even warier of people I know and he doesn't. His wariness is predictable, and while Andrew's execution of it usually isn't elaborate, it does make me relax a little.

"You weren't planning on eating with us?" you ask. It startles me. You're resuming your perusal of tender places: who I was in Utrecht, who I am today. Your presence connects stages in my life that seem so separate from each other they couldn't ever be brought into contact, but of course that's nonsense. They connect in me. I am their point of origin. Your being here reminds me, pulls me back into confusion. Andrew is no longer Andrew, or if he is, I never knew who he was from the start.

"Fran?"

I look up, remember what you'd asked. "The fridge broke down," I say, "and I'm running late on everything."

"Oh, just eat something first," Evan reiterates, and motions toward the chair that Andrew drew out. "Here, sit down."

I do. Andrew comes back with a glass, a plate, and cutlery. "Here you go," he says. Briefly, his eyes meet mine. I'm taken aback by the whorl of feelings and meanings I see in them, everything impossible to untangle. My mouth is dry. I can't think of anything to say. He sits down as well and I watch with sudden dread as he turns to you.

"You and Fran know each other then?" he asks. He's all nonchalance, but I can hear the edge in his voice. Evan glances at me, he can hear it too. I wonder if you can. You don't give anything away.

"That's right." You're polite as anything. "We studied together."

"So did we," Evan grins at you.

"A lifetime ago." You grin back. "When we were young, remember?"

"How could I forget? Darling, your friend here," Evan says to me, pointing at you, "bested me at every stage of my less-than-illustrious academic career."

The Dinner Party

"It wasn't hard. He just never bothered to do more than sod all. Still got a first, though, didn't you?"

Evan raises his glass. I try to picture the two of you together, the unlikeliest pair I could have imagined. You're no-nonsense, at your most extravagant in jeans and a shirt with a tiny, whimsical pattern, while Evan wears slick polo shirts with the collar turned up, trousers in ridiculous colors, bare feet in patent leather moccasins. For Christ's sake, he wears Ray-Bans whenever he's outside, even on rainy days.

"So you went to the Netherlands a few years ago?" Gerald asks you. He's still got his sweater draped over his shoulders, even though it's very warm inside.

"Seven, I think. Or six. I went there after I..." you search for words and smile as you finally settle on "...threw a wobbly." The others laugh.

"What happened?" Andrew asks. He's looking at you like he can't quite figure you out.

"I had a burnout," you tell him. "A few years back. Had to take some time off work, so I went to Utrecht and enrolled in the literature program, where I met Fran here."

"Anyone for a top-up?" Evan asks the room at large, holding a bottle of white.

"Please." I lift my glass and smile at him, grateful for his efforts to steer the conversation away. "Cheers."

"Andrew, mate?"

"No thanks." There are two red patches on Andrew's cheeks, but it isn't from the drink, I think, looking closely. Usually, when Andrew's had too much, the flush is higher on his face, and his eyes sort of flit everywhere, rapid-fire. Now his eyes are fixed on you — and besides, he's hardly had any.

"I know a few people who have had burnouts over the years," Gerald reminisces, turned to you. "Invariably, they suffered from perfectionism, and an inability, or even more often sheer unwillingness to listen to their bodies' signals."

A beat of silence follows this statement. I feel my cheeks flush but you just give Gerald an indulgent smile. You must have heard all this before. Evan wears a look of amused incredulity. When he catches me looking, he winks. *Can you believe this dick, darling?* No. I can't.

"Well." Andrew clears his throat and nods at the salad bowl. "Go ahead, please. Tuck in."

"It looks delicious," Gerald says, and gets up to take hold of the spoon. "Franca, can I get your plate? Ladies first?"

"Guests firsts," I say quietly. "Harry?"

"Sure," you say, and hand your plate to Gerald. We all watch as he carefully selects some salad leaves, mozzarella, tomatoes, and pieces of glistening tuna.

"Enough?"

"For starters, sure." There's nothing to be discovered in your tone of voice. You're cool but amiable, businesslike. A surface that reflects other people. It's not so hard to picture you and Evan at Cambridge now. You were open and warm in Utrecht, but here you're dispassionate and closed-off — friendly, but also unflappable and slick, like Evan. Perhaps this is what you're really like, and our time in Utrecht was a deviation. Andrew's not Andrew. Maybe you're not you either?

"So you were friends," Andrew says to you when everyone's been served. I roll my shoulders back, my spine, hear the cartilage crack, try to stretch off some of the growing tension. I don't want to hear your answer. I don't want the two of you talking, not about this, putting labels on something I do not understand myself.

"Yes, we were friends." You smile.

I struggle to swallow a mouthful of raw tuna. It tastes of earth and

The Dinner Party

creatures alive and growing, and the texture's all wrong: it's slick, covered in slime, too rubbery to chew.

"We liked a lot of the same things," you go on, "so we got along pretty well."

"Did you get your degree?"

"No," you say pleasantly. "I'd done two years, but..." you shrug. "Went back to work."

"Fran didn't either," Andrew points out. "Get her degree."

You turn to me, surprised, and give me the same look you gave me before, like I'm lost in translation. I fake a smile and swallow finally. "I didn't." My voice is heavy with embarrassment.

"Oh well," you shrug, kindly, drawing the others' attention away from my flaming face. "There's worse things. A degree only gets you so far."

"I know I hardly use mine," Evan agrees, and claps me on the shoulder. "I don't know about the rest of you, but I could do with another top-up."

"Yes." I get up gratefully. The back of my shirt is wet with sweat. Everybody looks up, as if startled out of an unpleasant reverie. Foreheads glisten with sweat, all except yours.

"I'm sorry if I — " I hear Andrew begin as I escape into the hallway.

"Oh, not at all."

"It's just, in the four years I've known her, Franca's never once spoken of you."

I stay in the cellar for a few minutes. I can still taste the fish. It must have gone off, I reckon, but everyone else was eating heartily. The box of white is in the corner. I take a bottle and open it, lift it to my mouth and take a sip, another. The ice in the wine cooler has turned to water, the chicken in its plastic wrapper is bobbing just below the surface. I

81

take another, longer drink, then lift the chicken from the water and let it drip.

"This is what it's come to then, is it?" I ask the chicken. "You on a polystyrene plate, arse on display, and me secretly slugging it away in the basement."

I remember frozen hands and feet and the endlessness of the heath. Sneaking into the kitchen afterward, the sound of the TV, Scotch in pink plastic.

"It's how it all began," I say to the chicken, but I know that's too easy.

I leave the basement and walk back into the dining room. "It's not as cool as it should be," I tell Evan apologetically as I hand him the bottle.

"Neither are we," Evan reassures me. "I'm sure it's fine, darling. Harry?"

"Sure, why not? It's the heat," you tell me with a wink.

"Fran, here." Evan pours some into my glass.

"Thanks." I take a sip and head out again. "I'll get the chicken in the oven, be back in a few."

"Okay, darling, but no more than a few," Evan says. "I need to rehearse my speech for tomorrow, and you're the perfect audience. You're the only one who hasn't heard what I'm about to say."

I leave the door to the kitchen open, just a crack. Their voices carry: Evan drawls, Andrew murmurs, Gerald's holding forth, and as for you? In this company of men, you must be listening — I don't hear you speak at all.

※

Dad had left a whole list of instructions. He'd chosen the music, the venue, the undertaker. He left a wife and an only child.

He wanted to be cremated. Mother put the urn on the bedside table. His side of the bed. Though not the bed he'd lain dying in. She

The Dinner Party

put him there, her hands gripping the stone for a moment, then went down into the kitchen. The cupboard, a bottle, cut crystal: two minutes, and the glass was empty. She put the bottle back where she'd found it.

"Are you hungry?" she asked. I shook my head. "Have you eaten?" I shook my head again. "You should eat," she said. "I'm just going to..." She walked past me, back up the stairs, out of sight. I heard the door to the bathroom open, close, the lock turn. She turned the shower on.

I walked to the foot of the stairs, looked up, listened. Apart from the sound of running water, I couldn't hear anything. I glanced back over my shoulder and saw the hospital bed in the center of the living room, sheets cleaned and folded into a neat pile on top of the bare mattress, fully reclined. I put a hand on the small dimple his weight had left, sniffed the pillow, but found no remains of his warmth or his smell. He'd gone, he'd left entirely. He'd never told me what was wrong with him. He'd never said goodbye. He'd always pretended he was fine. He'd lied. He'd never again tell me he loved me, never tell me I was doing fine, that I was all right the way I'd turned out.

I turned away. Sat down at the foot of the stairs and waited.

The sun went down. The whole house turned orange. Outside, in the garden, a cat slinked in and out of sight. Shadows changed. The house slowly turned dark. The water stopped running. Nothing happened for a long, long while. I was cold, had been cold for days. Dad was dead.

Mother reappeared, but not really. She wore black clothes, so I could only see her face, pale and drawn and without expression, nothing like my mother's face at all. I remembered my dad's plastic one, wanted to ask if she was going to die, too, but couldn't. The possibility that she would... I was reeling with the realization that I couldn't count on anything. I followed her back into the kitchen. She turned on the light over the stove. Her eyes were red but the skin around her mouth was very white.

She put a pan on the stove, cracked an egg, another one. She took a spatula from the drawer, then stood staring at the yolk. It hissed and spit.

"I can do it," I whispered. "Mamma."

"I'm going to bed."

"Mamma?"

"I'll see you in the morning. Mind you turn the stove off."

She dissolved into the dark, melted into it. She didn't make any sound as she went back up the stairs.

I turned the eggs. Put them on a plate. I ate them without tasting them. I was afraid to leave the kitchen, where the light was. All around me, the darkness loomed. It was endless. It would consume me. I stayed put.

※

It's been a while since I last wrote, Harry. I see Stella twice a week, and the stuff she's asking me about... It's clouded my head. She makes me work hard, you know, makes me look at things I've hidden from myself, silly playground scrapes, childhood bruises, the year after my father died. But I'm better now. I feel a little clearer. And the writing does help.

The years we spent together in Utrecht felt to me like one long summer. Previous relationships had taught me that people tend to like me in the beginning, but after a while there is something about me that's dissatisfying. I'd never had a friend like you, someone who wanted to see me every day, who didn't tire of me after a week.

We began with coffee, do you remember? That tiny bakery at the end of our walk. We went there after our first few lectures, too. I marveled at you, the way you talked, your accent, your poise. You were grown-up, but there was something vulnerable about you, too, small parts of you that were still unfinished. You were searching for some kind of completion, just like me, little bits and pieces that would make you

The Dinner Party

whole. I didn't know what shape you wanted to take, not at the beginning. I only realized later that you were hoping to go back to your old life all along.

But we began with coffee, and with tea, dollops of honey and a splash of milk for you. When we had a lecture later in the afternoon, we'd go for a drink afterward. One of the pubs lining the canals, or the bar of the tiny cinema opposite the five-star hotel. We progressed to glasses of beer, toasties, nachos to share, red wine to go with our mains. At night, the city was strung with lights reflecting the deep green of the trees and the black of the water and the dark red of the cobblestones, and we took tipsy walks that veered and swayed in indistinguishable patterns and felt the shells crush under our soles as we followed the park's footpaths. We ended up in another bar and drank too much but the headaches never lasted. I was young, slept like the dead, drank strong coffee in the mornings.

When it ended —

"Was that all?" Stella asks when she's read this part. I let her read some parts of this letter, Harry. Others, I keep to myself.

"Sorry," I say after a beat, taken aback. She's never commented on my writing before. She brushes back a lock of long blonde hair that has fallen across her forehead and looks at me expectantly. She's wearing a blue short-sleeve blouse and gray slacks that leave her ankles bare. Her feet are very slim and she's wearing high heels and it all makes her look like she's in her mid-thirties, though I know she's forty-five. "What do you mean, is that all?"

"At the time of the party," Stella begins, flicking through the pages I've printed, "you hadn't seen Harry for four years."

"That's right."

"But in your account of that evening, he takes a central place."

"*He* does?"

"Harry was — and still is, I think — tremendously important to you." Stella crosses her ankles, rubs a thumb over the arm of the chair she's sitting in. She's waiting to see if I contradict her, I think. I don't. My eyes again shift to the framed pictures lined up on the cabinet. Today, I'm drawn to a picture of a couple, him leaning on a cane, she on a walker. They're in some sort of hothouse, I guess: huge glossy leaves crowning their heads, and in the corner a terra-cotta pot sprouting bright yellow flowers.

"But the two of you hadn't been in touch?" Stella continues. "Since Harry left Utrecht, there hadn't been any phone calls or messages?"

"No." I'd never heard from you. And I hadn't reached out either. "Nothing."

My gaze shifts to the smallest picture, the one I can't look away from. The woman facing the sea, her back toward the camera and a huge black instrument case balanced beside her. Who is she?

"Do you play?" I finally dare to ask. Stella turns round to see what I'm looking at.

"That's not me, actually," she says.

"Oh." I feel embarrassed. "The case. It's for a...a bass?"

"A double bass, yes."

"Sorry, I didn't know the word in English."

"No problem." She gives me a benign smile. "She was my wife. We played in a quartet together."

"Oh." I take a moment to digest this, the implications of that past tense. I shouldn't ask anymore, clearly, but Stella doesn't speak, and I can't bear the silence. "What did you play?"

"The cello."

"Professionally?"

"Sort of. Not really. We did weddings, funerals, parties. No concerts or anything like that. But we earned our living."

The Dinner Party

"But you do this now?"

"I still play at home. Now and then we have a gig."

"You and your wife?"

"No, she died."

Fuck. This is why I never should have asked. Hell. I don't know what to say, and the silence is so awkward, so awful, and Stella just sits there in her chair like she's said it's going to rain tomorrow and don't forget to take an umbrella. "I'm so, so sorry."

"She got ill," Stella explains with a shake of her head that says I don't have to apologize. I see the woman on the shore, bare arms and bare legs and blonde hair that waves with the wind. "We were due to play on the quay that afternoon, but we got there a little early, so we waited on the beach. One of those golden moments." She smiles absently as her voice fades. Her gaze returns to mine. "A week later she had her first round of chemotherapy."

"I'm so sorry," I say again. I feel mortified: if I hadn't been so nosy she wouldn't have had to —

"No need, Franca," Stella says quietly, watching me. "I don't mind talking about her. It makes me feel like she's not completely gone."

I force my eyes away from the picture.

"Now, if you'll allow, there was something I wanted to put to you," Stella says. I nod. I'm listening. I'm not thinking about how the people who seem the most collected, the most put-together, have often built their strength on suffering you just can't see. "The way you've written down the story — how you met Harry, the friendship you developed... It's particularly stylized."

"What does that mean?"

"There's a certain detachment to it."

I frown. "I've told you everything so far. What happened at the start. What Andrew did."

"You have, yes."

"It's..." I shake my head. What did Andrew do? What words can I use? "It was — " I shake my head again, unable to see how I can possibly tell her more than I already have. "Just — how can't you know that I can't — "

"I do know, Franca." Stella's calm, and she sees everything, and I deflate like a flat tire. My hair hurts at the roots. "I know."

I look up at her. "You *know*?"

"I had an experience similar to yours," Stella says. "When I was about your age."

I grow hot in the face, and though Stella doesn't show any sign of feeling any shame at all, I feel it for her.

"It upsets you to hear this?" she surmises.

"Yes. How...how did you cope with it?" How can this cool, collected woman who has all the answers, whom I've grown to admire during the past months, how can she have gone through all this and still be who she is?

"It took a while."

"But you didn't — " I waved a hand at myself, my throat, my chest, my arms.

"Everyone is different. Every life is, too. What matters is — "

" — what we make of it," I finish. "Yeah."

"I'm glad you remember."

"Did you meet her after?" I ask, nodding at the picture.

"Yes. She was a bit older, and she knew what I was going through."

I get up — can't help myself — and place a hand on the windowsill, the other on the glass. How can this happen to so many women? And why does no one talk about it? And why am I the only one who has —

"I feel such a failure," I admit. I try to open the window, but it's locked, the handle won't move. "So many women go through so much

The Dinner Party

worse — I mean, look at you," I add, pressing both hands against the glass and looking down at the street. "And then, what I've been through, it was just..." I turn round, lean on the sill, thud the back of my head against the window.

"Yes?"

I force the words out. "Bad sex."

"We both know it was more than that."

"I didn't. I don't," I correct myself. "Did you, at the time?"

"Yes."

I nod. Stella's simple answer feels like a reproach. I feel like such a child. I step away from the window and sit down.

"As I was saying," Stella says after a while, and I force myself to look at her, "there is a distance to what you share, how you share it. Am I correct in saying that Harry was your best friend?"

"In Utrecht, yes."

"One of your only friends, in fact?"

"I did have friends in primary school," I defend myself. "A lot of them, actually."

"You found it easy at that time? Making friends?"

"Yeah," I realize. It's a surprise. I did find it easy when I was a kid. "But after Dad died, I stayed at home all the time. I didn't want to meet up with anyone, so I guess I lost them." I give a little shrug. "Wouldn't have lasted in any case, because we all went to different secondary schools."

"And you didn't make any new friends until you met Harry?"

"No, I made a few, mainly when I was doing English, but nothing that lasted."

"But Harry did?" Stella asks, but she already knows the answer. You didn't last either, not in any real sense. A four-year gap with no communication is generally not the kind of stuff that sustains a friendship. But even though you left, you stayed with me nevertheless...

"Look, I generally don't fit in, all right? Never have. I'm shy and I'm awkward and if I can't think of anything sensible to say I'd rather not say anything — except when I'm well oiled," I add after a moment's thought, "but er..." Let's leave that for another time. "Now if you asked my mother she'd say these are all signs that I've 'failed in my development' in some way. But Harry...My obsession with reading was overwrought and slightly ridiculous, but Harry was pretty 'out there' as well. We spent evenings, nights even, talking about David Wojnarowicz and Hilary Mantel and whether *Cosmopolis* by Don DeLillo was or wasn't aware of its sexism. We had arguments about it. We both thought these things were important, could teach you stuff you couldn't learn anywhere else. Harry was..." I shake my head and smile at Stella. "The *joy* of just being able to fucking *talk* to someone."

"I see." Stella smiles as well. "But you summarize your friendship in a few sentences. You drank coffee together. You drank wine together. You took walks and went to bars. This is more or less the sum of what you've told me, and what you've written. Yet you've spent more than two years together. This letter you're writing, you've addressed it to Harry."

"I won't send it."

"Nevertheless." Stella shakes her head, but smiles. She hands me back the printed pages, my words to you. "Do you understand what I mean?"

"Yeah."

"Now, next time we meet, would you be willing to tell me a little bit more?"

"About Harry?"

"Your time together."

I lick my lips and nod. Something to look forward to. Thinking about you hurts. I miss you. I regret everything.

The Dinner Party

"When I say that there's a certain detachment to your writing, to what you're telling me," Stella goes on, "what I'm getting at is that this also translates into real life. Social interactions. You keep people at a distance. There's nothing wrong with that. It's up to you how much you're willing to share with people you don't know particularly well. But — "

"I was waiting for the 'but,'" I say quietly.

"You keep yourself at a distance as well. Don't allow people to come near, and..." She shrugs and simply concludes: "Nobody comes near."

Stella lets the silence settle. Out the window, the tops of the trees are swaying silver-green. It reminds me of that night in Utrecht, when you were supposed to meet my mother, but she'd cancelled at the last minute. Blue, purplish light, the smell of slightly brackish water drifting through the canals, the smell of perfume wafting from the shops, luring people in, evening just beginning, lights strung up and twinkling in the trees, silver-green leaves, and your arm through mine. You'd put it there. I didn't mind.

"Now, next time," Stella says, brings me back, Stella's office, Berlin, spring edging toward summer, "we'll talk about Harry, if you feel up to it. What he meant to you."

I straighten and look up. "You know, Harry's not — " I stop and shake my head. Never mind. It's not important.

"I realize it's difficult," she adds in response to my expression, "but there's not just pain beneath the surface. There's treasure too. Tell the truth. Dive. And see what you find there."

※

There was the time when we'd been about to go for a drink with my mother, finally a chance to introduce you two, and she'd blown us off at the last minute. I felt such a fool, thinking she'd turn up, and you were there with your bright red hair and your jacket on, keys in hand, closing your front door, and I said I hadn't had any real friends since primary school and my mother knew that, told me every afternoon to make more of an effort with other people, to not spend so much time with my nose in a book, and you smiled and hugged me tight and said you're so bright, most parents would kill for a child like you, I know mine would have.

 Maybe that was why.

※

I turn on the oven. One-eighty degrees Celsius. Put the rack in the middle. I'll need a large pan that'll fit the chicken. We have tons of casserole dishes, most of them orange ones by Le Creuset, but they're too heavy: I prefer the plain porcelain one that's always at the bottom of the pile. It takes a while to get it out, but it's light, and big. The bird should fit.

 The cutting board's white stripes have turned orange from the chorizo. I put the chicken there. It's still in its packaging, plastic pulled taut against its pimpled flesh. The label says it had a "better life." Now its head's cut off, and its feet, its feathers pulled out, insides removed, arse on display, another hole where the neck should have been.

 I use a knife to cut the plastic wrapper around the chicken. The flesh is cool and glassy against my fingertips, surprisingly solid. I cut the string pulling its legs together. It's elastic, tougher than I expected, but it snaps eventually. Some particles fly free with the release of pressure, tiny bits of tissue or moisture or whatever. I lean back, but I guess some must have landed on my face. My stomach squeezes. The legs part a little, sink to rest against the chopping board. A few long strands stick out from the exposed joints, like hair but thicker, like flesh. The skin is dented where the rope cut into it: an "X" across the belly and the legs. A smell issues, one I can't describe, not strong or pungent but there, certainly. A reminder that here is what remains of a living, breathing creature, still subject to decay.

The Dinner Party

Nails dig into my trouser leg, cat climbing up my calf, my knees, paws scribbling pinpricks in my skin traveling through my arteries, nausea rising muscles bunching shivers up my spine nestling between my shoulder blades and the slime between my legs not there but there, still, a warmth on my hip and I pull it off and fling the cat through the kitchen door and out onto the patio, slam the door before it can get back in and watch it launch itself forward, throw itself against the door scrabbling up against the glass, a thud and a thud and a screeching sound I've never heard it make before and I'm about to vomit all over the floor when you come in and ask what is happening, and I breathe in, great gulps like I've been underwater for too long, can breathe again, see again, am again something that feels like myself, that knows I'm being ridiculous, making a spectacle, making you think I'm losing it.

"It's the fucking cat," I gulp. Another thud at the door, a screech. I wipe my forehead with my sleeve. It comes away wet. You're carrying all the dirty plates, the cutlery, staring at me like I've lost my mind. "It won't leave me alone. Crawling up my leg and — and *licking* my *toes*, it's disgusting." Thud. "Listen! Listen to it go on and on and on."

You put the dishes down onto the counter, let your eyes travel through the kitchen. "It's because you cut him off from his food. His water bowl."

"It can get in through the dining room."

"Hey, it's fine." You hold up one hand, reassuringly. "Don't worry. It's all good, see?" You open the door and pick up the cat. Smile. Your entire face transforms as it sometimes did in Utrecht, when you used to smile at me.

"Hey mate." You lift it, close to your face. "How are you doing? You're making a lot of noise, eh?" It pats your nose, gently. Purrs. It's completely calm now. I glare at it. Tonight, after everyone's left, I'll drive it to the woods ten minutes from here. I know a spot. It's dark and can't be reached by car and it takes a few minutes' walk through bracken and thorns to get there, and when I crouch down at the clearing nobody can see me. I'll put the carrier down and ignore the meows and the paws sticking out from between the bars, unlock the hatch without opening it and I'll run, run away. The cat's never gone beyond the garden. It doesn't know its way back, and it can starve for all I —

"You're a good chap, eh? There." You cradle the cat against your chest, but now your gaze rises to mine. "You're a love, aren't you?"

Pressure builds up behind my eyes. I press my lips together and take a shaky breath. The cat's just a cat, isn't it, but whatever the hell's going on in my head obviously isn't "just" anything...

"Are you okay?"

I force a smile. "Sure, why?"

"The scratches." You nod at my arms. I look down.

"Oh, they're from this afternoon. It jumped into the bin. I pulled it out."

"His nails are not that sharp, are they?" You take one of the cat's paws, peer at it. "Oh no, they're quite long." It pulls back its paw, gently. "You should clip them."

"I hate it," I admit, looking at the cat as it snuggles against the crook of your arm. Your smile fades.

"Of course you don't." A moment's silence. "God's sake, why?"

There's shame in my silence, but I can't break it.

"Why in the world did you get him then?" you prompt after a long moment.

"Andrew just came home with it."

"Really?" You raise an eyebrow.

"He told me it'd be good for me."

"Did he?" Your eyebrow goes up another notch.

"To have some company, when he's not around."

The Dinner Party

"Pff."

"And now it follows me around. Like, all the time."

"He's young. They do that when they're young."

"I don't give a shit about it being young. What, does Andrew think it's a practice lap for motherhood? I don't want — "

"You shouldn't be talking about this to me, Fran," you say quietly. There it is again, the awkwardness. For a minute, I'd forgotten everything is different now. We haven't seen each other in four years. I'm a different person, and so are you.

You smooch the cat on the head, then look at me. "You sure you're okay?"

"You know what," I begin, trying to release the tension in my neck, "why don't you get another bottle? I have to get back to this dinner, otherwise..." God knows when we'll be finished.

"Sure." You back off, actually hold your hands up. "Don't sweat it."

"Bottles in the cellar. And please, Harry." You stop in the hallway and turn round. "Close the door?"

"Sure."

"Keep the fucking cat out of the kitchen," I add under my breath as the door closes behind you.

The chicken's dead, a hole where the neck should be.

I check the recipe. "Season the cavity with salt and pepper, then fill with the chorizo stuffing."

I wash my hands. You come back with two bottles of wine and a few beers, which you put on the counter without speaking. You remember then: I prefer beer. You take the wine into the dining room. You're greeted with a cheer. I open a beer and take a slug and add a spoon of the fancy French salt onto a saucer, grind some pepper with the Georg Jensen stainless steel pepper mill, mix it in. I take another slug and spread the legs a little further. They give a strange little "click."

I try to widen the "cavity," and put two fingers in. The flesh is cold, and the bones inside are hard.

"Oh, for fuck's sake."

I pull back, wash my hands again, open the cupboard under the sink and pull on some disposable plastic gloves I'd normally use to clean the house. Then, I put a hand in, spread my fingers and pour the salt and pepper from the saucer into the chicken. I rub it all in, try to do it evenly. There are ridges — ribs — and a knobbly spine. The salt feels like rough grains of sand. I take my hand out and lift the chicken, arse down, to see if any excess salt falls out.

The bean-chorizo mixture's cooled. I briefly consider using a spoon, but it wouldn't work, would it, so I scoop out a handful and push it in, press it firm against the back — or the front, I guess. Extract my hand and do the same again. There's not much room. I press, push as much of the beans in as I can, but when the chicken's filled entirely, half the stuffing remains.

"Place a whole lemon at the cavity opening, tucking any excess skin over it."

I wash the lemon, squeeze it into the chicken's arse. I take the "excess skin" between two fingers and tuck it over the greasy lemon, tuck tuck tuck. There. A yellow turd sticks out.

Why the fuck would people eat this?

I wash the gloves I'm wearing. The bottle of olive oil is slippery. I pour some over the chicken, some paprika, salt, pepper, rub it all into the skin. It turns it brown and shiny. I lift the whole contraption carefully and put it in the casserole dish. Take the gloves off, put them in the bin. Wash my hands. Open the white and pour half the bottle in with the chicken. Add a glass of water, as the recipe says. I drink the rest of the beer, which tastes the way the chicken smells: of salt, oil, and pepper, but most of all of dead flesh. The kitchen tiles swim. I grab the countertop for balance and bend down, down, feel the blood rush back into my head. I feel behind me for a chair and sit. Take a deep breath. Another. I'm fine. I'm breathing. The tiles stop moving, and the worst of the nausea recedes. I wipe my cheeks, my forehead with the back of my hand. Another shaky breath.

The knife lies on the countertop. What did I do with it?

"I love you, you know."

The words are quiet but clear, clear as if Andrew's in the kitchen with me. He'd gone down on one knee and whispered them to me. I can feel his hand round mine again, his gaze fixed on my face. There'd been so many people there, and they'd all watched, and waited for my answer. "I love you, you know. Marry me."

Three months before the dinner party, Andrew drove us into Buckinghamshire for his parents' ruby wedding anniversary. I sat in the passenger seat and stared out the window. It was a cold day, late April, drizzly and gray. I'd received a few more rejections that week, jobs I'd been trying to get interviewed for, but I'd hardly ever made it that far. I was tired of the whole thing, bitter, and ready to give up again. So there I was, in the passenger seat.

Traffic slowed down. "Fuck's sake," Andrew muttered as we slid to a full stop, but there was no rush, really. We'd left early, even had time to pick up some tea to go on the way. I was about to tell him so when, to my left, a young woman in a black Audi pulled up. She was wearing glitzy sunglasses despite the weather, and she was talking on the phone, gesticulating with the hand that wasn't gripping the steering wheel. Every gesture the woman made exuded confidence, a no-nonsense focus. She wore a big watch on a strong wrist and there was a smooth blue ring around her index finger which made her seem able, competent. She was obviously working, talking to a colleague, and I estimated she was younger than me by a good few years. She reminded me of Evan, I realized, even though Evan hates fancy cars and prefers to travel by train, and as I averted my eyes and considered the flowery dress I was wearing, my own legs sticking out from underneath the hem, pudgy, and with thick knees, feet wedged into a pair of strappy heels that seemed to have been designed for people with three toes, what happened next became inevitable. I must have squeezed the paper cup of tea I was holding, or it must have slipped out of my hands because I yelped when burning water sloshed over them and soaked the front of my dress.

"Shit!" Slicing shards of pain shot from my hands all the way up my arms, and I took a shocked breath. "Ow. Fuck."

"Jesus, Fran." Andrew glanced at me as traffic began moving again. "How bad?"

"Fuck." My hands were red, and trembling worse than ever, plucking at the pale blue fabric of my dress. The Earl Grey was manifesting as a spreading brown stain. "It's ruined. Shit."

"I meant your hands, not the dress," Andrew said as the car in front of him sped up, and he did too. "Let me see."

"I'm fine."

"Are those blisters?"

Two welts had appeared in the bright-red skin of my left hand.

"Right." Andrew checked his mirrors and switched lanes. We'd been about to pass a service station, but he just made it onto the exit. The car behind him tooted. "Dickhead," Andrew murmured. "Here." He stopped at the entrance to the toilets. "Go on. I'll park the car and join you. Stick your hands under the tap."

"I'm not — "

"Did you burn your legs as well?" he asked, looking down at the soaked dress. "Shit. Go on, get your hands in the water, Fran."

The Dinner Party

I looked up. I wanted to cry, not with pain, but out of sheer frustration.

"Go on. Please," he prompted. I nodded, shakily undid my seat belt, and slid out of the car. "Tepid water," Andrew called as I was about to close the door. "Not too cold." He sped off when I stepped into the small cubic building.

I couldn't help it. I began sobbing as soon as I saw myself in the mirror, a girl in a woman's dress, tea spilled all over her front, a bloated face and a ridiculous attempt at makeup. I gripped the basin with my smarting hands and let the tears fall, and the door to one of the cubicles behind me opened and I could feel someone staring, but I ignored her, and she left without washing her hands. It might have been the woman in the Audi, disgusted by the spectacle I was making of myself, now squeezing her bottle of Purell, this woman who had a job and who seemed to be good at it, one of the practical people who'd been able to buy her own car. No dead father or boyfriend to buy her everything.

"Fran?" Andrew stood outside, knocking on the door. I turned the tap and stuck my hands underneath. "Can I come in?"

I looked round at the three cubicles, sniffed and tried to get myself back under control. "There's no one here."

Andrew seemed a little wary as he stepped into the ladies', but he forgot his embarrassment when he caught sight of me. I bit my lip and tried desperately not to let new tears fall, but when Andrew saw my distress and took a quick few steps to wrap me in his arms, lopsidedly so as not to remove my hands from the flowing water, I gave up. In a pantomime of adulthood, I bawled, heaves of grief and snorts and snot on Andrew's perfect suit jacket.

"What's this?" Andrew asked quietly against the top of my head. With one hand he rubbed my back, the other was soft against the side of my neck. I made to take a tissue from my pocket but Andrew took hold of my wrists and kept my hands under the tap. He kissed my temple. I rested my head against his shoulders, and smelled his smell — he smelled lovely, Andrew did then — and when I finally began to calm down and my hands were growing cold, we stood there, quietly, the classic pose, man and woman, like that picture of those two people in a crowded subway carriage.

I leaned away from him, looked at the ruin of my dress. I caught sight of Andrew, the lapels of his jacket sodden with tears and mascara and everything I'd painted my face with, all that pretentious gloss, and I started laughing, a chortle turning into great heaving cackles, seeing Andrew standing there in his ruined suit, shirt smeared and myself in similar shape, good god the pair we made, I couldn't stop laughing so hard my abdomen hurt with it and fresh tears trickled down my cheeks, imagine the two of us turning up like that at Andrew's parents', the face his sister Clem would make...

"You look ridiculous," I heaved, laughing laughing laughing so hard and Andrew joining in, a few good-natured chuckles from him, "I mean, look at you — look at me," I added, though I'm not sure if Andrew could understand anything I was trying to say at this point, he kept saying my name and I couldn't stop laughing, letting out all the stress of the past few months, *years* probably going by how long this was taking, "your suit."

"Never mind about the bloody suit. How are your hands?" I began to shake my head, but Andrew took my hand and lifted it. Three blisters were straining up against the skin of the hand he was inspecting. "Does it hurt?"

"Not so bad," I sniffed, and wiped my eyes with a paper towel. "We should go. We'll be late."

"What's going on?" Andrew interrupted quietly. "I know you just

The Dinner Party

spent ten minutes laughing your arse off, but you're not happy, Fran. What's wrong?"

"I can't get a job, Andrew." I shivered with a leftover giggle that I failed to suppress. My voice caught. "I've never had a job before. I never got my degree. I'm twenty-six and I — "

"Just give it some time, Franca. Just because you haven't yet, doesn't mean you'll never find — "

"But I'm not fucking good at anything," I cried, and the hilarity dissolved as quickly as it had set on. "I can't do anything like you can."

"You can write, darling. I know you haven't for a while, but — "

"I'm a dead end, and I — "

"Look," Andrew said and kissed my forehead again, both hands cupping my jaw, "you've chosen to study a subject that makes it difficult, this part. And for better or worse, I chose one that made it easier. Let me help you. I don't mind," he insisted, and gave me a smile, a small, kind one. "Really. Take your time to figure it out."

I returned his smile, watered-down. "My dress is ruined."

"Don't worry about it. I brought another dress for you."

"What? Where?"

"Suitcase, in the back. I've packed fresh clothes for both of us."

"Why?"

"I booked a room at this hotel. Just an hour's drive from my parents' place. Big garden and a good restaurant, five stars on — " Andrew flushed and shrugged. "It was meant to be a surprise. Never mind," he added, when I felt my face crumple at the realization that I'd managed to ruin something else. "It's all good, Fran. It's fine. We'll change our clothes here and be fashionably late, who cares. It's not a problem. Here, come here." He pulled me into his arms again. I hugged him, gripped his jacket with my smarting hands. "Talk to me, Franca, love. What can I do to help?"

"I just..." I pressed my face against his chest and breathed in, deeply. I didn't know. I didn't know anything about myself, who I was, what I wanted. I knew nothing about life.

"Shall we talk about it in the car, then?" Andrew proposed when I didn't, couldn't answer. "Would that work?"

"It would." I kissed him, through his shirt. "Thanks."

"I'll get our clothes, okay?" He squeezed my arms and let go. "But I'll just change in the men's."

"That might be best," I chuckled.

"Just a minute then."

I waited. I couldn't face the mirror any longer so I turned round and leaned against the washbasin. The floor and part of the walls were lined with small square tiles in a murky mint green. Dirt collected in the corners, under the basin, a milky substance caked to the tiles beneath the soap dispenser. The lamp, screwed into the ceiling, buzzed and flickered now and then. The smell was, well, exactly as you'd expect.

"Fran?" Andrew knocked again.

"Yeah."

"Here," he said, and hung a black polyester suit bag on the door of one of the cubicles.

"Which one is it?" I murmured, eyeing the bag. I owned only a few dresses: a necessary evil for the parties Andrew's parents threw.

"It's a new one."

"What?"

"I bought you a new dress," Andrew admitted. "Again, it was meant to be a surprise. Sorry, I thought you might like it, but if you don't..."

"No, it's — thank you. I'm sure it's lovely."

"Well." Andrew smoothed his hair. "Let's hope it fits."

"Is that your suit?" I asked, nodding at the bag still in his hand.

"Yeah. I'll just..." He made to step out the door, and stopped. "I love you, Franca."

It was the truth, and I smiled, and said I loved him, and that was true too. The door shucked closed behind him. The dress shimmered as I extracted it from the bag, a long and silky green swathe of fabric with a V-neck, high in the back. There was something a little disconcerting about how perfectly it fit me, Andrew's apparently very precise knowledge of the shape and size of my body, but mostly I was flattered. The hem touched the top of my shoes and complemented them, made me feel very slim and taller than I was. I dabbed at my face with a wet towel until I no longer looked so bloated, took the pins from my hair and brushed it with my fingers. I put the pins back in. There. I sniffed, and wiped my nose.

The door opened and a woman came in. She wore tight studded jeans and a top that displayed her décolleté. Her hair was piled high on her head, very shiny and secured with a couple of glittery clips. She was yelling into her phone in the kind of accent that a foreigner like me had trouble understanding: lots of swallowed vowels and the ends of words missing, swear words that I'd never heard before. She glanced at me, dismissed me, and slammed the door to the right cubicle. She never once stopped shouting.

I took a deep breath and dared a look in the mirror. I didn't look so bad. The dress made me seem a little older than I was, and my skin was smooth and clear, and if I wasn't the smartest or most successful person on the planet, I wasn't the most moronic underachiever either.

I know the logic of that conclusion is questionable. Everything I've written, and no doubt what I'll write after. It doesn't make me look good either — good as in a good person. I wasn't. I was arrogant and looked down on other people. But this is how I was thinking, or rather, what

I felt. I was a feeling creature then: what I felt was sacrosanct, and I allowed it to lead me. Should have had a knock on the head, probably, or someone to tell me to get on with it, put your feelings aside for a minute. Grow up. I'm an adult woman. Should have told myself that, but I didn't. If what you've read makes you think I'm foolish, then yes: I was every bit as foolish as that.

"You look beautiful," Andrew said when I emerged from the loo, and he gave me a crinkly smile. I kissed him, one hand on his lapel, the other on the swell of his bum.

"So do you," I admitted. "Thank you."

We didn't talk in the car. Andrew tried, but I was tired, and fine, now, I was fine, fine, I was doing all right again. I was comparing myself to the rest of the world, and believed I came out of that comparison favorably enough. I held Andrew's hand for the rest of the journey, nervous about his family, all together, and me trying not to make a fool of myself, but also excited to become part of that group again.

"What are you thinking about?" Andrew asked as he cruised through country lanes, and I said "my father" but what I was really thinking about was how you need a sense of belonging not just from the place you live, but also from the people you're living with.

We're going out. My mother's eyes, clouded. The way she'd walked past me, constantly walked out on me. *We're going out.*

I hadn't just lost my father when he died. I'd lost everything else, too, that childish thing you believe in as a kid that there are certain things you can count on, certainties that won't diminish with time, or crumble with the stupid mistakes you make. The idea that I was good enough. Deserved to be heard, seen.

The driveway to Andrew's parents' house was lined with gravel and flanked by old oak trees. The tires crunched, reminded me of holidays

The Dinner Party

in rural France. As to the house at the end of the driveway: Imagine the kind of English country manor you see in period dramas. The kind of place which, before I first met his parents, I hadn't realized still existed as homes that people really lived in. I'd been there dozens of times by that point, but it still disoriented me. The Dutch version of grandeur is not quite as ornate as the English one. It wasn't about how fancy the cars were (not all that fancy, really) or how expensive the clothes (some of the women that day wore beautiful outfits, but most of the men sported old-fashioned, slightly scruffy shirts and jackets) — it was about manner. Language, too.

The door opened before we could even ring the bell. "Andrew, you're late." Andrew's sister, a tall and teeteringly thin woman, drew him in for a kiss on both cheeks.

"Traffic jam," Andrew lied. "Clem. How are — "

"Well then, why didn't you leave early?"

"I was tired. It's been busy at — "

"Yes, yes, busy, tired. Franca, darling, how are you?" She kissed me as well, spotted my dress under my open coat. "Gorgeous outfit. You look lovely."

"Thanks," I flushed. "How are you?"

"Oh, fine. Come in. Daddy's about to make a speech, and Mummy's mingling has already put her on a straight course toward the liquor cabinet."

We handed our coats to the girl in a black-and-white uniform standing before half a dozen clothes racks.

"Where's your present?" Clem asked, watching the proceedings.

"We gave it to them last week. The actual date." Andrew straightens his cuffs. "Week for two in — "

"So you'd better step on through." Clem was already halfway down the marble hall, high heels clacking, wearing an ankle-length dress with a high neckline. Her shiny blonde hair had been twirled and twisted into an elaborate, beautiful construction at the back of her head. "Food's in the sitting room, speech will be in the library. String quartet's setting up, they were supposed to have started their first concerto or whatever fifteen minutes ago, but they, like you, also don't check for traffic updates. And Uncle David's here, he's already asked for you, so you'd better see him first. You know how he gets." Clem opened a door and held it open. "You want a drink, hunt down the staff. They're going round with champagne."

"Will do, Clemency," Andrew said. Her eyes narrowed.

"Step on through."

"Thank you." I smiled up at her and followed Andrew into the room. It was crowded. The guests were of all ages, shapes, and sizes, the men in suits and the women in dresses, and there was a buzz of conversation, groups of three and four, champagne glasses, canapés on silver trays. Nobody had noticed our entrance yet. This was good. I could have a few moments to get used to it, feel daunted by the crowd, and then the exhilaration would set in. It did so already, as always. The warmth of so many people standing close together, the buzz of voices and the fuzz of champagne and the feeling that this was something I was lucky to be included in, and how many people weren't here, and I was, and how fortunate I'd been, meeting and loving Andrew, who had a family.

I followed Andrew, catching snippets of conversation, drawn-out vowels, sharp T's, everyone speaking English in a way I'd never be able to.

"Okay?" Andrew asked me quietly, putting his hand on the small of my back. "Champagne?"

"Sure." I took the glass gratefully, took a big sip, stepped a little bit closer to him. Andrew watched me.

"You sure you're well?" he asked.

"Yeah." I bit my lip. "Sorry about before. I'm just nervous."

"Why?" Andrew sounded surprised.

"Your family's big and...posh and kind of...you know. They pronounce 'issue' with two S's instead of an H."

"Andrew!" a voice boomed. A big, portly man in a black suit was smiling broadly and wrapped his arms round Andrew, clapping him on the back.

"Uncle David."

"How are you, my man? Still making millions?"

"Oh, just a few."

"A few? Whatever's the matter? Spending all your time with this lovely girl by your side?"

"Franca, this is my Uncle David. He's my mother's younger brother."

Through heavy horn-rimmed glasses, a pair of dark eyes met mine.

"Splendid to meet you," Uncle David boomed. His hand was very fleshy, but soft and dry too. Reminded me of my grandmother's.

"Likewise."

"You're the last to meet her, Uncle David," Andrew remarked.

"Oh, you've met the rest of the family?"

"Just once or twice," I said, "most of them. We visit Andrew's parents more often."

"So you know everyone's names?"

I blushed.

"Oh, not to worry." David grinned and looked round the room. "I've been coming to these shindigs for sixty-three years and I still don't know half the people here by name. It is a large..." and here he paused for effect, "extended family, and it must be hard to be a newcomer."

"Andrew!" Clem called from the other side of the room. Andrew squeezed my waist before letting go, and made his way toward her. His hair had been cut the day before, exposing the back of his neck beautifully. There was some tension in his posture, across his shoulder blades, but his stride was long and confident.

"So?" I looked up and found David looking at me questioningly. "Is it? Hard to be a newcomer?"

"I don't know." I sipped from my glass. "In smaller groups, it's not so difficult. Parties like these..."

"Yes?" David prompted when I didn't finish. I emptied my glass.

"The British have this wonderful expression," I said. "I'm sure I won't get it exactly right — "

"Oh, never mind."

" — but I feel as awkward as a pig at Parliament."

David's laugh boomed through the room. "Exactly right, dear girl." Several people looked round, and I flushed a deeper red. "Sorry, sorry," he chuckled, noticing my discomfort, "apologies. Can I get you another?"

"Yes. Please." He took my glass from me and I waited, at the edge of the crowd, and watched them all milling about. Whenever someone passed close by, a whiff of perfume followed them. Pearls shone, diamonds glittered. In a side room, the string quartet began to play. A nocturne by Borodin, the one they'd used in the film of *The House of Mirth*.

"It doesn't show, you know." David held out a glass of white. I took it. "Your...self-consciousness."

"Oh, you're *very* kind," I scoffed, rolling my r's and attempting to sound as old-fashioned as I could.

"It's true." David smiled. He *was* kind, I realized as I looked up at him. "You seem quite at ease. And you've a quick tongue. A sharp intelligence. I can see why Andrew likes you. And you him, of course."

"I met him before he sold his company," I felt obliged to point out, stung, as always, by the familiar inference.

The Dinner Party

"Oh, that's not what I meant at all," David protested. "No, no. Andrew's a dreamer. We've always said so. His parents, his sister, too. From a very young age, Andrew wanted to believe in things. Father Christmas, at first, and storybooks, things like that. But when he was older, he wanted to believe in something bigger."

"Bigger?"

"The universe. Stars. Planets. Galaxies." Uncle David pronounced these things like they were admirable but implausible fantasies. "Couldn't speak of anything else for years. Wanted to be an astronaut at an age when he should have grown out of it. Oh, I tease him, and he's a good boy," he admitted readily when he saw my face, "but what I'm getting at is that he wanted something to believe *in*." He looked at me meaningfully. I nodded to show I understood. "And you, with your literature degree, choosing to pursue your studies in a field like that, while the arts, the humanities, have been squeezed tighter and tighter for years and years, misunderstood and undervalued..."

"I'm not a torchbearer," I said.

"Well, no, I'm not saying you are at all. But when you made the decision to read books for three years, you knew there was a slimmer chance of easily finding employment afterward than had you chosen to study, say, marketing or international business."

"My father died a wealthy man. And my mother's — I could afford to make that choice."

"But you *did* make it. You believed it was important to read books, that it was a skill you wanted to hone, that every writer, past and present, could teach you something valuable."

"Suppose," I said uncomfortably. I tasted the wine he'd given me. It was light and fruity.

"Well, Andrew dreamt of becoming the new...oh what's his name, the new Stephen Hawking. But when the time came to make his choice..." Uncle David shook his head. "He didn't quite dare, you see."

"He chose computer science," I pointed out, feeling defensive on Andrew's behalf.

"A fine choice, yes, by all accounts, but what he wanted, what he dreamed of, was to have done what you did. He admires you, Franca. Your courage."

I frowned at him. David smiled affably. "If you'll forgive me," he went on, "Andrew went to Harrow. His parents own three homes in central London alone, and outside it — "

"I know his family's much richer than mine."

"What I'm trying to say is Andrew needn't have felt constrained by his...career prospects. His parents were prepared to give him time. He would have found his way eventually. But he — "

"Sorry to keep interrupting you," I said, "but Andrew's parents were the ones who touted his career prospects. They told him he needed to earn his own bread."

"Did Andrew tell you this?" Uncle David frowned.

"Yes."

"Oh." David nodded, and I had the feeling he wasn't exactly surprised, but still hadn't expected this. He tried to hide it, though. "Well, he must have remembered it differently. It was a very long time ago."

"It was."

He smiled. "Water under the bridge. Ancient history."

"Mm."

We both looked at the other guests, chatting animatedly. Outside, rain dribbled against the windows, blurring the view of the grounds. A knife was tapped against the side of a glass, repeatedly. The chatter died down.

The Dinner Party

"Dear family, dear friends," the voice of Andrew's father boomed out from another room, "if you'd all join me in the library. I'd like to say just a few words."

"Well then." David smiled at me, but it was awkward now between us, and we moved forward silently. Andrew found me in the doorway and squeezed in next to me, his hand around mine.

"You all right?" Andrew whispered, studying me. "You look — " but he cut off as his father began his speech. I don't remember what he said. I didn't really listen, and what he said wasn't as interesting as what happened next. We all raised our glasses and drank to the happy couple — Andrew's parents really did seem happy with each other, as far as I could tell, and not just at these big parties — but before anyone had even begun to file out of the library and the string quartet could resume, Andrew sank to one knee in front of me and took my blistered hand in both of his.

He didn't make much noise, nor make a fuss, but somehow everyone in the room turned toward us and their gazes fixed on the ring he took out of his pocket. He whispered his proposal to me. I heard the words through a throbbing in my ears. The diamond glittered in the light from the chandeliers. Everyone was looking at me, and at Andrew, and the ring, and they clapped when we kissed, and cheered, and Andrew hugged me and turned toward the room at large as they raised their glasses, and he raised his hand in thanks, beaming.

Summer

I MOP THE FLOOR. I buy a can of oil and try to apply it evenly. Rub it out afterwards. The result is slightly splotchy, but the wood's got a richness to it now, a deep shiny color. It creaks a little when I step on it, like in old country houses. There are gouges in the wood, scratches, marks of the people who lived here before me. The building's old, there must have been many. They might have had a wife or husband, or, like me, they might have lived here on their own.

The smell of the place is one I created, though. Polish and paint and lavender multi-purpose cleaner. A hint of bleach. My deodorant. The tea I brought in, sip from as I sit on the floor and look out the open window at the treetops hiding behind their leaves, warm raindrops dripping quietly.

There was the night with the blue purplish light and your arm through mine when my mother had blown us off but we'd gone to the restaurant regardless. She sounds like a peach, you said, your mother, and I said she's a prince among men, but don't judge her too harshly, grief changes people, and you retorted she never visits you, and I said I never visit her, which was true, and rooted through my bag for the pack of cigarettes. You're a much better person than me, you said, giving everyone a chance, and I said she's my mother, and you said yes, and you deserve much more from her. I'd found the pack by then, lit up, and you asked what I was doing, you don't smoke, gaped at me, a little circle of dots buffering in and out of focus. Whenever my mother calls I only smoke the one, don't worry, I said as I inhaled, and you said please don't let her get into your head like this, she's getting into my lungs, I argued, not my head, I lived with her until I was twenty-one, and you said then she should know what a wonderful woman you are, please see that, even if she doesn't? I know it hurts a lot because she's your mum and she made you, you continued, but that doesn't mean she holds the truth of you, too. I'd lowered the cigarette and, after a moment, began to grin, let the grin grow bigger and bigger and bigger, such a little thing to think of and yet nobody I knew had ever thought of it, least of all me. You know, I'd smiled, and perhaps I'd fought the urge to cry, I think I just needed that pointed out to me.

Maybe that was why.

※

"Why did you say no?" Stella asks today. "To Harry?" she clarifies. I've just told her a little about how it began to end between you and me.

"You'll laugh at me," I say.

"I doubt it." She presses a button on the remote control. The air con whirrs on. "Why don't you take the plunge?"

"I want you to like me." The blood rushes to my head. "And you won't, when I've finished."

"I doubt that, too. Go on."

"If you'd asked me at the time, I wouldn't have been able to put it into words." Cool air wafts over the top of my head. It's a relief. I pluck at my shirt, pull it away from my sweaty skin. "They were just feelings then, suspicions, a...a tugging in the back of my mind."

"And now?"

I let go of my shirt, lean back against the chair, still clammy. "I'm a coward."

Stella frowns. "How did you come to that conclusion?"

"I thought about my future a lot, after Dad. Not immediately, a few years after, I mean. The kind of life he lived, the kind of life I'd want, what kind of relationship he'd had with my mother, what kind of relationship I'd — the person I'd have wanted to have a..." I pull a face, rub my eyes.

"Yes?"

"I thought that getting a boyfriend, a partner, was, like, one of the most important prerequisites to being an adult. Being in a long-term relationship, the first sign that I'd grown up."

"And right now you don't believe — "

"Of course not. Fuck's sake. And when I came to Utrecht and did my first courses, read the books, wrote the papers, listened to the lecturers, and generally just absorbed other ways of seeing the world, I was already beginning to question my presumptions, but..."

"But?"

"Well. 'Beginning.'"

"What did your future look like, in your imagination?"

"A very specific kind of man." I look away, can't look Stella in the eye any longer. To admit to my greatest imbecilities...I force myself to go on, to speak, to say these things out loud. "He'd have worn shirts in light colors, rolled-up sleeves, crisp collars." My voice sours, tilts, turns snide, sarcastic. "He'd have been tall, and thin, fine hands, broad shoulders, fucking hell," I say again. Snort at myself, and my left hand grips my right wrist, and my thumbnail presses against the skin there.

"Do you remember the three-step strategy we practiced when you first came to me?" Stella asks. She's looking at my thumb, resting against the old scars.

"Yes." My thumb presses in harder. It begins to hurt a little. I try not to find this comforting.

"I'd like you to close your eyes and go through them."

I do as she says. It's hard, but it works. It works almost every time. A hand on mine. Stella's. I slowly release my wrist.

Harry, why did I turn you down?

"Harry was the opposite," I whisper as I open my eyes. "In every way I could think of. I deserved it."

"Deserved what?"

"I deserved what happened. With Andrew, and all... all of this. A fool deserves to be confronted with her foolishness. A coward with her cowardice."

"What form does that confrontation take, in your experience?" From the tone of her voice, I know that Stella disagrees with my conclusions. She's decided to pursue, though, not argue.

"Loneliness," I say without a moment's thought. "Or, no. I mean, to be alone."

"Is it a punishment?" Stella frowns.

"No." I'm sure of this. "It's a blessing."

"Why is that?"

"It's the only way out. You can't know which way to go if you don't know where you are, if you don't know yourself."

"I see." Stella considers me. "Can you tell me a little bit more? About why you and Harry began to drift apart?"

Sure. I nod. I'll tell her more. I'm used to it by now.

The Dinner Party

"I don't know any of these," I remarked, lying on your couch, skimming through the pile of books on your coffee table.

"You don't?" you asked from the open kitchen at the far end of your living room.

"I don't," I admitted quietly, taking the next book from the pile to stare at its cover, and on the back the author photograph. First and last names I couldn't pronounce. I read the blurb, rifled through the pages, ended up at the author's portrait again.

"She's very pretty, isn't she?"

"Who?"

I held up the book.

"Oh yes. Of course." You turned back to your pots and pans. You were making spaghetti, tomatoes, zucchini, onions and garlic and lots of creamy cheese. It smelled delicious. I took a sip of my tea and settled back against the armrest, comfortably ensconced on your couch that smelled of old polished leather, a fire in the grate and the stereo humming in the background, fifties' crooning. I'd spent a lot of time there, on that couch of yours, hanging out after classes. You'd invited me into your home straight after we first met, said I was welcome to pop by as often as I liked.

I remember it well, your home. It was that of a grown-up, a regal townhouse with antique floors and beams and high ceilings and an even higher rent. Your furniture was grown-up, too, a sofa and a chaise longue and two leather armchairs before the fireplace. In my student's room I didn't have a couch because it wouldn't fit, and the shared kitchen looked like it hadn't been cleaned in the past quarter-century. Everything in your house was clean, neat, but the rooms never so tidy as to lack personality. You'd collected plenty of little doodahs, art, received gifts and postcards, plants, bought so many different books, and everything offered a satisfying little glimpse into who you were.

"Is she any good?" I asked, still considering the woman's gorgeous face. She wore black teardrop earrings that fit perfectly with the shape of her face.

"Well, I never had her before," you scoffed. I rolled my eyes, and you smiled. "Yes. She's fantastic. All her books are."

"All of them?" I frowned. "She can't be more than twenty-five. How many has she written?"

"Three."

"Hell." I dropped the book on my lap, her perfect face staring up at me.

"Don't look so discouraged," you said as you put two steaming plates onto the coffee table and handed me a set of cutlery. "If you wanted, you could write one book a year and you'd be in her shoes by the time you're twenty-five."

"Only with a face like hers," I grumbled as you lifted my feet off the yellow velvet cushions and sat down next to me.

"You're kidding, aren't you?" you said with a raised eyebrow.

"Point taken." I held a hand up. "Apologies."

We put the plates on our laps. On the stereo, Doris Day sang about stars shining bright above her lover.

"Do you want to, though?" you asked after a minute.

"What?"

"Be a writer? You've talked about it, I know, but..."

"What?" I asked again, feeling the heat rise to my cheeks.

"I can't work out if it's something you *really* want, or if it's what you *want* to want."

"What does that mean?" I attempted to scoff, though I knew what you were getting at.

"I was the first in my family to go to university." You swirled the spaghetti around your fork. "I wanted to make it count, make it worth

The Dinner Party

their effort, and the only way I thought I could do that was by getting terrific grades, getting a high-level corporate job, great pay." You chewed and shook your head. "I thought I wanted to be the next, best new thing in marketing, but really I just wanted to please my parents."

My father, beside the water, book in his hand. A smile on his face.

"No, I do." I frowned, wishing his smile away. "I want to write. It's probably the only thing I could become good at."

"Great," you agreed easily. "If it's what you want, go for it."

We ate the rest of our food in silence, listened to Julie London lilting about what spring is like on Jupiter and Mars. I'd been chewing the whole thing over, the fire smoldered, you got up and put your empty plate on the coffee table, threw another log into the grate.

"I mean, I won't write for a while, though," I confessed.

"Why not?" You turned toward me.

"If I start now, I won't have anything to say. Doubt I'm smart enough yet."

"Of course you are," you said.

"Who'd want to read anything I have to say?" I scoffed, feeling snappish suddenly and taking both our plates to the kitchen to avoid saying anything I didn't mean. But you followed me, leaned against the fridge and watched.

"I would." The earnestness in your voice was unmistakable, and it compelled me to glance at you as I filled the sink with water, soap. "I'd love to hear what you have to say."

I stared at you and found that same frankness everywhere in your expression, your stance, the way your hand was open around your wine glass as if to ask why anyone would ever think otherwise.

"I mean," you went on as I started scrubbing plates, mugs, the pans you'd used, "it wouldn't have to be a book. Hell, even if you became some right-wing hack on TV, I'd listen to you."

"Really?" I rolled my eyes, couldn't help but grin back. "Very unlikely, I'd say. Although," I offered as I put the pan on the rack to dry, then turned the kettle on, "my mother would love that."

"What, is she a right-wing —"

"No, no. She's just always thought I was an idiot." I filled our mugs and carried them to the fireplace, set them down beside the two armchairs and settled in. It was a cool evening, we were halfway through our second year in Utrecht, and I felt like we understood each other perfectly, like you'd been my friend since primary school. "Just never been clever enough for my mother."

"And your father?"

"No, he..." I cleared my throat, swallowed noisily. "*He* wanted to hear what I had to say," I said, and to my mortification felt a tear escape.

"He sounds like a wonderful dad."

I shook my head, felt more tears escape and scrambled to my feet. "Sorry, I'll just..." I rushed to open the double doors and stumbled onto the balcony. The air smelled of dead leaves and warm rain cooling and the wind turning it into a fine spray that clung to my eyelashes.

I'd felt a bud growing inside my chest ever since you'd said you'd want to hear what I had to say. A strange little bud fluttering to spread its leaves against everything I thought I knew about myself. The bud burst into flowers now, and the leaves were strong and glossy and curled until they filled my entire chest.

"Sorry," I repeated over my shoulder when I felt you join me on the balcony, "I just need a moment."

"No worries." You put a glass of wine on the edge of the railing and squeezed my elbow. "Have as many moments as you like." I turned and gave you a watery smile. You smiled back. "Here." You put a box of tissues next to the wine, gave my elbow another squeeze and left me there.

The Dinner Party

I watched the city hide under a shroud of mist and rain, the bell tower close by but barely visible, eighteenth-century townhouses casting gold through open windows, shining eaves and below, heels clicking on cobblestones, bikes rattling past, students sozzled already.

"Better?" you asked when I stepped back in. You were sitting on the couch, legs folded up beneath you, leafing through the biblical tome we had to get through for our course on literary theory. Your house smelled of vanilla pods and vaguely like the cognac you drank sometimes, late at night, right before bed.

"Yeah." I swallowed. "Sorry. Just..." I looked round the room, the large palms you misted every other day, the Van Gogh print on the wall, the lucky cat on the mantel that didn't fit in at all. "Ghosts from the past."

The phrase didn't do it justice. You'd given me something I couldn't name yet, but which felt momentous, a kind of strength I'd have to hold on to for the rest of my life.

"What other ghosts are there?" you agreed, smiling. You were kind: you pretended not to see my confusion, my turmoil, the way my insides were rearranging and flowers bursting everywhere. I sat down next to you and drank my wine and tried to slow my heart down. "You can do anything you want, you know."

"You're really lovely, Harry." I smiled. "Lovely to say that, but let's be honest. I read a lot, and try to catch up, and I listen in class when people make clever arguments, or say things in a beautiful way, and I try to figure out how they do it so I can try, too, next time, but my grades are average." I felt awkward, saying all this. I'd been trying to compete with you, if only a little, follow your lead — but you got straight A's for every paper you turned in, graduated from Cambridge, for pity's sake. "I'm really not clever or astute or observant enough to become a proper writer, you know."

"Oh, I'm not talking about you writing." You frowned. "You could be a plumber, or an accountant or a forester, whatever. No, I meant you can do something you *want*. Not what you're supposed to want. Or what you think...other people might want you to do. I did that for years and it's easy to lose your way, eventually." You hesitated, took my hand and pressed it for a moment. "Ghosts aren't here anymore."

You began to read the excerpt of Gloria Anzaldúa's *Borderlands* we'd been assigned for our next lecture: "A Tolerance for Ambiguity." I opened my bag and took out a book of my own. I was already halfway through, though I'd only got it yesterday. *Victorian Suicide: Mad Crimes and Sad Histories*. A whole new world — I'd felt like that so many times since starting school in Utrecht.

I didn't read a word. I watched you underline sentences with a thick black pen. You didn't bother with pencils. You trusted what you thought was important: you wouldn't need to erase anything. I watched you, and watched you, and you noticed, but you let me.

"What?" you asked at length without looking up. "What is it?"

"Thank you."

Now you did look up. "For what?"

"Earlier." I flushed, and shrugged. "It means...it means the world to me."

You smiled. Went back to reading. I did the same, heart thrumming warmth through my entire body.

"Do you have someone?" you asked after about half an hour.

Now you were watching me.

"A boyfriend?" you clarified. "Girlfriend?"

"You've known me for a year and a half," I pointed out. "If I had a boyfriend, you'd have known by now. *Or* a girlfriend."

"Oh, I know. Just — well. We've never talked about it, have we?"

The Dinner Party

We hadn't. I'd been waiting for this for a while. "Do *you* have someone?" I asked. "Waiting for you at home or something?"

"No, no, no." You shook your head. "My last relationship broke down a while ago. I was working all the time and she'd had enough." You shrugged. "Quite right, of course."

"I'm sorry."

"I wasn't, at the time. Goes to show you."

"Show me what?"

"What a shit I am." You smiled. "How about you? Any exes we should watch out for?"

"A few flings. Nothing long-lasting."

"How many?"

"Just the one, before, and then a few here."

"Here as in Utrecht?" You frowned.

"Yeah."

"A few?"

"Yeah," I said again. "Why?"

"I never noticed." You looked so surprised, I began to wonder whether I should start feeling offended.

"It was mostly just overnight," I said, and shrugged.

"Just men?"

"Yeah." I felt a little embarrassed now. "Just men."

"Where did you meet them?"

"Cafés." I shrugged again. "Clubs."

"How does that work then?"

"It's not like I made a plan or something beforehand. I just went and had a drink on my own. That's how you meet people, isn't it?"

"I see." You settled back against the couch's armrest. "I feel so old now."

Viola van de Sandt

"You're not. Men are just...easy that way. Young men especially."

"Whew." You whistled and gave me a leery grin. "Look at you. Who knew, eh?"

"Don't embarrass me," I pleaded.

"No, sorry," you said in your normal voice, still grinning. "Well, I'm rubbish at it."

"At what?"

"The casual thing — just sex and nothing else. Too old for it."

"No you're not."

"I am," you maintained. "I'm of an age where I don't just want a good time. I want a good life."

"So...no relationship, no sex?" I concluded.

"More or less," you admitted.

"How did you meet — what was her name, your old flame?"

"Chris. Friend of a friend of a friend. Old-fashioned way." You paused. "When was the last time that you...hooked up with someone?"

"Six, seven months ago?" I estimated. "End of our first year." It had been hot, that summer, so hot I hadn't been sleeping.

"Was this when I went back home?"

"Yes." You'd been visiting your family. You'd had a family to visit, people who wanted to see you. I'd stayed behind and written papers and when the papers were finished I'd spent three days in my room, drinking and drinking and when the bottles were empty and the headache hit and the walls were about to swallow me I went to a pub just so that I could feel noticed, seen.

"It wasn't good?" you asked quietly. "You look so sad, suddenly."

I shook my head. "It wasn't good. Not really," I admitted. "It did help, a little. Just for the day. But afterward, I..." I'd felt lonelier than ever, and I'd promised myself I'd never do it again.

"Fran?"

The Dinner Party

I looked up. You'd leaned in very closely without me noticing, and now you kissed me.

Just the once.

Closed lips. Not a statement, or a declaration of intent. Just a question.

There was a tiny spot in the iris of your left eye. I'd never noticed it before. You were so close now, it was obvious, as was the question you were asking.

Yes?

The echo of my father's voice inside my head, a tendril of a memory I'd forgotten until then. *Don't be childish, Franca.*

I froze. I'd never thought about kissing you before. You were beautiful, my best friend — I'd never even considered you might want more. You were older, more sophisticated, more mature. Did you want me to kiss you back? Me? Sex, and then, presumably, from what you'd just told me, a relationship? To be your girlfriend, partner, whatever? To sleep in your bed and cross the street holding your hand and to introduce you to my mother? To spend my life with you, and everything that would entail?

You exhaled, your breath warm against my cheek. Not a second had passed. I couldn't wrap my head around the idea of you wanting me like this.

You'd been watching me carefully, and now your face crumpled. "You're saying no, aren't you?"

"I — " I looked down at my lap, leaned away a little bit. You drew back immediately. "I'm sorry — " I began.

"No, no. I shouldn't have — sorry, I'm an idiot."

"Of course you're not. It's about me," I said, but didn't know if I meant it. Didn't know why I drew back, didn't kiss you in return. All I knew then was that it was too far removed from anything I'd been expecting, been envisioning my life to be. Beyond that, I understood nothing. Only how much this was hurting you, and that I'd ruptured something.

"I *am* a lot older, I guess," you said at length in a calm, reasonable voice.

"No." I frowned.

"Ten years."

"That's not what it's about."

"Then what is it about?" you sighed. "And don't start with 'It's not you, it's me.'"

"I'm sorry," I repeated quietly.

"It's fine." You'd caught sight of my expression. You'd retreated already. You looked me in the eye but some familiar part of you was missing. *"I'm* sorry. I shouldn't have — "

"I like you."

"Well," you huffed, but in your annoyance you became familiar again, "I shouldn't think that was an impediment."

"No, I really, really like you." I blushed, and felt ridiculous, a child. "More than anyone."

"But?" you prompted.

"I don't know. I'm..." Christ, what to say? I'm a girl, I'm a child, I haven't figured anything out, I have all these expectations? "What I said before, my last...whatever. It wasn't good."

"Of course."

"I just want to be more careful," I said, and knew that I was lying. I didn't want to be careful at all.

"I understand." You pressed your lips together, nodded to yourself. You withdrew even further, sat straight on your end of the couch. Patti Page was dancing with her darling to the Tennessee Waltz.

"I should go, shouldn't I?" I asked after a moment.

The Dinner Party

"Probably," you agreed with a painful smile. I got up and began to gather my things. Your eyes were on me the entire time. I avoided meeting your gaze.

"I'll see you tomorrow?"

"Nine-thirty," you agreed as I slung my backpack over my shoulder. At the front door, I turned to you, and hesitated. "I really am sorry."

"Don't be. Really."

"I'll see you tomorrow."

"Sure." You opened the door for me. "Don't worry. I'll see you in class."

"Great." I paused. You stood in the doorway, holding the door, watching me. It felt too much like goodbye, this. What had just happened? Had I made a massive mistake?

"I — " I began, but you shook your head.

"Look," you said. "Don't worry. It's — " You stopped short. It wasn't fine. You weren't going to lie. You rubbed your forehead, the crown of your hair. You looked me in the eye. "You were the first person, ever, who's never judged me. When I told you how I'd lost my job, you never..." You sighed and tried again. "You never rolled your eyes. Not once. You never insinuated I should just, I don't know, man up. You never once made me feel like you looked down on me, or — " You held your hand up, high as your throat, horizontally. "I've never felt ashamed of what happened, you know that."

"Of course."

"And you never tried to make me." Your eyes were still on mine, hardly blinking, and your face was red but deadly serious. "I am," you continued slowly, "*so* grateful to you for that. It's meant more to me than you'll ever know, so just. Don't worry." You gave me a small unhappy smile. "We're fine. I was so alone, and I... I owe my life to you."

I was hot all over, about to cry. I nodded, tried to smile. "Okay."

"So good night."

"Good night," I repeated.

I crossed the courtyard and heard you lock the door behind me.

We were good at pretending it hadn't happened. Acting casual, being exactly as we'd always been, it took up so much of our mental space, we had no room left to feel awkward in. I mulled over my part constantly, still do, trying to see if I'd made a mistake. I don't know if you were doing the same, and for a while, in the beginning, I thought it was all fine. But within six months you had left Utrecht, and I thought I'd never see you again.

※

I open another bottle of beer. Take a swig. Try to focus on the fucking chicken. Move over Harry, here I come: the disillusioned housewife and the burnt-out young professional, two clichés on a couch.

Never mind. The recipe. "Roast for one hour in the preheated oven."

"Fran, darling, get out of the bloody kitchen and come join me outside for a fag," Evan drawls. He has a glass in one hand, an unlit cigarette in the other.

"Give me a minute." I open the oven door and put the chicken in. I wash my hands again, for good measure, dry them on the dishtowel, take the beer and follow Evan out the kitchen door onto the patio. We sit down on the bench. Evan lights up, offers the cigarette to me. I take a drag, then a swig. Evan exhales loudly as he lights one for himself. He looks tired, the skin beneath his eyes paper-thin and crinkly.

"Long day?" I ask. The sky has turned an older, faded blue, and the sun's touching the treetops. Day's finally beginning to end.

"No worse than usual." He blows the smoke out of his nostrils and turns to look at me. "Why?"

The Dinner Party

"You seem sad."

Evan pauses, fag halfway to his lips. "I do?"

"I know you've been joking all evening, all cool and, and *suave*, as usual."

"Evening's barely even begun, darling."

"But your heart's not in it. Something you said..." I shake my head, trail off. "What's wrong?"

Evan watches me closely for a moment, then says: "I could ask you the same."

"Why?"

"Because Andrew hasn't looked you in the eye all evening and you're hiding in the kitchen, ostensibly to stuff a bloody chicken."

I take a drag from my cigarette, and another. The stub burns my fingertips, but I don't drop it.

"Fran?"

"I don't like it," I admit at length. "How rude Andrew's being to Harry."

"Oh. Well." He squeezes my hand, then lets go, lights up again. "Man gets jealous. Could be worse. My mum used to complain that when other men flirted with her at the club, Dad wouldn't even notice."

"You know, every time I see you, I just get more curious about your childhood."

"Father was absent, Mother was distracted." Evan shrugs. "Very familiar state of affairs to a great many people, I should think."

I open my mouth, close it again. "It is, actually."

Evan studies me. "So, you and Harry...?"

"No, no. Nothing like that."

"Really?"

"No. We were good friends."

"Then why are you so on edge?"

"Oh fuck, I don't know. It's just — strange. It was a long time ago, I feel like a different person now."

"Different how?" Evan asks.

"Um, let's see. I've no degree. I'm twenty-seven years old, have never had a job, and I don't even have a fucking hobby. I drink too much — "

"Name me someone who doesn't, darling."

" — and instead of doing something meaningful with the luxuries I have, I can barely get out of bed in the mornings and spend the rest of the day watching fucking Netflix."

"I thought you spent all your time reading and writing?" Evan sounds genuinely surprised.

"Not for a long time." Not since I left Utrecht.

"Andrew says you still do."

"Well he's never here, is he?" I ask irritably.

"It's a childhood dream of his, Fran, this project. A bloke he went to school with was on the team building the spacecraft."

"I remember." Andrew had jumped on the opportunity. Couldn't shut up about it.

"So why don't you write anymore?"

"Don't know."

"Come on."

"I barely ever wrote things down, to be honest, even before Andrew."

"Andrew's put you off?"

"No, no. He just... he asked me to come to London with him, so I had to pack up everything, and then we moved here and I..." I trail off. It's not at all convincing, not even to me. "Fuck, I don't know. I thought I'd find a job, do something real, but when I didn't, whenever I did write something I felt like I was wasting time. Now that it's been a few years, the idea of getting back into it is terrifying. Even less credible than it seemed before. Besides, these days I've the attention span of a toddler."

The Dinner Party

"That'll be the Netflix."

"D'you have another fag?"

"Sure, darling."

We sit there, puffing, for a few minutes. The light's gone mellow, sun dropping, everything easier on the eyes. It's very, very warm still, but at least the burning oppressiveness has gone out of the evening. I remember the ferns, white with frost, even though it's been more than a dozen years. Beside me, Evan's sadness is a tangible thing.

"Is it something to do with Rosalie?" I ask carefully.

"How'd you guess?" Evan sniffs, confirms my suspicions. He wipes his forehead with his hand, wipes his hand on his trousers.

"How is she?"

"Buggered off."

"What?" I turn to him. "When?"

"Last week. Three years — " he waves a hand, wriggles his fingers to mimic something scattering in the wind.

"Shit." I put a hand on his shoulder, shirt wet with sweat. "I'm so sorry."

"Hmm."

"I liked her."

"She was...earnest," Evan says. "Sincere. Not a good match for me."

"Oh, come on. You're lovely."

"Thank you darling, but you said it yourself. I *act* all cool and suave."

"That's not a bad thing."

"But I coat all my working-class insecurities in upper-middle-class arrogance and pretend it's inherited, then top it off with a fine veneer of self-depreciation and irony and pretend I don't mean any of it. 'It's impossible to know me,' apparently."

"Well, she's wrong. Just because her eyes are up her — "

"Darling."

"And you know better than to do that upper-lower-middle-working-class thing with me. I don't understand any of it."

"Ah yes, your Dutch sense of equality."

"The Dutch have no such thing," I protest. "We just don't have the vocabulary."

"Well, she has a point." Evan stares at me, dares me to contradict him. "You know I was bullied, as a kid." I didn't know this, but Evan isn't asking. "I wasn't always the tall, rugged, *manly man* I am today."

I laugh, and he goes on: "Way I behave, it's become a kind of habit, maybe."

"Has it?"

"Difference is, you saw that immediately when Andrew first introduced us," Evan continues, and I remember, and know it's true. "Rosalie only found out last week."

We both take a drag from our cigarettes. Light spills through the open double doors to the dining room. Gerald's delivering a lecture: he goes on and on, a steady drone. A buzz like a dentist's drill, soft but burring in the background and impossible to filter out. I need to focus to make out the words.

" — you cannot read a page in Plato without being a better man for it."

"I don't know about you, Gerald," your voice rings out clear from the dining room, "but for me, trying to become a better man has always proved a fool's errand."

"Naturally," Gerald proclaims, "but you can't deny that engaging with some of the world's best literature improves your — "

"Fuck me, that man talks." Evan drops the butt of his cigarette, steps on it with his heel.

"I thought he was a literature professor?" I ask doubtfully. The way Gerald's been talking, the patently stupid things he says...

"Did Andrew tell you that?"

"Yeah."

"Well, he's not. Not really."

"Who is he then?"

"You don't know Gerald Wiltern?"

"I don't, obviously," I sigh. "So?"

"He's like... He's like Dr. Phil."

"What?"

"Surely you have heard of him?"

"Who, Dr. Phil?"

"Well, I'm sure the good man got a degree somewhere, four decades ago, but now he's more of a TV personality. Gerald's the one they interview when the Nobel Prize in Literature is awarded, or when... well..." Evan struggles to think of another example.

"I get it."

"Gerald's the kind of TV personality who speaks in sound bites, one-liners, sentences taken directly from books — "

" — but only the books he cares about," I finish. "So why didn't you get a proper professor?"

"Andrew invited him."

"Andrew did?" I stare at Evan. "Really?"

"The man's on TV. Andrew thought it would get the project some extra attention. And it has."

"Oh." I try to let it sink in. "I see."

"It's an issue?" Evan frowns.

"It wouldn't be if he hadn't told me the exact opposite. Said he insisted on getting a real professor, 'someone with credentials and experience,' but you wouldn't hear of it. Insisted on 'the dinosaur,' as he calls him."

"Oh did he? Ha." I'd expected Evan to be irritated by what I'd told him, but I can hear only amusement in his voice. "He's just trying to impress you. He's always telling me 'Fran's the real deal, you know, she knows what she's talking about.' He'd be embarrassed if you knew."

"For the love of..." I shake my head. "I'm a dropout, and he's acting like I've got two PhDs."

"He thinks the world of you, Fran," Evan says, and pauses. "Again, I'd say, count your blessings."

Unexpectedly, my eyes fill.

"Kindness, darling." Evan's watching me. "What with degrees and money and careers, it's horribly underrated, but you've got it in abundance."

"That's not a —"

"You noticed."

"What?"

"And you asked. No one else did." He squeezes my hand. "Seems a small thing, but it isn't."

He wraps his arms around me. He does this, once in a while. It's unexpected every time. Behind Evan's flamboyant facade, there's a surprising warmth. I hug him back. I don't cry.

"Come inside, Franca," Evan says as he draws back. "I know we're a crummy lot, but we're company. Better than being alone, at least."

"Is it?" Perhaps, if I'd been alone, hadn't met Andrew, stayed in my room, stayed miserable, I would have done something. Been someone. But right now, I feel exactly as I did just after you left, so alone it's crushing me.

"After the week I've had, I can say, unequivocally, yes." Evan gets up and holds out a hand. "Company is better." He smiles at me, finally a smile that touches his eyes, but it's a sad smile, too. "Besides, it isn't an

The Dinner Party

occasion until there's a speech, and I suspect I've had just about enough to drink for a rehearsal."

※

There was the first time you smiled at me, and the last, and all the smiles you gave me in between. There was the first time you spoke to me, all our chats, everything you told me about yourself, all the things I told you. There was the trust, mutual, to which all this attested. There was the way you allowed me to be shy, awkward, introverted, hesitant. There was every time you wanted to see me. There was your kindness, pure *and* simple.

Maybe that was why.

※

I didn't go to school the day after. The day after my mother had come home with the urn, cracked the eggs, melted into the black. I could have. I'd been going to school on my own for years, my parents both too busy to take me.

But that day, I waited. I waited for my mother to get up, emerge from her bedroom. She didn't until noon, and then she looked like she hadn't slept at all. I hadn't either. I'd spent the night in the kitchen. When she came downstairs, she looked at me, but absently.

"You should take a shower," she said. She opened the kitchen cabinet, took out the bottle, the glass, filled it, drank slowly. I took a shower. Put on the clean clothes I had left, a T-shirt and a long sleeve shirt over that. Dad would've said I wasn't dressed nearly warm enough, would have told me to wear a sweater, but he did neither. The water hadn't warmed me. I was cold down to the marrow.

"We're going out," my mother said when I came down. Her eyes were red again. I suspected she might have downed another glass or two while I was upstairs. Her breath when she walked past me confirmed it. She put her coat on, so I did the same. My dad's coats still hung on the rack, and they still smelled of him. She went into the bedroom and came back with the urn cradled against her chest. She put Dad in the back, twisted the seatbelt round him, sat behind the wheel. I hesitated, then sat down in the passenger seat. I didn't want to sit next to him, but as my mother drove, faster than she should have, I kept looking round to check if the urn had fallen over, cracked and spilled Dad all over the backseat. He ought to be kept safe; I ought to have kept him safe.

When I realized where we were going, I remember feeling relieved. My dad's favorite trail...this was where we might, maybe, feel close to him. After more than a week's absence, Dad would be with us again, his warmth and his approval and his love for me, and my mother would come back to herself. Things would get better from now on.

The car stalled as Mother parked. She forgot to put the handbrake on, so I did this as she got out. She'd parked across two spaces, but it didn't matter. There was no one else around. It was very cold, after all, and the forecast said it might start snowing early evening.

We followed the trail. Mother led the way, the urn again cradled against her. Our breaths made clouds. Mother walked too fast, but she didn't notice, didn't look back, and I had to jog to keep up. The trail led through the heath and into the forest, where the ferns were white with frost, sloped up and down again and twisted toward a kind of dell where flowers grew in spring. Now, it was bare brown earth and the gnarled roots of trees bubbled up and tree trunks led up to bare branches. We stopped in the center, and the ground rose steeply all around us, and the dell seemed like the bottom of a hole. There was a large rock that Dad and I used to sit on, he on this side and me on the other. This was where we used to read to one another.

The Dinner Party

"Sit down," Mother said, her back to me.

I didn't want to. I looked at the rock and never wanted to take another look at it, wanted to forget this rock this place this love for this man had ever existed.

"Go on, we'll be here for a while."

I sat down. The stone was damp. Dad's warmth was missing at my back, but when the wind turned I thought I could smell him, just a whiff of old coffee against wet leaves. Mother stood gazing at the treetops, still cradling the ashes. The roots of her hair were peppery gray, the rest was still red but dry like straw.

For a long time, Mother turned round on the spot, still looking up, I thought, but after a while I saw that her eyes had closed, and that there were tears rolling down her cheeks. I walked over to her and put my hand on her sleeve, but she didn't respond.

I sat back down. Put my hands in my coat pockets, drew my knees up to my chest. It was too cold to be sitting still for this long. I tried to imagine my dad behind me, putting his arm around my shoulder, kissing the top of my head, letting me steal some of his warmth. I didn't remember if he'd ever done something like that.

The light was fading fast. My mother moved, finally, looking down at the urn in her arms, held it in one hand and opened it with the other.

"Mamma?"

The wind picked up, and she lifted the urn, and in the dusk thin trickles of him blew away into the blue-gray air.

"Mamma."

She was throwing away the very last we had of him. I hurried to her side, perhaps with the intention of stopping her, but he'd gone already. The wind was strong.

She should have waited. I wasn't ready yet. He'd been her husband, but he was my father too. I was on the verge of telling her this, but then my mother sank to her knees and from the very core of her produced a kind of animal wail I'd only ever heard on TV. There was no room for my loss, my grief, my memories of my dad in the midst of grief that manifested like this. I shrank back, watched with a hammering heart as she bent over and let the urn drop, put both hands into the frozen leaves, and the skin on her knuckles seemed to split with her mourning, the earth itself crack under the huddle of a winter coat and a bleeding body that had been my mother and now was some...some *thing* else entirely. I began to cry too, but silently, and put my hands over my ears, squeezed my eyes shut and turned away, scurried up the slope, away, away. I stumbled, reached out to steady myself, and was surrounded by the most impenetrable darkness I'd ever experienced in my young life. I thought I'd gone blind, the world had become a bath of Indian ink in which I'd been submerged entirely. I couldn't breathe. I couldn't hear my mother, couldn't hear the wind, the rustle of the forest. I thought I'd died and this is where Dad went.

 The panic made me slip and I slid down, my clothes catching on tree trunks, and when I hit the bottom of the dell with shaking hands I reached out for the rock I'd sat on before. I was trembling with relief when I felt the smooth stone and pressed myself against it, and after a while I could see my mother, merely a few meters away, and although she was no longer making those animal sounds I could hear that she was breathing fast, and when she moved the leaves beneath her rustled, and the forest was full of sounds and echoes and dark but muted colors, a whole range of grays and browns.

 I didn't dare move after that. Didn't speak, and my mother didn't either. I listened to her breathing, which eventually became calmer until I could barely hear it at all, and kept my eyes on that silvery strip of hair that stood out in the darkness. I was terrified my mother would

The Dinner Party

leave this place without me, not look back as she hadn't for a week now, and simply disappear like Dad had. I waited.

It was the longest night of my life. I dissolved that night, lost every sense of time, of self, of love and belonging, only knew that it was dark, and so cold that I could barely feel it after a while. I tried to think about something other than my mother or my dad, about school, the classes I'd missed that day, what I'd say if anybody asked me what my first year in secondary school was like. It didn't help. I tried to think up endings for the stories in my head, but the cold made me forget, unable to concentrate. Mother sat in the center of the dell, still breathing, not speaking. My father became a dread thing then, not a loss or a lost love but a specter that had robbed me of something valuable and left me alone, my mamma gone, in its absence.

Mother stood up. She looked around, seemed to search for something. I realized it might be me and I stood up shakily. My legs hurt, and my back. My eyes were dry. I'd been afraid to take my eyes off her, had been afraid to even blink.

Mother began to walk, back the way we came. I kept on her heels, my dry eyes never straying from her back. My nose ran, and I couldn't feel my feet, which made the walking difficult. The forest had become silent again, and so had the heath, and I began to think I was stuck in a nightmare that would never end.

But then the car was there, and Mother unlocked it, and it hurt to open the door with my frozen hands. The heat that blasted from the vents was painful, made me shake worse than ever, and the car smelled of my dad still, and his sunglasses lay on top of the dashboard, and when we got home I went straight upstairs and curled up under the duvet.

I was ill for days. Mother took care of me, brought broth and plain rice and took my temperature to confirm the obvious, but didn't speak. I burned and burned and burned until I was a pile of clanking bones, no better than my father, and in my mind my mother burned with me.

I stayed in my bedroom for six days. On the seventh, I chanced a trip down the stairs and into the kitchen. Mother looked up from where she sat on the sofa, watching TV with the sound on too loud. Her eyes traveled over me and drifted back to the screen. Again, she held a glass of cut crystal, filled with about a centimeter of amber liquid.

It seemed to help. I remember thinking that, as I climbed onto the countertop as quietly as I could and opened the cabinet. Took a pink plastic beaker and poured two centimeters of the stuff into it. Put the bottle back, tiptoed to bed on socked feet.

By rights, I should have been sick all night. Two fingers of Scotch for a twelve-year-old who'd never drunk before? But I sipped it, very slowly, as my mother was wont to do when I was looking, and the jagged edges leveled and the warmth spread from my throat through to my toes.

"So it started with the Scotch," Stella concludes. She sounds rather more light-hearted than I would have expected.

"It's the only thing we had in the house. I hated it. Still do. Couldn't stand the taste, the smell even."

"I'm going to go out on a limb," Stella says with a small smile, "and posit it wasn't the *taste* of the Scotch that attracted you to it as a child."

"Fair point."

"How often did you drink?"

"Every day, I think. A glass when I came home from school. Sometimes in the evenings, too."

"And for how long?"

The Dinner Party

"A year. I stopped when Paul came along."

"How did your mother come to meet him?"

"He's a bereavement counselor. I think my mother's bosses made her go see him." I consider this for a moment. "She can't have been very good at her job that year. If she behaved the same at work as she did at home."

"Your mother truly didn't speak for a year?"

"Well, no, she did say some things. Like, she told me to get dressed, get ready for school, go to bed, eat up. That kind of thing." *Mind you turn the stove off.*

"I see."

"She wasn't neglectful or anything."

"But other than that, there were long periods of time — hours, I would imagine — when your mother was uncommunicative?"

"Yes."

"Did she ever talk about the death of your father?"

"No."

"Did she notice you were drinking alcohol?"

"If she did, she never said anything."

"You don't think she did?"

"That was half the thrill of it. I put it into teacups. Mugs. I spiked the hot chocolate. I drank it right under her nose."

"This excited you?"

"It was thrilling. Addiction's delicious when it's new."

"Were you addicted?"

"No." I don't think so. "I'm sure, if I'd gone on drinking... But I stopped immediately after Paul came, no problem."

"Yes, you mentioned this. How did this happen?"

"She'd invited him to come for dinner. I was sitting at the kitchen table with my homework and a glass of 'orange juice'. The bell rang. My mother went to get it and suddenly she was talking again." I shake my head. "I could hear her, in the hallway, *chattering*."

"How did you feel about that, at the time?"

"Oh, this isn't a modern interpretation of *Hamlet* or whatever, if that's what you're thinking of. Forget jealous, I was..." I rub my tired eyes. "By that point, she could have brought fucking Rambo home, I'd have been happy for the commotion. Anything to end that silence. That year."

"I see."

"So he came into the kitchen and introduced himself. Shook my hand. Sat down next to me and just... Chit-chat in that kitchen, in that house." I smile at the memory. "I must have gaped at him for minutes on end. And my mother, making conversation. I mean... *what the fuck*," I mouth.

Stella waits patiently.

"I don't think it took him more than half an hour to realize there was booze in my orange juice."

"Did he say something to you?"

"No, no. That only came later. It was his first time home, you know, and he wasn't my dad. I think he must have smelled it, though, or seen something in my eyes, my behavior. I was on my second glass by that time. He kept looking at it."

"How did you — "

" — feel about that? I felt... there. I was there. He asked me questions, about school and my hobbies and stupid stuff like that. I answered. He listened. He smiled. He looked at me."

"He was her counselor, you said?"

"Yeah. Bit inappropriate, that. But these things happen." I shrug. "And Paul is like the most principled, moral man I've ever met."

"That's a lovely thing to say."

The Dinner Party

"It's true."

"So you welcomed his presence in your mother's life, in yours?"

"As I said, I'd have been happy with any sap, as long as he'd make some noise. But Paul is... the best man she could have chosen."

※

There was that evening in the café when you'd gone to the loo and this guy sat down next to me, looked at my tits and put his hand between my legs, grabbed my neck as I made to get up and get away, and I began to shout at him to draw the attention of the other patrons and he shouted back that I just needed a proper shafting to set me right again, which is when you emerged from the loo and decked him, a schmuck just about twice your size, one punch to the side of his head, rejected the mores you'd been born with and made me think I could do the same.

Maybe that was why.

※

There's much about that evening's dinner party that I think I'll remember to my dying day, but Evan's speech? The one he made after we ate the salad, when everyone was already beginning to get sloshed — do you remember that speech? Jesus, that was something else.

When Evan and I step back into the dining room, the cat is on your lap, purring loudly as you stroke its spine, the sound like a stomach grumbling, limbs all relaxed, head lolling, and under your hands it turns over and exposes its belly, the white fluff there, which you brush obligingly. Gerald's droning on about something or other, and you're listening, one corner of your mouth slightly pulled down, one eyebrow curved ever so slightly upward. Your whole expression screams "Everything you're saying is so misguided, I can't even," but Gerald doesn't notice, and continues explaining things in an amicable fashion. Andrew's distracted, he glances at me as I pass him. I finger the collar of my blouse, pull at the hem to straighten it. I sit.

"Now then," Evan says loudly, "if you've all had enough of a ding-dong — "

"No ding-donging happening here," you say. "Gerald's been telling me why the expansion of the canon would mean its destruction."

"Oh, we've heard all that before. Gerald, old man, stop your mansplaining — "

"I'm not doing anything of the — "

" — and listen for a few minutes. Got your glass full? No. Harry — "

"It's empty," you say.

"Sweetheart, that's just — " Evan grabs the bottle, holds it up to the light. "Fran, where's — "

"In the cellar."

Evan strides into the hallway. The cat meows as you rub its belly, paws playfully at your fingers, which makes you coo at it. I scratch the skin on the inside of my wrist. I want another cigarette. Andrew's looking out the window. I look at him. He must feel my gaze because he begins to turn, but I quickly look away.

Evan returns with three new bottles, twists the cap off one of them and pours. "There we go." He takes a big sip and smacks his lips. "So. Harry, if you don't already know — "

"You're to give a speech tomorrow and as there will be a large audience of people whom you've never met before, and whose interests and principles, you suspect, are very different from yours, you want to rehearse and hear our comments."

"That's the gist of it," Evan agrees. "Fuck me, I hate these things."

"Dinners?"

"Speeches." Evan looks strangely vulnerable for a moment: the sincerity of his statement has stripped away much of his glossiness. His

The Dinner Party

recovery, though, is as quick as the onset. He moves to the opposite end of the table and clears his throat.

"Well then. Good evening to you all." He sends an ironic little smile our way, draws us into the show. "'We're about to begin a journey through the cosmos. It's a story about us, how the cosmos has shaped our evolution and our culture, and what our fate may be.'" He pauses, then goes on:

"Forty years ago, two phonograph records were put aboard the Voyager 1 and 2 spacecraft. Their original mission was to study Jupiter and Saturn. As I'm sure you all know, they have now ventured far beyond..."

The cat is dozing on your lap. You stroke its back and sip your wine, and seem to actually listen to whatever Evan's saying. I turn my head, feel like it costs a lot of effort, like the muscles in my neck have atrophied. Andrew's put his hands on the tabletop and is staring at them like he can't believe they're his. I get that. I can't believe it either. Andrew's got beautiful hands, but right now the sight of them disturbs me.

Laughter breaks out. I join in. Ha ha. Very funny, yes. The audience tomorrow will be in stitches.

"Go on," Gerald prompts.

"The words with which I began what I promise will not be too long a talk were, of course, the legendary Carl Sagan's. In 1977, he and a small team of scientists selected 115 images and over ninety minutes of music, spoken greetings and sounds of the earth, and engraved them onto two gold-plated copper records. Images were encoded in analogue form using vertical lines, while the audio — "

"This might be too much information," you pipe up. "Who cares about — "

"They're all scientists," Andrew says. "*Proper* space nerds."

"Sure man." You wink at me the way you used to. I smile back. Perhaps you and I haven't changed that much after all. I empty my glass.

145

"Splendid," Evan says good-naturedly, "okay. Tonight, after the successful start of a new ground-breaking mission — " Evan lifts his glass, and we all do as he asks and toast with him — "we have sent a third 'Golden Record' on its way to interstellar space. Our approach is slightly different: the original records didn't include any literature, paintings, or sculptures. In that spirit..."

Should I have said yes to you? I've been asking myself that over the past four years, though I've never wanted to admit it. The way you left, I couldn't build a life with a person like that — and yet... What would it have been like, my life, if I'd been with you instead of Andrew?

"Ladies and gentlemen," Evan continues, in full flow now, "the chances that this spacecraft will in the infinite expanse of interstellar space encounter any form of intelligent life at all are astronomically small. The conclusion might be drawn that this is a canon for ourselves: 'a signal to down here, not up there,' and that our record is therefore meaningless, obsolete. I believe the opposite.

"This canon has given us a rare and priceless opportunity to take a careful look at our planet and our species — to take stock. It affords insight into how we view ourselves: what stories we tell, the characters, shapes, details we include and, by necessity, exclude. This record represents the lives, dreams, and abilities of 7.5 billion people. The Mission of Interstellar Space Exploration represents the very best of our species' capabilities, one of the most breathtaking voyages of exploration ever attempted."

"Are these all quotes or something?" I ask. I wasn't going to intervene — everyone's looking at me now — but it wouldn't be fair to Evan.

"More or less," Evan admits. "Why?"

"The superlatives make my ears hurt."

"I've toned it down already."

"Can't you use your own words? It's just such a lot of grandstanding."

The Dinner Party

"It's part and parcel, isn't it?" you say. "They're sending a bloody rocket into space. They'll send back pretty pictures of the planets, glossy globes, color them in. The entire business is pandering to our vanities."

"Really?" Andrew frowns. "That's a bleak assessment of an *entire* branch of scientific research."

"And not *entirely* fair, I'm sure," Gerald adds.

"All right," you give in. "Apologies. But my point is, the language, they'll like it. The grandiosity." The cat's woken up. It jumps off your lap, digs its nails into your shoes and stretches. "Carry on."

"'We make our mark on the cosmos by exploring it,'" Evan continues, "'surely one of the most positive acts by the human species in all our history.'"

"Jesus," I groan.

"Fran, darling, pull your socks up and stop interrupting."

"It's imperialism on steroids, this. Check your notes, Evan," I tell him, "and if there's the word 'exotic' or something similar anywhere in there — "

"Next paragraph, actually," he says under his breath, looking at his cards. You burst into laughter.

"I'm taking a break." I get up and hold a hand out. "Spare me a fag?" Evan hands me the packet.

"Since when do you smoke?" Andrew frowns at me. I turn away from him.

"Is 'exotic' really in there?" you ask Evan, still laughing. You lean over the edge of the table to peek at Evan's cards.

"Right here," he murmurs. "'Worlds with exotic alien landscapes.'"

"God almighty." I take a cigarette from the packet and the lighter, step out the double doors and onto the lawn.

"I don't get what the big deal is," I hear Andrew say as I light up. "They *are* exotic."

"'Like mountain climbers, making discoveries,'" you quote, and laugh again. "It's a humanities thing," you say, presumably to Andrew. The smoke burns in my lungs. I keep it in as long as I can. The bruises on my hipbones hurt a little. The sun's just a little sliver behind the tree trunks. The sky's turned pink, lilac, pale blue growing deeper. I listen as Evan continues his speech.

"Sagan and his team eventually explained their decision not to include any artworks not just by saying that they didn't have enough time — "

"Oh, of course," Gerald says.

" — but also that extraterrestrials would have enough trouble interpreting the photos of reality that they *had* selected: pictures of bridges, satellites, human beings, rivers, the planets. Including photographs of paintings — interpretations of reality — would unnecessarily complicate matters, they said. But in an effort to show that there is more to human beings than science and reason, to show that we are feeling creatures — "

"Not sure they were, actually," I hear you joke. "Is this their attempt at reasoning that there is more to life than an MRI?"

I snort and flick the ash of my fag onto the ground.

" — they decided to include music on their record. Some of the aesthetic principles of human art forms seemed based on 'physical constants' and the 'mathematical order of nature.' And they concluded from this that this might make the music of Johann Sebastian Bach, for example, more intelligible to extraterrestrials."

"Oh, you just can't make this up, can you?" I shake my head at the cat as it slinks through the double doors and onto the lawn, eyes on mine as it pads toward me, awkwardly, like it finds the touch of the grass unpleasant, and I find myself mirroring its self-imposed restriction, shoulders climbing up to my ears, blades of grass prickling at the bare skin beneath my sandals, vertebrae locking up so I can't move my neck,

The Dinner Party

my back, can only watch as the cat sits down on my feet and licks at my heels, the weight of it pushing my feet down into the ground, through the grass and into the warm earth beneath, between the roots and tendrils just starting to grow and my legs in it up to the ankles, two foreign, unstable things that make me wobble, weak-kneed, and with the dregs of command I have over my arm I lift my fag to my lips and take a drag and let it drop, ash falls but the red-hot tip falls faster, hits the cat and burns an angry welt through its fur. It screeches, bounds off across the lawn, and the sound frees me, and the butt of my fag drops down onto the grass, and the blades it lands on sizzle, brown, whither, and the fag dies out. Evan is still speaking.

My foot hurts. I look down and see an angry red welt in the skin between my sandal straps, right where the cigarette must have landed.

"You're trying too hard," I say as I walk back into the dining room and sit down. The cat wakes up at the sound of my voice and blinks at me, curled up safe on your lap, your hands on its belly.

"Well, I am trying bloody hard," Evan says, but I've forgotten what he was talking about. Can't keep up. Might be the booze, or the language, or both more likely. My mind's stuck on what I did to the cat just now, with the cigarette, remember it like it was someone else who did that, fuzzy and the angles all distorted, memory or fantasy? I smelled the hair burning, charred flesh, smell it all again, nauseating, but you're stroking its smooth and unmarked fur, and I feel faint with relief, grip my right wrist tightly in my left hand and rub my thumb across the skin.

"Ladies and gentlemen, it only remains for me to congratulate you all on the very successful start of the Mission of Interstellar Space Exploration, and to wish you the best of luck in this and all your future endeavors. Thank you."

We cheer. I'm a little late but nobody notices. Evan drains his glass and makes a show of being glad that it's over at last. My thumbnail rakes the skin of my wrist and the stinging helps me focus, makes me feel rather happy, truth be told. Andrew looks happy, too, happier than he's been all evening. He's sitting straighter, and claps Evan on the back. Oh, it's drugs, this evening, just like that: we're sloshed and now we're all very happy with ourselves. You cradle the cat against your chest and turn to me.

"You never told me," you smile, looking down — and the smile makes something in my stomach turn as Evan and Andrew chat about tomorrow's schedule, and the cat meows again " — what's his name?"

※

I can't remember the cat's name. Of all the gaps in my memory, it's this one that disturbs me most, more than the thing with the knife, even. The cat had been with us for a few weeks, after all. I'd looked after it for twenty-two days, fed it, petted it, took it to the vet. I should remember its name.

I don't though. I remember when Andrew brought it home, three weeks before the party, lifted it from a brand-new carrier with bars and flaps like a tiny little caravan and set it down on the kitchen floor.

"Oh my god, what's this?" I asked, and had to work very hard not to make my voice sound too forced.

"Surprise," Andrew cried, and we both looked down at the meowing bundle of fur at our feet, two large and nervous eyes. I felt a trickle of sweat glide down my back. It was hot then, too, and it hadn't rained in weeks.

"It's a cat," Andrew said.

"I can see that."

"I wanted to surprise you."

"Well, you certainly did." We watched as the kitten gave another sad meow and hid beneath the cupboard. "It's scared," I concluded.

The Dinner Party

"It'll get used to us before you know it."

"Should we give it some water?"

"I thought you're supposed to give it milk?"

"No, that'll give it the shits," I told him.

"Oh."

"Put a lot of thought into this, eh?"

"I wanted to cheer you up," Andrew said defensively.

"Cheer me up?"

"You've been..." He hesitated, flushed.

"What?"

"Different. You've been different."

I crossed my arms across my chest. "Different how?"

"You seem sad. I mean, you look sad, when you think I'm not looking."

He does that, you know. Andrew. Well, he did. Just whenever I'd decided he was too busy and self-absorbed to look anywhere but forward, and think about nothing but himself and his company, he'd look round. Right into my eyes, right through me. He'd been noticing. He'd been paying attention. I loved him, after all.

"I'm fine," I said after a moment. "I'm just feeling..."

"You've been on your own here for a while." Andrew took my hands. "And I haven't helped. Working such long hours — "

"It's not that." I shook my head, watched his long fingers intertwine with mine. "I don't mind being here on my own."

"I just thought," Andrew went on, "since there's still three weeks to go before the launch, and me at the office all the time, I just thought that — "

" — you'd buy me a cat? You know it'll live longer than three weeks?"

"I know. I just thought it might be good for you."

"How?"

"You'd have something else to think about. Something to care for."

I stared at him. Glanced down at the pale eyes now peeking out at us from beneath the cabinet. Looked at Andrew again.

"Tell me this isn't a step in some insane plan to get me to want children."

"Christ, Fran," Andrew murmured, "no, it's not an exercise in child-rearing. How do you even come up with this stuff?"

"Because we had an argument about it?"

"For the love of — no, it's not that." Andrew carded a hand through his hair. "And you said 'yet.'"

"What?"

"You said you didn't want to have children *yet*."

I gave him a disbelieving look.

He sighed and closed his eyes. "For fuck's sake, Fran, you've got too much time on your hands." He shook his head. "What is going on inside your head?"

"That's the problem, isn't it?" I snapped. "I've no fucking clue what's going on inside my head. Half the time I've no idea what I'm doing, where my life's going, what I want even."

My honesty disarmed Andrew. He hadn't expected me to own up to the puerile state of my inner life, my shortcomings, the greatest of my failures.

"Look," Andrew went on in a gentler voice, and now he was looking at me in a way that dropped into my stomach like a brick, "if you don't want him..."

"It's a he?" I croaked. I found it difficult to swallow.

"What?"

"The cat, it's a he?" I did my best to sound like a rational human being, take it back, all of it, everything I'd just told him. I didn't want

The Dinner Party

Andrew to think what he was obviously thinking of me, didn't want him looking at me like this for a second longer: like I was a damaged, pitiable thing, about to have a mental breakdown. For a second, I thought of you, unbidden. Your gorgeously wild hair, your lips.

"Yeah. Why?"

"D'you have the food he's used to?" I could be an adult. I could. Watch me. I went on: "A bowl or something to put it in? A... I don't know the English word, a box it pisses in?"

"A litter box. Of course." Andrew was relieved, I could hear it plainly, see it. The look on his face had changed into something more familiar. He preferred this kind of conversation, knew where to stand. "I bought all that on the way."

"Great."

The cat meowed again. Andrew squatted down on his haunches and carefully held one hand beneath the cabinet. A pink nose sniffed it. A white paw touched his palm. I stood straight and watched.

After a while, I dared to point out: "You know, if you wanted me to get out of the house — "

"I never said that," Andrew interrupted.

" — you might have got a dog."

"What?" Andrew looked up.

"It would have needed walking. Training. Much more attention. Cats usually just do their own thing."

"A dog," Andrew repeated. "If you react like this to a cat, can you imagine the scene if I'd brought home a *dog*?"

"Fine." I held up my hands. "Fine."

"Good. Well." For a moment, Andrew looked at a loss. Then he rallied. "I'll get the litter box." He strode from the kitchen, down the hall and out through the front door.

The cat crawled out from under the cabinet, sat down at my feet, meowed up at me.

"Fuck's sake," I murmured, and bent to pick it up.

The cat proved metaphorical. It slept between us that night, burrowing for warmth against Andrew's back and mine. It didn't piss in the bed, or rip the sheets, or any of the things I'd been expecting. It just nestled and slept. I felt it breathing. Its paws were soft and touched my neck now and then. It got up a few times and used the litter box. We gave it a name the next morning.

※

There was the hour after the guy in the café had grabbed me, when you took me to your place and turned on the lights in the bathroom and insisted on a proper perusal of the damage, the bruises on my neck. I bruise easily, I said, but you shook your head and spat a range of expletives I hadn't heard yet and railed against the dicks that did this kind of thing to women all the while touching my skin so gently like my very being was a drop of caster sugar left out in the rain.

Maybe that was why.

※

"Do you think I should have seen it coming?" I ask Stella after I've told her about the day Andrew brought the cat home. Were there signs that might have predicted what he would do at the beginning of the evening?

"What do you think?" Stella asks.

"He wasn't a bad guy," I argue. "I mean, it's tempting to think in terms of saints and villains, but Andrew's neither, and most of the time he was kind and caring."

"I'm sure he was."

The Dinner Party

"I thought I fell in love with him because he was, in the beginning."

"From what you've told me, yes."

"I read this book about the humanities this week. It was by Martha Nussbaum, d'you know her?"

"I do."

"So she said that the arts teach us to be empathetic toward other people."

"Mm." Stella's waiting, I think, for me to connect these ramblings to the issue at hand. I've been talking to her for about a year at this point, have managed to relax a little, go off on tiny tangents.

"I'm paraphrasing, obviously, but basically she said that people often see one another as just a body, which they then think they can use to their own ends, but that art allows us to see a soul in that body, and makes us wonder about its inner world."

"I know the quote," Stella nods. I flush.

"And Andrew..." I go on, and then don't know how to continue.

"Had he ever assaulted you before?"

"No." I scratch my elbow. "I don't think so."

"Do you believe that excuses his behavior?"

"Of course not. But I'm thinking... What with you saying you'd gone through something similar, and so many other women — don't you wonder how many guys are doing this kind of thing? Because there's statistics about how many women this happens to," I go on, more quickly now as Stella makes to answer, "but you never hear about how many men are guilty of this."

"And how do you — "

"It's just, it was the way he did it. Almost," I frown, "nonchalant, casual, like it didn't really register on any scale, I mean, not until afterward and he kind of became aware of my reaction. And even then..."

What words to use? How to choose them when I don't even know what to say, what to think?

"It was like it was normal," I try eventually. "And if you think about it, one in three women and girls — that's the UN number, you know — experiencing sexual or physical violence at least once in their lives, and the real figure is probably even higher because nobody wants to talk about it... and that's not even talking about the boys, the men who get assaulted..." I look up at Stella. "It *is* normal, isn't it?"

Stella gets up, squeezes my shoulder, and makes us both mugs of tea with a lot of milk thrown in.

Autumn

I MEET SOME OF my new neighbors. They're from all over the world, have come to Berlin for many different reasons. Some are reserved, greet me quietly on the street, others invite me in for hot chocolate, tell me to knock on their door whenever I need something. I ask for the location of a second-hand furniture store. I take a bus, spend an hour rummaging for a wardrobe, a bed frame, bookshelves, two chairs. Two men in a van bring them all in and put them down where I tell them to, the places I've chosen. I order a mattress and a sofa from IKEA, a duvet, pillow covers. I fix the bookshelves to the wall myself, unpack the boxes sent over from the UK. Clothes, mainly, some books. When I'm done, the shelves seem emptier than they were in the beginning.

I buy a plant and put it on the windowsill. White flowers quivering against the glass to the bright blue cold outside, persisting.

※

I don't know if I answered your question. I must have. It wasn't a complicated matter then: the cat had a name, and I could have said it, easily. But I don't remember. And I still don't remember what I did with the knife. I just know the aftermath.

We're all still seated at the dinner table, Evan's just finished his speech and the chicken is in the oven for at least another half hour. The cat's still in your lap.

"Evan, mate," you say. "About this canon of yours. Can I ask a question?"

"Course, darling." Evan's all smoothness again: his unexpected nervousness about public speaking has dissipated as suddenly as it began. Things change quickly, in everything. I scratch my wrist.

"Those...aliens, whoever you think might find this canon of yours — what makes you think that they'll be interested?"

"Well, who wouldn't be interested to see something that they themselves hadn't made flying around in space?" Gerald says as Evan opens his mouth to respond. "They'd wonder about us."

You rub your index finger over your lips, look at Evan expectantly.

"What?" Evan asks, clueless as to why you're goggling at him.

"Oh, never mind." You wave a hand, and that small gesture of resignation tugs at me.

"You meant it's a bit like imagining your own funeral, right?" I speak up. Everyone stares. Andrew seems surprised, and I know why — I've never criticized his work before — but this is important to me. Resignation doesn't suit you. The Harry I knew was passionate about what you believed in, and willing to defend your views. You want to persuade people. Teach them something, even, though you know how condescending that sounds, and how futile it usually is. You're earnest. You argue your side until you drop. You don't just change the subject, shrug, and back down. You care, simple as that. You never backed down, so why are you doing it now?

"What?" Andrew frowns at me.

"Like," I scramble for an example, "picking the music they should play at your own service. Imagining who will be there, how much they'll

The Dinner Party

cry, how they'll realize as the songs play that they never saw you for who you are. Your untold depths. You'll all miss me when I'm gone, that kind of thing."

"Well." Andrew clears his throat and sits back in his chair, purses his lips. He's angry. I've insulted him, his work, belittled it. I've thrown him under the bus, he'll say later.

I shift in my seat, and the bruises hurt. Whatever I broke just now, he broke it first.

You smile at me. It's a grateful smile, isn't it? It makes me feel better, for sure, like I've just found a small part of myself that I hadn't known I'd lost.

But it's a fantasy: I'm different now, in so many ways. Below the tabletop, I scratch my wrist. The skin's wet, now, and the stinging has intensified.

"Are you all right?" You frown at me. "You've gone really pale."

It sounds real, your concern. You sound like you mean it. You always did. I trusted you the moment we first met. Your open, friendly face, and all the kindness in your eyes. But the way it ended...

"Fran?"

"I think...I think the tuna disagreed with me." I force a smile and push my chair back. "Excuse me."

I lock the door of the upstairs bathroom and hurl into the toilet bowl, the tuna, slimy and slippery, disgusting. Finally I'm rid of it.

I wash my face. It's hot, but the water is cold. I brush my teeth but the taste of rot remains. I feel like I'm about to cry, or scream, and don't know why. Deep breaths, shuddering, my emotions up and down all evening. I don't understand any of it. I pour some alcohol onto a cotton pad and clean the burn on my foot, hiss at the sting, clean the abraded skin on my wrist. The cat meows from the doorway. I open the door and pick him up carefully, cradle him against my shoulder, feel his familiar weight.

"I'm sorry," I whisper into his soft fur. He puts a paw on my chest. I stroke it with my forefinger. "I'm so sorry." I kiss his small warm head, and carry him downstairs.

"I feel fine," I hear you say from the dining room when I pass the half-open door. "Do any of *you* feel ill?"

"No," Evan answers. "The tuna was delicious."

"It's not the tuna," Andrew says when I've put the cat down. "She drinks a lot, these days. Starts in the afternoons, and — "

"Perhaps you shouldn't talk to us about it," you cut in, and I can feel myself turn red. "If your girlfriend's drinking much more than she used to, perhaps you should — "

"Fiancée, actually," Andrew says. I freeze. In the dining room, a beat of silence.

"What?" you ask.

"We're getting married in the summer."

"Andrew, mate — " Evan begins.

"Congratulations," you say.

I step out onto the patio, around the corner into the little alley where the dumpster stands. I open the lid. There are the rabbits, smelling worse than ever, bloated in the plastic bag, green and yellow and reddish brown. The rabbits' paws are discernible, and their teeth, too. They move in the liquid, heads going up and down, just a little, and a paw, too. Their eyes are open, and they stare at me imploringly.

"Do you want to go to Andrew?" I ask them. They blink. I pull the bag out of the dumpster. The cat flits away. The bag drips. "Andrew likes rabbit, too, you know. With red wine and mushrooms."

I hold the bag up higher, at eye level: grand pose for a soliloquy, but I don't have any words. The blood and ooze glisten. He likes eating the fancy stuff, Andrew. There's a prestige in food for him. Sole. Pheasant. Partridge. Rabbits. Serve him these instead of the chicken and he'll be shitting and barfing for days. I like the thought. It's petty, but it would fucking serve him right.

It took a while, but it ended. Three months before you left, we spent an hour in a pub together. By then, we saw less of each other than we'd used to: you'd had an email from "the firm," as you called it, like a husband in the 1950s. They'd offered you a few minor projects to cast your eye on.

"It's really nice, actually," you said over the top of your pint. "It's nice to try my hand again. Dabble a little." Your cheeks had a rare rosy glow and your eyes were brighter than usual, and you sat very straight.

"You sound surprised," I remarked, watching you closely. Something was up. You were going to tell me something.

"I *am* surprised," you admitted. "I was nervous, you know, to get back to it."

"Yes."

"But it wasn't hard. It's really easy, actually. I mean, I know they only gave me the simple things, and only a few of them, but still."

"That's great." I smiled cautiously. "It must be really nice to know that you could go back to it. If you wanted."

"Yeah." You beamed at me like I got your point completely. It wasn't very hard. You just missed mine. "That's it exactly. I mean, they should ask a woman, because the gender balance at that place is fucked, but still..." You took a long drink and looked inwards, cherishing your victory. I watched, and watched, and waited. A man with a beard reaching down to his sternum sat down at the table next to ours and began to set up a checkers set, humming something that vaguely sounded like "La Marseillaise" under his breath — but all my focus was on you.

"Would you?" I prompted at length, trying hard not to believe what I was seeing in your face. "Want to get back to it?"

"You know, I never thought I would." You touched your earlobe, rubbed the skin behind it.

"That's not a no, is it?"

My question brought you back to earth. "I'm not sure."

"Well, that's a change."

"Is it?"

I took a slug of wine: a white Bordeaux, which I'd never known was a thing. It wasn't nice, what I was going to say, but I had to: "Two years ago, you said you'd have to be dead and buried before you ever went back to work there."

You laughed. "Well, yeah." You took another big sip. "I did feel like that. But — " your eyes finally met mine then, and what you saw made you pause. "Well, in any case, I'll get my degree first."

"Mm." I pressed my lips together and nodded. "Good idea."

The bearded man beside us had begun his game of checkers, shifting both the white and black pieces across the board.

It was definitely "La Marseillaise."

You checked your watch. "I'll have to go soon."

"Oh?"

"Yeah, I've got these reports to finish."

"I thought you'd done them all?"

"I had, but they sent me new ones."

"Oh." I shouldn't have been surprised, but I was. Mainly about how fast this was going, the speed with which I'd be losing you.

"What?"

"Nothing."

"No." You'd reddened. "What?"

"Nothing, really. It's a surprise, that's all."

"I'm not saying I'm going back."

The Dinner Party

"You're not saying you aren't," I pointed out.

"But why's that surprising? I worked there for a decade."

"Yeah, and over Christmas you told me how deluded you felt you'd been, needing affirmation from 'a pack of puffed-up liars whose greatest professional victory was to sell pork as the other white meat.'"

The bearded man looked up, but you didn't notice. You gaped at me. "You're remembering everything I've ever said now?"

I thought about this, then nodded. "Yeah." I wasn't going to be embarrassed about this.

Your embarrassment was obvious, though. "Wow." You looked at my empty glass. "Um. Another?"

I watched you chat to the bartender, flirt a little with her, and felt a hundred things I couldn't name. When you came back, a glass in each hand, you didn't say anything. I didn't either. We nursed our drinks and watched the other patrons. They chatted and laughed and shuffled past each other toward the bar, or the loo, or the terrace for a fag. The bearded man had gone back to his game. He was now humming the "Wilhelmus." Your silence reminded me of the white ferns, the freezing heath, the night in the forest.

"My mother didn't talk after my father died."

You looked up, startled out of whatever reveries you were having that would take you away from me.

"I remember," you said cautiously.

"She didn't speak. Not for a whole year." I looked at you. You blinked at me. I swallowed half my glass in one go. "It was like I'd disappeared."

You cleared your throat. "You were twelve."

"I was." I crossed my legs, ankle over knee. "I can still remember the smell."

"Not from the... surely?"

"No, no." I shook my head. "But you know when someone's ill, and you can smell their sickness? In the house, I mean. Smell they're dying? You've ever smelled that?"

"No." You licked your lips. "I've never watched someone die like that." You took hold of your glass, but didn't drink. "Did it get better, afterward? With your mother?"

"Yeah, she managed. Got quite... practical about it, after a while. She met Paul and it got a lot better, but it never really went away."

Silence turned to clay and then to bricks and made a wall between us. And I'd spent the rest of my life, every day afterward doing everything I could to never hear that silence again, only to have it follow me everywhere.

"I had that," you told me in a low voice, "with friends. Well, not exactly, I don't mean that, but — that silence settling in between?"

"Yes."

"When I couldn't work anymore, friends and family would visit me at home. I hadn't made much time for them over the past years, so it was weird from the beginning. Most of my friends had never even been inside my house. I'd open the door and probably looked different, and you could see how thrown they were, but they didn't say anything. Ever."

"They didn't ask you about what happened?"

"No, never. They assumed I was ashamed of it. So we'd sit there for an hour, drinking coffee, not talking about *anything*..." You sighed. "Longest hours of my life. I just wanted them to leave, and go back to bed." You shrugged. "I lost a *lot* of friends."

I nodded. I was about to lose my only friend. That prediction was the sum of everything you'd said tonight, your excitement, your body language.

"That's not going to happen," you said suddenly. I frowned. What? "That's not going to happen to us," you clarified.

I smiled. "Oh no, of course not." I drew figures in the condensation on the glass. People squeezed past us on their way to the bar. In the

The Dinner Party

corner, a couple had been sitting together in total silence for over half an hour. One man wore a white shirt with a peacock pattern, while the other wore bright blue trousers and a hot pink shirt.

"So what are you up to these days?" you asked. "I haven't seen as much of you as I'd have liked."

"You've been busy," I pointed out. In the beginning, we'd seen each other every day, but you didn't have time for all that anymore. We met twice, three times a week now. Every time you blew me off, I'd been reminding myself that that was still quite often.

"And what have you been doing?" you asked.

Here's the thing. I could have been honest with you. Perhaps it would have turned out different. I could have said I spent every minute when I wasn't with you back in my own room. I'd been having one of my "sulky streaks," as my mother used to call them: weeks in which I let some amorphous strand of sadness grow until I was afraid to leave the house, to talk to people. When I had to shop for groceries, the looks the cashiers gave me became loaded with a whole range of indeterminate meanings, all of them amounting to rejection. I could have told you all of this, but I was too ashamed to. Of course I was.

So what I said was I'd been working a lot. I said I wanted to get to a 4.0 average and graduate with honors. I said I was taking two extra courses, reading all the time, preparing properly for every lecture. You hadn't done that in a while. I was priggish about it, I'm afraid. I might have implied with no great subtlety that *I* was serious about getting my degree. *I* wasn't about to go back to the place that had ruined my life just to feel important. *I* knew what I wanted to do with my life — even though of course I had no idea.

Or maybe I'm making too much of this. What I actually said, when you asked me what I'd been doing, was: "I've been working, papers mostly. Want to get a 4.0. Graduate with honors." That's all. Did I really imply all the rest? I felt it, certainly, and thought it, too, but did I communicate all this to you?

Perhaps it all would have happened anyway. Maybe you just wanted to go away.

So if the beginning of our friendship was like someone had struck a match, the ending was a slow quenching. You worked on more and more projects for the firm, showed up for fewer and fewer lectures, didn't do the reading, didn't have any time for tea, no, sorry, you had to finish something for the firm. You were slipping away, but you saw it as a recovery.

Apart from all that, what hurt me most is this: you knew you were my only friend, and still you left.

Stella says it's easy to lay everything at your feet. I can blame you for leaving the day after my mother dropped her little bombshell, and I can blame you for setting the stage so perfectly for the life I had with Andrew. I shouldn't. These were my decisions, my responsibility. You had your own life to live. And no matter how it ended, you gave me two fantastic years and were the best friend I'd ever had.

So when Stella asks what brought me here, the worst times of my life, I always tell her something different. But when she asks me about the best of times, I've learned enough by now to recognize that when things end, they don't necessarily become mistakes. So I say it's you, Harry, always. I say your name.

MAIN

I get back into the kitchen. The rabbits' smell follows me in. My hands are covered in clods of grease and who knows what else. I'm shaking with anger. Andrew had no right, none at all, telling everyone I'm an alcoholic. Who doesn't fucking drink in the afternoons?

I push the packet of ready-made mash in the microwave. It pings a few minutes later, and I spoon the stuff into five bowls. Make sure to stir Andrew's, get the lumps to melt a little.

The chicken's in the oven. I check the time, but I've forgotten when I put it in. The skin's turned brown already. I open the door. Fluid's bubbling at the bottom of the dish. The lemon's fallen out of the chicken's arse, and there's an indent in the bean-chorizo mixture. I stare for a minute. It looks disgusting, and I've no idea if it's done, or if the flesh is still raw.

"'The lady had a most respectable husband,'" you say, appearing once again in the doorway.

"What?" I frown. I prod the chicken with a fork, but I'm hesitant to break the skin. That will make it dry, won't it?

"'But to tell the truth he knew nothing.'"

"Who wrote that?" I ask, sliding the chicken back into the oven and closing the door.

"René Depestre. 'Face à la Nuit.' Well, a very loose translation. Forgive me for not knowing the original. French is a nightmare."

I straighten from the oven and turn to you. I'm not in the mood for riddles. I'm fucking livid. "And what do you mean by it?"

"I know you heard what Andrew said, Fran." I make to deny this, but you hold up a hand and go on: "I saw you pass the dining room, and you didn't close the kitchen door until afterward."

"Great."

"I'm just saying, don't take it to heart. Andrew doesn't possess the truth of you."

"You've said this before," I remember. "About my mother, I think."

"He isn't always right about you. Even if he is your fiancé." There is an edge to your voice, and the look you give me is inscrutable. "Congratulations."

"Thank you." I turn away, stare at the chicken for want of something better to stare at. You hurt me, the way you left. A fucking text. There's no reason to feel guilty. You moved on, and so did I.

"What the hell is this?" you ask. You're turning a small figurine of a squirrel over in your hands.

"It's a nutcracker," I say.

"What?"

"You put the nut between the arms and jaw and press down on the tail."

"Is it gold?"

The Dinner Party

"Of course not." I frown. I can't remember who gave it to us. One of Andrew's aunts, I guess, on his mother's side. "It's brass."

"Of course." You put it down, survey the rest of the kitchen. "So that's not gold either?" You point at the mortar and pestle standing on the end of a shelf. The pestle's also made of polished brass, glinting in the light, while the mortar's shaped out of white marble.

"Fuck's sake, no, of course not. What do you take us for?"

"Couldn't fault me." You shrug. "KitchenAid mixer," you point out, "a — what does it say? — Cuisinart waffle maker, a Vitamix Ascent blendery thing and a Lavazza coffee machine?"

"Andrew has more money than he knows what to do with," I murmur, and turn back to the chicken, still in the oven.

"Do either of you ever use this stuff?"

"The coffee maker, sure."

"But nothing else?"

"Do you see me making waffles?" I snap, opening the oven door again.

"No." You sound amused. I'm glad I'm entertaining you, albeit at my own expense. You come to stand beside me. Your eyes are on the oven as well.

"If I were you, I'd just carry it into the dining room and let one of them carve it."

"Can't you do it?"

"I've only ever seen it done on TV."

"More than I've seen," I murmur.

"Why *did* you decide to make a chicken?" You still sound amused, the tension between us dissipating a little. "You never answered me."

"Gerald wanted rabbits."

"You know he's on this talk show? Weekdays. A table of six people finding themselves desperately interesting. He does book reviews, I think."

"He's an idiot," I murmur.

"A numpty," you agree, and we share a smile that makes it feel like it used to, you and me.

"You know, if I'd known you were coming, and if I'd known what Gerald's like, I would have told Andrew to keep the two of you well away from each other. This whole thing, the two of you together, it can't possibly end well."

You laugh. "Here. Let's put it on the chopping board." You use two spatulas to lift the chicken from the dish, then put the little bowls with mash onto a tray. "I'll take the chicken in. You take the tray and the knife."

I do as you say and follow you into the living room. The three of them have got started on another bottle, a white again.

"Gerald," you announce, "Franca here was hoping you might do the honors." You put the chicken down in front of him.

"Ah, can't leave this to a lady, eh?" Gerald jokes, pushing himself up to sit somewhat straighter. "Well, Franca, dear, it looks fantastic," he gushes. "I'm a bit of a game aficionado, as Andrew knows, but a roasted chicken just never goes amiss."

"Great," I murmur, handing him a bowl. "Bit of a last-minute thing, but I hope it's turned out all right."

"I'm sure it has, Fran," Evan says, taking the bowl I offer him in one hand and putting it down next to his wine glass. "Sit down, darling, you're looking peakier by the minute. Have a drink."

"Cheers," I murmur as Evan fills the glass still standing by my plate. "Harry." I offer you a bowl.

"Thank you."

I've got two bowls left on the tray. I look at them. They both look fine to me, exactly the same. I sniff surreptitiously, but there's no difference.

"Andrew." I pick a bowl and put it next to his plate. I don't meet his eyes, but I can feel him looking at me. His glass is full. "Where's the cat?"

"Outside. Trying to scoop a goldfish out of the pond."

In the distance, through the dusk beginning to set in, the light a tired blue and gray, a small bundle of fur is pressed close to the bank, shoulders sticking out, ears flat.

Gerald gets up and takes the knife in hand, then looks at me. "You've let it rest, I assume?"

"I — "

"Of course," you pitch in effortlessly. "Naturally. Lady knows what she's doing."

Gerald nods at you, turns back to the chicken. "You see, it's important to allow the juices to settle, making sure the flesh remains moist. Additionally, giving it at least fifteen minutes to settle will allow the fibers in the flesh to relax, which in turn will make carving easier. Now, one usually has a carving fork to steady the bird — " I make to get up, but Gerald holds up a hand " — but one can just as easily use an ordinary fork. I promise you all," he says to everyone at the table, "I haven't used this fork before."

I meet your eye. You wink at me.

"Now, to carve a chicken is really quite easy, actually. You just insert the knife right here — "

"Evan," you say, turning to him, "can I see the list?"

"The list?"

"The selection you've made. Your canon."

"Oh, yeah." Evan takes his phone out of his pocket and fiddles with it. At the other end of the table, Gerald has cut both the legs off, speaking now to Andrew, who's less than barely interested. I watch them hazily, chicken turning into carcass, swallow another mouthful of wine. You were right. Fuck Andrew. Give me one person in this room who doesn't drink too much. There. Stick that up your pipe and smoke it.

"Harry, here you are." Evan holds his phone out. "We start with books, and then the next document is paintings, the next sculptures."

"Great."

You start scrolling on Evan's phone. Gerald resumes his work on the chicken. Stuffing spills out. The lemon falls out again, this time onto the tablecloth, leaking yellow onto white. I make to pick it up, but it's soggy and disintegrates as soon as I touch it. The stain grows.

"Shit."

"Can I help?" you ask, looking up from Evan's phone.

"It's fine. I'll get a cloth." I hurry back into the kitchen, but as soon as I get there, my phone rings.

"Frannie," my mother says as soon as I pick up. "It's your mother."

"Yes. I know."

"I thought you might not recognize my voice. We haven't spoken in such a long time."

"We lived together for over twenty years. Of course I recognize your voice."

"Now, how are you?"

"I'm fi — "

"Imagine this, Franca. Last night, as Paul and I are celebrating our tenth anniversary — "

"Congratulations."

"Well meant, I'm sure," my mother says dryly. "Now, as the band strikes up, as they say — "

"Do they?"

" — I get into a conversation with George Acorn. You'll remember he's got a cottage in the Chilterns — "

"I hadn't."

" — or Shropshire, Berkshire, oh who knows, can't remember — "

"Someplace," I finish, dry as I can.

" — and he tells me he's been to a similar party three months or so ago, where my daughter apparently made quite the decision."

"Ah."

"Ah, indeed. So at what should have been a very happy occasion, I was forced to confront the fact that my daughter has engaged herself to this Andrew — "

"To Andrew, yes."

I hold the phone up with my shoulder and wring out a dishcloth.

"So?" my mother demands.

"So what?"

"Tell me about him!" Her exasperation's palpable. "You've got engaged to a man I — "

"I've been living with him for four years, you know."

"Well, I've never met him, have I?"

"No, you haven't."

"Why don't the two of you pay us a visit?"

"Andrew's just a bit busy at the moment. He's working on this — "

"Berlin's nice in summer."

"It's nice here, too."

"Have you set a date already?"

The sound of footsteps distracts me. I turn round and watch you walk into the kitchen, opening the cupboard under the sink, bending down to peer inside. I touch your shoulder and hand you the dishcloth. You smile in thanks. Your fingers touch mine as you take it.

"Frannie?"

"Next summer, probably," I say into the phone, but keep my eyes on you. "We're looking at venues." Something changes in your eyes, a vulnerable thing that hardens. You make to retreat, but I grab your hand. Wait. "I have to go," I tell my mother. "I've got guests over."

"I'll call you back tomorrow," my mother says, as I knew she would. This degree of understanding comes to her exclusively when there are guests to be entertained. "But tell me one thing now. Is he good to you?"

"I — what?" I ask, though I understood perfectly well. Cold sweat collects on my forehead. There's a tingle in my fingertips that spreads down to my palms, burrows in deep until the bones themselves start to hurt with it. A delicious ache fluttering in my belly. You're watching me. Your red hair catches the light. Your lips are very red as well.

"Does he make you feel good about yourself? Make you feel like you're someone worth loving?"

"I — I mean, he — "

I can't keep talking about Andrew while the touch of your hand is searing itself into my palm.

"Franca?" I remember the black, like India ink, the feeling of being submerged in it.

"I've got to go," I say and hang up.

"What is it?" you ask. You look uncomfortable. I let go of your hand.

"I just…" This thing I'm feeling, it's obvious but unnameable. Inappropriate, and years too late. I know nothing about your life now, what you've been up to. I search for the words. What do I mean? Four years later and I still don't know what I mean, what I meant when I said no to you.

You turn. You're about to leave, you've lost patience with me, and I blurt out the only thing I can think of.

"I'm glad you're here."

You stop. Look at me over your shoulder.

"Despite, you know," I go on, "how things ended."

"We were never more than friends — "

"Oh." I flush. "No, I mean, I didn't — "
" — were we?"

I stop short. You're studying me, ruthlessly cataloging every aspect of my reaction.

"We were best friends," I say eventually. "Well, you were mine. But you left."

"Was that your mother?" you ask. It's so far from the response I'd been waiting for, I don't immediately understand. "On the phone?" you clarify.

"Oh. Yes. She lives in Berlin now."

"What's she doing there?"

"Paul's got a job."

Do you have someone?

You asked me this back in Utrecht, and now I want to ask you the same. I've been wondering all evening. I've been wondering for years. Did you find someone else after you left? Do you come home to someone now?

"Food's getting cold," you say quietly.

Right. I join the others. Keep going.

"How's the chicken?" I ask Gerald, who's putting the knife down.

"Carved, and looking delicious. Franca, shall I serve you first?"

"I'm sticking to mash," I say as I sit down. "Vegetarian."

"Ah. Harry, then?"

"Sure." You pass your plate. I remember my confusion about the mash and sniff mine. It smells fine.

"Thanks, that's enough."

"So what did you make of it?" Evan asks you as Gerald takes his plate. "Our canon?"

"I was wondering how you'd made your selections."

"Well, we didn't. Andrew and I, I mean. We realized that with regards to art, we were something rather less than experts, so we enlisted the help of those who are. Gerald here made the literary canon."

"Literary excellence," Gerald announces grandly, sits down and picks up his cutlery. "That has been my criterion of selection. Franca, dear, it looks delicious." He takes a bite of the filling. "Mmm. And it is."

The others take it as a cue to tuck in as well. Andrew and Evan's eyes are on their plate, but yours, I notice, are on Gerald.

"You can't be serious," you say at length. Gerald, who'd been about to take another bite, pauses and lowers his fork.

"Why?"

"Well, for starters, all anthologists give the same answer."

"Well then," Gerald chuckles.

"But more importantly, you truly feel you know what 'literary excellence' actually *is*?"

"Look," Gerald says, and pauses to chew, "you've seen my list, haven't you?"

"What I've seen is forty-five books written by white men, three by white women, and only two by male writers you'd describe in your TV appearances as belonging to ethnic — "

"You can't deny the works I've chosen are all great literature."

"I'm not denying it," you say, smiling. "What I'm talking about is all the other works of literature which could just as creditably have been selected."

"Well they couldn't have." Gerald shrugs. You stare at him. I sigh and swallow a mouthful of wine to stop myself from interfering. This is your fight. And people like Gerald, they're never going to be convinced of something they just don't want to believe in. "These books are the very best of what has been thought and written throughout the world."

"But why?" you cry. "You keep saying that these are great books — fine, that's your opinion, and I have no interest in arguing about that —

The Dinner Party

but *why*? I'm asking what 'great' means to you, and you just don't give me an answer."

"Look, in order to exercise any lasting power of fascination, books must truthfully represent man's experiences, those of a general nature. Only then will they attract a large readership, and prove themselves to be more than just passing fads."

"So, it is definitely as I remarked before," Evan drawls as you move to retort, looking increasingly exasperated, and Gerald's smile has turned particularly self-satisfied, "that Andrew and I are about to send a collection of old codgers into space?"

"Didn't you check beforehand?" I ask him. "Check the list, see what kind of books are on there?"

"I did," Evan counters with a shrug. "Seemed fine to me. Heard of most of them. Read some. Thought they were fine," he says again. "The *Iliad* and *Odyssey*, obviously, *Beowulf, The Canterbury Tales, The Faerie Queene, Leviathan, Robinson Crusoe* — "

"Oh, they're all fine," you mutter, and push up from your chair. "Of course they are. Spare a fag?" you ask Evan. He takes a pack from his pocket, opens it to find it empty, gets another one from his bag. "Good thing I stopped for petrol," he murmurs.

"Are you angry with me?" Gerald asks you.

"Oh no," you say, though I can see how annoyed you are. "I just need some fresh air."

"Hence the cigarette."

"You know," you say as you're about to step through the French doors, "the thing that strikes me most is that you truly seem to believe in some kind of general experience. What did you call it? 'Man's experiences of a general nature'?"

"Yes I did."

You smile, and light up. The smoke drifts into the dining room, but I don't protest. I want you here.

"We all have our preferences," Gerald concedes, "but I never quite take to the writings by authors of interest groups."

"Interest groups? That's half the population. Much more than half." You shake your head and step outside, into the dusk. The light's blue gray, the tip of your cigarette a brilliant gold. It casts a glow on your face, its strange angles and their unexpected softness, still surprising me.

I swallow, shift in my seat. The leather squeaks. "The last course Harry did in Utrecht was 'Debating the Canon,'" I say quietly to the three men sitting around the dinner table.

"Ah," Gerald says like that explains everything, and perhaps it does.

※

A girl saunters down the third-floor hallway and sinks into the chair opposite mine. She's tall, very, very tall, wears a short dress over bare legs despite the autumn chill. Can't be older than seventeen, I guess. She pushes her sunglasses up into her long blonde hair and nods at the nameplate on the door beside which I am sitting.

"She's good, isn't she? Stella," the girl says. Her voice is surprisingly low and gravelly. "Mine's crap," she goes on without waiting for my answer, nods at the door opposite Stella's. I squint to read the nameplate. Dr. Peter something German. "Looks like a pedo and talks like a politician. Never gives a straight sodding answer, but he gets annoyed when I do the same. Tries not to show how it drives him up the wall, but he's crap at that, too. You new?"

I'm a bit slow on the uptake. The sudden torrent of words and information — the girl speaks in very quick German, barely pausing for breath — has taken me aback. Just as I open my mouth to reply, she goes on: "I'm not. Been here three years, not the blindest bit of difference.

The Dinner Party

Keep telling them there's nothing wrong with me, but hell if they listen. Might as well not say anything. Drives them crazy," she says again. She rummages in her handbag, extracts a single cigarette. "You should try it. Got a light?" She starts to plow through her handbag again before I can tell her I haven't, and flicks the cap of one of those old-fashioned lighters. Blows the smoke in my direction, seems to see me for the very first time.

"Want one?"

I shrug to myself. "Sure."

She produces another fag — does she have them loose in her bag? — and lights it for me, leaning in, her hand cupped around mine. I murmur thanks.

The smoke's heady, light in my head and heavy in my lungs, sour. It's been a while.

"What you in for?" the girl asks, in English now, as she leans back in her chair. The move makes her dress ride up a little, expose a bit more of her legs. I feel particularly dumpy in my oversized jumper, my sensible trainers made to withstand an autumn in Berlin. "Why are you here?"

"Bit of trouble at a party," I say. She flicks the ash onto the floor. "You?"

"I was on the radio."

I stare at her for a moment. "And that... bothers you?"

"No, no, no, that was why they sent me here. Well, a few other places first, but — there was this program on the radio a few years back about some teacher they'd arrested." She cocks an eyebrow as she looks at me, and I know what kind of teacher she's talking about. "My father called in, all emotional, on national radio, mind you, told the whole fucking country about how he'd stepped out of the shower one morning, years ago by that point, when his youngest daughter — that's me, hi! — caught sight of his dick and said that it looked just like the PE teacher's."

My throat goes dry. "How old were you?"

"Seven."

"Jesus."

"So who fucked you?"

I freeze, stunned.

"Go on," the girl prompts with a smile. "I won't tell anyone."

"I'm — I'm not — "

"No? It's kind of obvious though."

"Is it?" I breathe, beet-red.

"A teacher put his hand up my skirt and made me touch his dick. It's obvious to me. Besides, Stella specializes in this kind of thing."

"I wasn't — that wasn't what happened to me," I mumble. "It wasn't that..."

The girl leans in. "Did it hurt?"

"I — " I shake my head. "It — yes. It did."

"It didn't for me," she says simply. "Still fucked me up, though."

The door swings open. I turn my head. Stella's looking down at us with knowing, unsurprised eyes. "Thought there was a smell." She sounds disapproving, but there's also a trace of amusement in her voice. "No smoking inside, ladies."

I feel myself go, if possible, even redder. Hesitate for a moment, then lift my foot and squash the fag against the sole of my shoe. Drop the butt in my palm and close my fingers around it, hiding it from view. The girl just sighs and takes another drag.

"You too, Sandra," Stella says calmly. The girl sighs again, then drops the fag onto the floor, where it smolders on the tiles. Leaves a mark.

Stella visibly decides not to comment, turns to me. "Franca, come on in."

The Dinner Party

I step inside, close the door behind me. "You can drop it in here," Stella says as I dawdle a little, wonder what to do with the fag in my hand. She points to the bin beneath her desk.

"Thanks."

"Please, sit down." She does the same, both of us in our usual places. "You've met Sandra, then."

"Yeah." The sleeve of my jumper smells of smoke, unpleasantly. "She told me what happened to her."

"Did she?" Stella doesn't sound surprised.

"She said you specialize in that sort of thing."

"Amongst others, yes."

"So why am I here? I mean," I quickly go on, "I know what I did with the knife was — I know I need help. And I don't mean I don't appreciate — it helps. It's helped a lot, talking to you. But I just, I just wondered if, what the girl, Sandra, what she was talking about..."

"You wonder if what happened with Andrew," Stella helps me out, "is altogether comparable with what Sandra went through."

"Yes."

"Why would it have to be?"

"Well, she was a kid. Seven years old, Jesus Christ."

"I understand your consternation," Stella allows. "The abuse of children is in many ways far more nefarious than any other crime."

"But what happened with Andrew," I maintain, "that's nothing like what happened to her."

"I can see how your experiences might differ, but why do you find this so important?"

"Well," I splutter, wondering how on earth this couldn't be self-evident to a woman as clever as Stella, "she was only seven."

"A child, yes, as we've established."

"She couldn't defend herself. Not against a grown man."

"Is that where the vital difference lies, then, in your mind? Whether a woman who goes through this kind of experience is able to defend herself?"

"I — no…" It's ridiculous, of course, to even suggest this, hearing what it sounds like. "No, you're right. Just — what happened with Andrew…" I shake my head. "It's nothing compared to what a girl like Sandra has been through."

"The circumstances were different, yes. But I ask again: why should a comparison be made?"

"Well," I finally burst out, "because I'm here, and so is she, and you're looking at me with pity like there's a big flaw in my thinking but you can understand why I'm thinking like that, because you've heard all this before, seen it from so many women."

"I have," Stella concurs.

"What happened to me," I go on, "it doesn't warrant — " I wave a hand at the office, Stella, myself " — all this."

"I disagree." It's the first time she's said this, directly disputed something I've told her. "And instead of telling you why, and giving you a long and patronizing lecture, I'd like you to think about it."

After a beat I say with a small smile: "That's also a little patronizing, to be honest."

"Nevertheless," Stella allows. "And again, I'll ask you to write about it." She pauses. "You look worried."

"I don't want to write anymore," I admit.

"Why not?"

"It's never-ending." I rake a hand through my hair. "I've been writing about that goddamn evening for over a year now and we're still only eating that fucking chicken. I'm getting bogged down in that endless discussion about the fucking canon, like it matters."

The Dinner Party

"Why, you must believe it does. You remember a lot about it."

"Well of course it matters in principle, but none of it is going to help me in any way now, don't you think?"

"I think," Stella says, "that you should write about whatever occupies your mind. Especially," she holds a hand up as I'm about to interrupt, "at times you feel like this, when you think you'd rather stop, that it's impossible to keep going. When things are tough to think about, to discuss — "

"It's for a reason," I summarize with a sigh.

"That's one way of putting it," Stella allows. "Now, you've talked a lot about the silence that you feel follows you everywhere."

"And you want to know why I'm so scared of it, yes?" I'm getting the hang of this, Stella's methods.

"It's an important question. Generally, only the things that scare us tend to pursue us."

"Yes, well, that's a great turn of phrase but it doesn't bring me any nearer to an answer."

"Put it this way. What do you fear will happen when you stop reading books, watching movies?"

"You mean what do I think I'll hear when I stop running from the silence?" I ask skeptically.

"Yes," Stella says.

"It's a lopsided question."

"I am aware."

"I don't hear anything at all. Of course. Like that night in the forest, there's just this blanket of thick, heavy silence that keeps out every kind of sound. I can't hear traffic, or the neighbors, or the kettle switching off, can't hear myself breathe, even."

"How do you — "

"It feels like being buried alive."

We continue eating. Evan picks up his cutlery. I eye the stretch of lawn I can see from here. It's very nearly dark now: I can only see shadows, hints of movement.

"I do not see what the problem is," Gerald admits quietly, and uses a spoon to scoop some of the mash from his bowl onto his plate. It's lumpy, I notice. "You cannot truly hold that... *Twilight* should take the place of Homer."

Andrew laughs. I roll my eyes. Evan says, "I don't think that was Harry's point."

"It wasn't," I agree, watching you outside, your face thrown into relief by the end of your cigarette. You wander toward the patio, out of sight but closer.

"To read is to be in the company of great souls," Gerald goes on, for fuck's sake. "And these new writers, I mean, whatever their merits — "

"Can we talk about something else?" I ask. And can I *write* about something else, too.

"I'm so sorry, my dear," Gerald offers affably, "we must be boring you."

"It's not that," I assure him. "It's just that you're going round in circles."

"Am I?" Gerald asks.

"Yes, 'cause — "

"Fran," Andrew begins, but there's a crunch of gravel from somewhere outside and I catch a glimpse of your red hair, so I ignore him. You're listening, I know you are. I can practically feel you standing just around the corner there. The least I can do is show you I'm not like these men, not entirely.

"You're going round in circles," I tell Gerald, "because you show a

The Dinner Party

marked inability to understand that the books you selected…" I hesitate. What are the right words?

"Yes?" Gerald prompts.

"They reflect who you are," I tell him. "Your views, your background."

"And what's wrong with that?"

"Well," I huff, "nothing, as long as you're *aware* that you're pale, male, and stale — "

"Franca — " Andrew says again.

" — basically, an old windbag who's been at the top of the food chain all his life."

Evan inhales his drink, coughs uncontrollably, tears streaming, shoulders shaking with laughter. Andrew looks apoplectic. Gerald's turned red. "And Harry's not saying that Homer isn't worthy of being included. That's not the fucking point."

"Franca, will you come with me into the kitchen," Andrew tries.

"It's the process of selecting these books that's inevitably colored by your own personality," I go on. "And once you understand that, you'll see that there's no actual, rational basis to this idea of 'greatness' in books. None at all." I take a swig and shake my head. "It's hot air. Complete drivel."

You appear in the doorway, but the others don't see you: they're all goggling at me like I'm a stranger. Have I been that passive, this whole time? Or that quiet? They all stare, and you're grinning at me like the cat that ate the what — the parakeet? That's not quite right, is it? Never mind.

"Someone wrote an essay." Evan smirks and salutes me with his glass.

You turn away and drop your fag. I can't see your expression, only the slant of your back. It doesn't tell me anything. You wander off, back into the darkness of the garden. Evan drops his fork to the ground.

"I'll get you a new one," I say, and push my chair back. Andrew gets to his feet, too.

"Need the loo," he says, but follows me into the kitchen and carefully closes the door behind him.

"So," Andrew says. "What is it, Franca?" he asks.

For a moment, I'm floored. He doesn't sound angry, or annoyed even. That's the least I'd expected. That he'd be irritated. But he isn't. He looks at me like I'm a stranger who doesn't speak the same language.

"What's going on with you?"

"What?"

"What are you doing? Saying Gerald's canon is complete drivel — "

"I never said — "

"What's that about?"

"I never said his canon's drivel. I said the idea of literary greatness — "

"What's the damn difference?" Andrew sighs.

Oh, come on. I take a moment to try and parse what he's saying, the implications of it. But really. Come on. "So you're allowed to talk about him like he's a flatulent fool farting out old prejudices, but when I disagree with the man and tell him why, straightforward, to his face, that's not okay?"

"Look, I don't like it any better than you do, but Gerald's here, for better or worse — "

"No no no, stop, just stop it." I shake my head and hold up a hand. Take a breath. Push the anger out of my throat and speak in a clear calm voice. "I know you're the one who wanted Gerald to make the canon. You're the one who invited him onto the project. Not Evan."

Andrew blinks. It's like someone's put him on pause, like I've told him I killed the cat and dressed it up as a chicken and he's just eaten his own pet. I watch him. It's a bit excessive, really. How convinced would he have to be of his own brilliance, how many times would people have told him, growing up, that he was clever, to be this surprised that I've seen through one of his lies? "Evan told you that?"

"Now, I basically don't give two shits — "

"You're drunk, aren't you?" Andrew says quietly, but he sounds too ashamed for it to come off as an accusation.

" — who invited who, and yeah, I am a little," I admit, "and thank you for telling your friends I'm an alcoholic, by the way, really classy, but what I'd really like to know is why you'd lie to me about Gerald."

Andrew looks at me for a minute. Then he looks away. "Gerald's a name. He brought publicity. Gave us a lot of exposure."

"Sure," I snap, "but why did you lie?"

"Because I knew you'd be like this!" Andrew shouts, and his face suddenly has turned red.

"I'd never even *heard* of the man before tonight," I cry. Andrew's anger is contagious. "Like I'd never even seen that bloody list because you treated it like it was a state secret."

"Well forgive me," Andrew goes on, even louder now, "for wanting to build something. For wanting to provide for me and you. You know we can't *all* just study a subject like 'Victorian female suicide' that will never bring bread to the table."

"You're hardly just bringing home the bacon," I snap, waving my arms at the kitchen, all the gadgets we'll never use.

"Yes, and there's no fucking shame in that!" Andrew shouts. "I make a lot of money! I work hard! Not all of us can afford to — "

"You could," I butt in. "Even before you started the company. Your parents would have been happy to let you study astrophysics — "

"Well unlike you, Fran, I don't want to spend the rest of my life being dependent on somebody else."

I take a shallow little breath. He's hit that tender spot. He knows it's there. Obvious as anything. The hurt reverberates. I flex my hand against the ache.

"Fran..." He looks like he regretted the words as soon as they left his mouth, but they're out now. They're right here, lodged inside. I take them with me.

"You offered," I say in a low, quivering voice. "You offered. You said I could — "

"You barely looked for a job, Fran." He sounds regretful, but honest. He's being honest. This is what he thinks. I realize I was wrong to think he's regretting hurting me: he's driving the stake in deeper. "And then you called it a lost cause. I know people who sent letters for two years, and they didn't — "

"Please stop."

"It's comfortable for you," he cries. "It's easy. And you look down your nose at people who — "

" — who silence their own insecurities by supporting others." I'm trembling with anger, fury blowing capillaries, streaming from my fingertips. "You could have studied astrophysics," I seethe, "like you told me you wanted to, right when we first met." Andrew's expression flickers. "Your parents would have been happy with — "

"Sorry, but how do you think you know this?"

"Because your fucking uncle told me!" I yell. "And again, you told me the exact opposite! How great it must be for you, having someone in your house every day to reassure you that you've made the right choices. Look at Franca. Look at where I'd be if I'd done what she did. It's a very nice gesture and all," I go on mockingly, loud, loud, too loudly, a ringing in my ears, "supporting me, but it's all about you, isn't it?"

Andrew deflates, turns away, rubs his face with both hands.

The Dinner Party

He turns back to me. Licks his lips. His eyes are bright, his hair is messy. His ears are red. The cat appears on the windowsill, gives us a look beyond its years as it steps onto the countertop and makes a beeline for my hand and time slows down, Andrew's saying something but I can't hear, can barely see his mouth moving as my vision contracts again and every edge turns black, muscles bunching, my hand clenched around the handle of the cutlery drawer so tightly my fingers hurt and the pain travels up my forearm to my elbow and all my blood collects in my head and then seems to disappear entirely so that my feet leave the ground and I'm floating three inches high, tethered to the earth only by my grip on the drawer and when the cat licks my wrist disgust slithers up the length of me, I take a knife in my free hand and swoop down flesh tears and bone splinters blood spreads out, a pure circle in a gorgeous color, shiny and rich and glutinous like glucose thickening — who knew a cat this small had such a lot of blood in it? — and this must be what it feels like, I think, to be stronger than something, to be able to end things, impose my will, my vision of what the future should look like: power. Is that what it was about? They always say that, don't they?

It all leaves me, as quickly as it came, the rush, and the illusion, the disgust: all of it overblown, sure, but felt sincerely nonetheless. There's nothing now. I cover my mouth with my hand. It's shaking. I am, too. The cat meows. I've no idea what's happening anymore. I killed the cat, but it pads across the counter, perfectly whole, and Andrew picks it up carefully with both hands, cradles it against his belly. When he looks up again, his eyes are watery, and he takes a step forward.

"I didn't mean to," he begins, and puts his hand on my waist. Something crawls along my spine, and I step away.

"Fran?"

We both look round, and you're there. You've opened the back door without making a sound.

Viola van de Sandt

I turn my back on them, slowly, step into the hall, take my purse, sling the strap over my shoulder.

"What are you doing?" Andrew asks.

My heart's starting to beat faster. I open the front door, step out onto the path. My vision fades at the edges.

"Fran!" Andrew shouts. I don't turn round, speed up instead. I'm shaking all over now, can barely see, bits of gravel scraping my ankles as I teeter onto the street, lights flickering or perhaps that's just me, trying to breathe, trying to see, lurching down the pavement, turning left toward the bus stop my bag slapping against my thigh, my bum, shirt wet with sweat —

"Fran!"

There are the ferns, white because it's freezing, and the dark trunks of trees all round me, and that silver strip of my mother's hair, the crinkle of the heath, and I run, I run, fast as I can. The bus stop is a ten-minute walk away, a bench in the center of nowhere, a bus comes every half hour, once an hour maybe at this hour, whatever the hour is, I've never even taken the bus here and the wine's shot my stamina and why didn't I just take the fucking car keys?

A hand around my arm, pulling me to a stop, not letting go. I whisk round.

"For fuck's sake, Andrew, I said — "

It's you. You're breathing hard, red in the face. The alcohol hasn't done you any favors either.

" — no," I finish in a dry whisper.

You let go of my arm. Hold your hands up, like you don't want to threaten me.

Dizziness hits me. I bend over, hands on my knees, and try to breathe.

"What are you doing?" you ask.

The Dinner Party

I raise my head, take in the empty street, the dark husk of a house to my left, the dark field to my right. There's a horse there, I think, there in the distance, a smudge of white.

"Fran?" you prompt.

"Taking a walk," I finally say. I've run straight past the bus stop, ten meters away, and never noticed.

"This time of night?"

"It's only — " I stop. I remember I don't know the time.

You check your watch. "Nine-thirty."

"Thanks."

"Okay, just..." You hold out your hand. Don't touch. No man's ever done this: kept his distance. "Just, let's sit down?"

I follow you back to the stop. The bench is slightly damp, hard against my back. You sit down next to me, a warmth against my side. Up ahead, the horse is crossing the field, slowly coming closer. The pavement's still warm from the day's sunlight.

It's the complete opposite of that night in the forest. It's warm, and I can see, and you're beside me, you're calm and steady, you followed *me*.

For the longest time, you don't say anything. The horse reaches the fence, finally, cocks its head. I open my purse and count the cash I have. Barely enough for a bus ticket, and I didn't even take my phone. I get to my feet, agitated into motion, incapable of stillness, check the timetable affixed to the street light. Next bus in... fifty-three minutes, fucking hell.

"Nice evening for it," you comment as I sit back down with an irritated huff. I've a stitch in my side.

"Nice for what?" I grumble.

"Running away," you say with a smirk.

"Oh bugger off." I cross my legs and arms.

You give me a look, hard to decipher in the gloom. "You all right?"

"Oh, I'm dandy," I scoff. "Just... tip-top."

"Of course you are." You don't even bother pretending to be convinced. I stare at the horse, munching on the grass.

"What did you mean, earlier?" I ask after a while.

"What did I mean by what?"

"'The lady had a respectable husband,' by René Whatever. You distracted me."

"I answered you. I said you shouldn't hold yourself to Andrew's opinion of you."

"That was only half of it, wasn't it," I say. "It always is with you. You think I've settled or something?" I press. My voice has gone cold without my permission. I know I'm putting words in your mouth, that really I'm the one who thinks these things about myself, but I can't help it. "I can't bear to be alone so I just shack up with the first guy to offer a smile and a wink?"

"Look, it's none of my business."

"It isn't," I agree. "Because you left. Without a word."

"I sent you a text."

"Oh great. A text, after two years."

"You shot me down," you say, and I know you're not talking about our last aborted meeting now.

There's a pause, and for a moment I'm not angry. Here we are then, that moment I never dared think about, never dared discuss again even when you were still around. You were always much braver than me.

"Is that why you left?" I ask. "Because I said no to you?"

You look pained, but your eyes are on me. You don't speak.

"Because you disappeared," I go on. The anger's there again, fueled by your silence. "You'd been the first person in years who said, yeah, of course, come round whenever you like, I like talking to you. You wanted to hear what I had to say, the first to say I should do what *I* wanted to,

The Dinner Party

not what everyone else would want me to. When you met me, I was as pathetic as that makes me sound: I had nobody. And forgive me for not spelling it out to you, but you knew that."

"And you just walked straight into the arms of Mr. — "

"I met him *after* you left." It feels ridiculous, having to say this, but as I do, something resolves itself between us, some of the distance melting, and it's heady, watching some of what we were rebuild.

"I loved you." You say it, finally. "I *loved* you. I was head over fucking heels. Forgive me for wanting to leave after you turned me down." You slump a little, your knee touches mine.

"I loved you back," I admit.

"Then why?"

"You were like the *opposite* of what I'd planned." I groan. "Don't. I know how ridiculous that is."

"It's not," you say, too reasonable.

"It's the regret of a lifetime."

Your dark eyes find mine. I try to smile. There it is.

"Want to go back?" you ask after a long, long moment. Your eyes glisten in the dark. I hesitate. "You can leave, Fran," you go on, "if that's what you want, but like this?"

I sigh. Can't disagree with you there.

"What happened?"

"Oh, just a spat," I sigh, shaking my head. "You heard most of it, didn't you."

"Didn't sound like the kind of spat that would make you walk out like this." You say this carefully, wait for me to reply, continue when I don't. "You're sure nothing else happened?"

"Will you stay tonight?"

"What, with you and Andrew?" Your knee, still touching mine.

"I'll put fresh sheets on the bed in the spare room."

"So grown up," you scoff and hold your hands up again when you catch sight of my expression. "Sorry."

"You don't have a spare room or something?" I ask grudgingly.

"In Cambridge? Prices are like London's."

"You've got a good job."

"And you're spending too much time with Andrew's clan. Not all of us played in the grounds, instead of the garden. My parents didn't even have a yard."

"What did they have?"

"A miserable little flat. And four children."

"Oh." I didn't know this about you. How come? What did we talk about in Utrecht?

"And I don't have a job anymore," you go on. Your voice is all brittleness and vulnerability.

I gape. Can't help it. "What?"

"I had another burnout." Your fingers twitch, and you hide them in fists. You're shifting your weight, turn ever so slightly away from me. You're bracing yourself, I realize, expecting me to mock you. Fuck. Fuck me. I know I've hurt you tonight, more than once, and I hurt you four years ago, but do you really think I'd twist the knife when you're like this? You've just told me you've lost the future you'd chosen for yourself, the career that was your everything.

"I'm so sorry." It's a platitude, my words are insufficient. The horse turns its back. I try again. "When did you — "

"Two months ago. They kept me on, but I quit last week." Your eyes fill, but you're keeping it together.

"Fuck." It's all I can think of. "Was it like..."

"The last time?" you fill in. "Yes, exactly like that. Couldn't step into the car, couldn't eat, couldn't get out of bed eventually. Everything the same. *Weeks* spent trying to get up the courage to step out the front

The Dinner Party

door, get the post." You sigh. You're so, so tired. You're exhausted. I see it now.

"So I made a calculation," you go on. "Perhaps not the most sensible thing to do, but then..."

"What was it?"

"I'd had that job for ten years when I had my first breakdown. Came to Utrecht, had a two-year break, went back to it. This time, worked for four years, and bam, same thing happens."

"So you calculated..." I prompt after a moment.

"Yeah. I calculated how long it would be, if I went back to work and the curve would hold, before the third one would strike."

"You speak of it like a bombing," I remark.

"That's what it feels like. Complete paralysis. I couldn't go through that again. So I quit."

"Shit."

In the dark, I search for your hand and find it, warm and dry, hold tight, your fingers interlocking with mine.

The horse bristles — neighs? — whatever horses do in English. Your life is in ruins — that's how it feels to you, I realize, and mine's on the verge, isn't it? What did Andrew do?

"What now?" I ask.

"Well..." You rub your face. "I've started giving language lessons to refugees. People who went up a mountain pass in the dead of night, got into a ramshackle boat, survived a shipwreck, and walked across a continent that'd rather see the back of them."

We sit at the edge of a field waiting for a bus that won't come for another half hour, a bus we won't get on.

So I got fucked. So you lost your job. So what.

Look at us.

You squeeze my fingers. Nod at me. "Go back?"

Viola van de Sandt

I hesitate. Know that I should. Don't know if I want to.

"Will you tell me about it?" you ask, and get up, you stand close to me. "What's going on with you?"

Why did I run? What do I want? What did Andrew do?

"Later tonight, maybe?"

I turn and begin to walk back. You fall into step beside me. Your hand is still in mine.

Winter

I GO TO GALERIA Kaufhof and buy the cheapest frying pan I can find. A stainless steel pot, a plastic spatula, two thin chopping boards, two knives, one large one small, a ladle for soup, a box of cutlery. A bowl to beat eggs in. A filter coffee machine. A kettle.

It's unbearably warm inside the bus. The windows are fogged up by the chatter of the other passengers. When I get off in the quiet neighborhood I'm soon to call my own, I take a moment to breathe the frigid air in, listen to the stillness of the midwinter morning, and despite the weight of the shopping bags, the hurt in my shoulders, the nervousness that comes with knowing I will go to a room where no one's waiting for me, I feel okay.

※

"Do young people see the world more clearly?" My time with Stella is nearly up. I put this to her anyway.

"Parts of it, perhaps," Stella answers. She's holding back.

"You know, I've been young all my life."

"Yes." Stella fights back a smile, I think.

"But now I'm in my late twenties, inching toward thirty — people start seeing me differently. *I* see me differently. I'm not a girl anymore. Not like the girls at work."

"How old are they?"

"Sixteen, seventeen. People expect different things from me. And I'm beginning to see how the decisions I made years ago are going to work out in the rest of my life."

"Just your decisions?"

"It's not about blaming myself," I assure her, though in part of course it is. "It's also things that just happened, things I couldn't help."

"I imagine you've described a few of them in your letter."

"Yeah." I pull the sleeves of my woolen jumper over my hands. *Feel like a kid still, sometimes.* "Do you think that you stop being young when you see your past play out into your future?" I ask.

"What do you think?"

"I think it's more a matter of when things happened."

"Things?"

"The bad things." I shrug. "Life."

"By that account you have grown up very early," Stella concludes with a raised eyebrow.

"I was thinking I came rather late to it, actually."

"Your father died when you were twelve. And your mother — "

"Yeah, but — other kids go through all kinds of traumas, much earlier and much worse than mine."

"You remember we discussed the limited helpfulness of comparing one life with another in this manner." For the first time, Stella sounds stern.

"Some kids are assaulted when they are seven," I press on regardless, knowing I'm wrong and yet feeling I'm right, "I got to wait until I was twenty-seven. Makes me fucking lucky, in a way."

"Franca — "

"If I'm in this state now, can you imagine what I'd been like if Sandra's story was my own? It's a godsend," I say. "Really. I don't mean

The Dinner Party

this at all cynically or... or in a self-deprecating way. The only thing I want to say is thank fucking Christ it didn't happen to me then. It's the one stroke of good fortune to come out of this whole damn thing."

※

Near the end of my "academic career" in Utrecht, my mother came to see me. She'd rung the week before to tell me she'd booked a table at the restaurant of the poshest hotel in town. You and I had joked about getting a room there once, remember? We'd take a holiday but would get to pass on having to catch the right train, getting to the airport on time and squishing all our toiletries inside a bag that barely fits a deodorant stick. We'd walk. Fifteen minutes, there we'd be: on holiday.

But by the time my mother came to see me, that was long ago. You'd stopped coming to lectures. You were barely answering my texts. I'd seen you, once or twice, hunched over your laptop in coffee shops, your eyes small and your face pale and pinched. Work was swallowing you slowly: a mouthful every day. The first few times I'd crossed the street and gone in, said hello, what are you doing, what are you working on, are you forgetting me? But you'd been distant, your voice had had a sharp cool quality, and I'd learned quickly that you didn't appreciate it, me, butting in like this. You'd told me all about it, losing friends because of your work. And now you were getting back to it.

But anyway, my mother had booked a table at seven, she said over the phone.

"Will you drop by and come see my room first?" I asked despite myself. "You could see where I live?"

"You know I'd love to, Frannie, but I've got a meeting at four that afternoon and I can't leave until afterward. It's a nightmare, driving down the A12 on a weekday, so I'll have to go straight there."

"Okay."

"You turn on the radio for traffic updates and all you hear is Utrecht, Utrecht, Utrecht, jammed in all directions. Roads at Lunetten are congested in this direction, that direction, and don't get me started on the city center. Why *did* you decide to study there?"

"It's a nice place," I told her. "And the traffic's not that bad."

"Well, it's not as if I've had any say in the matter."

I closed my eyes. My tiny student room disappeared from view. "Can't imagine The Hague is much better?"

"What, the traffic? God no. But your father had his work — "

"Don't call him that."

"Darling, I wish you'd stop carrying on like Paul is some kind of — "

"No, Paul's fine, that's not my point. My dad is six feet un — "

"Yes, Franca," my mother said, and then said nothing at all. I waited. I bit my lip.

"So, I'll meet you there at seven?" I asked at length.

"Yes. The reservation's in my name."

"Dad's or Paul's?"

"*My* name. I'll see you there." She hung up before I could say anything else.

I got there at ten minutes to seven, and she was already seated at a table by the window. The room was large and airy, high-ceilinged, with windows along one side and a large old-fashioned fireplace on the other. The floor was lacquered, and in the center stood a big black cabinet with a huge vase of white flowers on top. I followed the waiter to the table and stood to the side while another waiter filled my mother's glass with Pinot Grigio. She took a sip and nodded in approval, and only then looked up.

"Frannie," she exclaimed, "there you are." I leaned down and kissed her cheeks. She put a hand on my upper arm, but remained seated. She smelled of perfume and her breath smelled of wine. She wore a skirt and

The Dinner Party

a sleeveless top, both of a stiff, silvery-gray fabric, a string of pearls and earrings that glittered.

"Haven't seen you in a long time," she went on as I sat down and the waiter filled my water glass. Sparkling.

"Can I offer you something to drink, miss?"

"Glass of wine, please."

"Would you like to consult our wine list?"

"No, that's — glass of white, please. Dry."

"Certainly."

"Have you been here before?" my mother asked as she took a sip from her own glass.

"No." I glanced at the gold chandeliers, caught a glimpse of deep-blue plates carried by a waiter, cubes of food carefully arranged, color-coordinated. "Not really the student fare, this."

"What *is*?"

"Burgers?" I guessed. For those eating meat, at least. "Burgers and beer?"

"Pity," my mother said with a grim smile. "I pop in here every time I have to be in the city."

"Do you?" I asked in surprise.

"Meetings, you know." She waved a hand. "Once, twice a month. Business lunches. The perch here is delicious."

"Is it?" A familiar bruised feeling spread through my abdomen. Embarrassment and anger made my teeth clench.

"There's a private room just to the side," my mother went on. "For the kind of conversation that shouldn't be overheard. The staff's always obliging."

I looked round the room. Only a few other tables were occupied, and the patrons talked quietly, the inquiries of the waiters muted.

"So you come here twice a month?" It came out strangled, the hurt all too obvious.

"Frannie, don't be like that." She held out a hand. The waiter slotted a menu in. "You know how busy I am."

"I've been living here for two years. You've never seen my room."

"I'm sure it's lovely, but I simply haven't the time."

"It's a fifteen-minute walk away."

"Time's money," my mother chirped jokingly.

"And twice a month you're having lunch in a place where the 'Wagyu A4' with onions and taters," I consulted the menu, "costs sixty-nine quid."

"That's the beef, Franca."

"*Money* doesn't seem to be an issue."

"The lamb's only thirty-five. And thirty-two for 'Cappellacci,' whatever that is."

"Order and see."

"Burgers and a...a beer, wasn't it?"

"No, no," I said to the waiter, who had been about to put down my glass of wine and was now hesitating, "the wine is fine, thank you."

"Will you need another few minutes with the menu, miss?"

"I've decided," my mother announced.

"I need a minute." I took a sip of wine as the waiter retreated.

"Yes," my mother said in a wistful tone, "you always did need a minute."

"How's work?" I asked, my tone making it clear I didn't care particularly.

"Same old. Terrible business, board meetings. Terrible bores, too, all of them."

"How's...Harmen?"

The Dinner Party

"About to retire, thank the lord. Becoming a nuisance."

"And Jan-Peter?"

"On the mend."

"Oh?"

"Gout," my mother said succinctly.

"I didn't think anyone got that anymore."

"Old people get everything, Frannie." She took a large sip from her glass. "Especially the men."

I smiled. "And Johan? How's he?"

"Same as always," she frowned. "How do you know the board's names?"

"I don't. Every board in this country is made up of the same old men. Ronald. Herman. Frank. Rijkman," I drawled, and rolled my eyes, "my favorite. The occasional Marja, of course," I nodded at my mother, "but really, what's the difference?"

"Well, that's put me in my place." Mother hailed the waiter. "I'll have the mackerel, then the perch. Make up your mind, Franca. I haven't got all evening."

"Gazpacho and the celeriac."

"Tomato soup and a root vegetable," Mother summarized as the waiter took my menu. "Is it too early to conclude two years of living on your own haven't made an adult of you?"

"Quarter-century hasn't made a mother out of you."

We stared at one another. My retort had left a bad taste in my mouth.

"So," I tried. "Why did you want to meet? If it's just so we can mock and berate one another, I'd rather skip dessert."

"I haven't berated you. You've berated me: I haven't visited, I married Paul after your father died, I'm stingy — "

"I don't care about your money."

" — with my love." She held up her hands. A silence fell.

"Yes. Well." I sat back from the table. "Just remembered why I'd decided not to make a fuss anymore."

"A fuss?"

"Ask for more from you."

"More of what, exactly?" my mother asked.

"Exactly." I swallowed the wine. My hand was beginning to shake. "I used to *beg* for your company, after Dad died."

"So you've concluded it's better not to ask for anything, I see." She nodded. "Is this why you haven't answered any of my calls?"

I put down my glass. "You haven't called."

"I certainly have. Your phone must not be working right, because I've called and called — "

"Mamma — "

" — many, many times, and you never — "

"You've never called me," I said as steadily as I could, taking care to enunciate each word. "You know you haven't."

Our eyes met for a moment. My mother looked away.

She was silent until the starters came.

"That looks nice," she tried, nodding at the small glass bowl of soup that had been placed in front of me on a very large green plate.

"It's good," I agreed quietly. "How's the mackerel?"

"Tarted up with peppers and beans. Lovely, as usual."

Outside, the sun was going down. In the courtyard, the white parasols turned pink. Beyond the open gate, the street grew busy. Light was fading, shops acquired an orange glow. People going out for dinner, drinks, a movie.

"How's school?" my mother asked when we'd both finished our starters and were waiting for the main.

"It's good."

The Dinner Party

"What year are you in now?"

"Nearly finished the second."

"And there's four in all?"

"Three."

"And you'll be..."

"A BA. Bachelor of Arts. I might do a master's."

"So what exactly is this program you're enrolled in?"

I cocked my head. "Are you fucking serious?"

"Franca."

Under the table, I gripped my wrist with my left hand. My thumb began to scratch the skin. "Comparative literature." When she didn't reply, I went on: "It's basically just studying how different cultures use literature to examine the — "

"Sorry," my mother waved at the waiter, who came over immediately. "Could I have another glass? Shouldn't drink too much," she said in an aside, "I've got the car."

"Another glass of the — "

"No, I'd prefer a glass of whatever goes well with the perch. This wouldn't do."

"I'll speak to our sommelier." The waiter took her glass away.

I stood up. "I need the toilet."

"Down the stairs there."

In the mirror above the washstand, my face looked long and thin, and my skin had a gray tinge to it. I tried on a smile, but my teeth were yellowish. Something pained was in my face. I tried to make it look indifferent, but all it did was look the same.

My phone buzzed. The text was from you: *I'm leaving in the morning. One last drink?*

I stared at the phone for one long minute. At the edges of my vision, everything was crumbling down. My fingers shook as I typed.

Dinner with my mother. Later tonight?

I waited for your response, gripping the edge of the sink for stability. Blood thumped at the back of my head, pressure grew against my temples.

Nine? I can't make it any later.

Fine.

I took a deep breath, washed my hands again, dried them very carefully with one of the wafer towels, and went back upstairs.

"You took your time," my mother said when I sat down again. "I've ordered another glass for you."

"Thanks," I said, and drained it in one go.

"Oh," my mother exclaimed. "Trouble with the boyfriend?"

"I don't have a boyfriend," I muttered.

"A girlfriend, then?"

Again, my father's voice rising up from a long-forgotten memory. *Don't be childish, Franca.* I shook my head, replaced the memory with anger: my dad wasn't here anymore.

"God, is that why we're doing this?" I snapped. "So you can ask if I'm having sex?"

"Well," she said, grinning, "it *is* my role as a mother, isn't it, to ask if you're being safe?"

I huffed and shook my head.

"You don't look well," my mother commented with a frown. "Your skin's clammy."

"I'm fine." I looked out the window and thought I saw you crossing the street behind the courtyard.

"But why are you sweating? The air con's on full."

"Look, just tell me why we're doing this. You don't ask me to dinner unless you want something. Just get it — "

"The celeriac, miss, with green apple, lovage, artichoke barigoule,

The Dinner Party

and black garlic. And for you, madam, the perch with a puree of carrots, lobster, coconut, daikon, and mango."

"Thank you," my mother smiled.

"Another drink for you, miss?"

"Yes," I said distractedly.

"The same?"

"Yeah. Yes — please. Thank you."

"Enjoy your meal."

"So?" I repeated, watching my mother reach for her cutlery. "What's this about?"

"You're rather direct," Mother said, raising an eyebrow. "That's what they teach you here, up north of the rivers?"

"I just tried to tell you what they teach me here, but you were more interested in ordering your wine. Aren't you embarrassed that after two years you still don't know what I'm studying? Dad would have known before I even — "

"Don't bring your father into this."

"He's my father. Why shouldn't I talk about him? Thank you," I added to the approaching waiter, and took the glass of wine off his silver platter, ignoring his look of irritation.

"D'you know," I went on after a long stretch of silence, after all the rancor had gone from my voice and in its place was something soft and painful, "I hardly remember his face."

"Oh?"

"The sound of his voice. What he smelled like." I tried to call it all back for a moment, but as ever, nothing came. "I only remember his hands were soft. The skin loose and wrinkly."

"He was gentle. Patient," my mother added, and she sounded softer too. "Everyone who spoke to him — they'd get his undivided attention."

For a second, our eyes met, and then, as one, we both looked down and began to eat our mains.

"You were right, though," she said when we'd halfway cleared our plates. "I do want to discuss something."

I looked up.

"Paul has had a job offer. An offer he's accepted."

"Congratulations."

"Thank you. He's delighted, of course. He's always wanted to work in Berlin."

"Berlin?" I repeated, watching my mother with a sense of belated realization. "And you're joining him?"

"Of course. He can't drive there and back again every day, and we both think it's important to stay together. We've found a lovely apartment."

"You've bought a house already?"

"An apartment."

I put down my cutlery. "When's all this happening?"

"Paul's there already, but I'll leave tomorrow."

"*Tomorrow?*" I felt the blood rush to my head.

"Don't look like that, Frannie. I just thought you should know beforehand."

"*One day* beforehand." Under the table, my thumb had rubbed my wrist raw, the thin upper layer of the skin scratched away.

"You *can* visit, you know," my mother reasoned as I extricated a hand from under the table and angrily wiped a tear away. The wine seemed to have curdled while my mother had made her announcement, and now it was sticky and sweetly bitter, too warm to be swallowed. I thought of you, packing your bags at this very moment.

"Eat up, Franca."

"I'm finished." I wiped my lips with my napkin and pushed my

The Dinner Party

chair back. "You've saved two years' worth of visits, I'm sure you can manage the bill."

"Franca!"

"Have a good trip." I strode from the room, ignoring the waiters and refusing to look back at my mother. As I strode across the courtyard, I took my phone from my pocket and wrote a text to you.

Can't make it. Good luck in Cambridge.

DESSERT

By the time we get back to the house, the others have nearly finished the chicken. You make our excuses as we sit down at the dinner table — something about you feeling the need to stretch your legs for a bit — but I barely hear. I can feel Andrew's eyes on me, know without looking that they're confused and fearful, that there are splotches on his cheeks and his leg is jittering up and down against the table. My insides roil and my stomach squeezes every time I swallow. When I shift in my seat, I feel a wetness against my lower back that I know isn't there, and when the cat meows — it wants some chicken too, I think — and looks at me and looks at me, a pitifully small thing scratching at the leg of my chair, big eyes and bigger ears, scratch scratch scratch, my thumbnail on the inside of my wrist, I resolve to put it in its carrier tomorrow, take it to the animal shelter, will step out of the BMW and say I'm unable to take care of this cat, and I'll be shamed, scratch, with people looking at me sideways, asking stern questions which I'll answer inadequately, or I'll fake an allergy, and I'd be rid of it and I'm sick with relief at the thought, feel like it's already happened, scratch, get back into my car and know I'm free to go anywhere, come home as late as I like, to not come home at all, to leave everything behind, and for a moment it's tomorrow and today can be forgotten, everything that happened tonight is left behind, and I'm alone again, nothing to my name, no home to go back to, and I can't tell if I'm desirous of the prospect or terrified out of my mind.

Your voice breaks through the low-level haze that's like the hum of a plane engine drumming inside my skull, and your tone has changed so much, gone from veiled irritation to open anger as you go in from another angle, asking Gerald why he chose to include only Western authors. Gerald replies along familiar lines. I only half listen. The alcohol's risen to my head, but when Evan refills my glass I don't stop him. The cat slinks out onto the lawn again.

" — the list is long enough as it is."

"Really?" You empty your glass. For the first time I see something impulsive in your movements, a growing exasperation you can't control. "I actually cannot *believe* you're saying these things."

"Let me put it this way. This list is a reflection of the fact that most people hardly know anything about their own literary traditions. To add Eastern authors to a list that would prove a challenge to most people as is..." Gerald shrugs. "Well, the most important thing is to know your own tradition, before turning to anyone else's."

"So call your list the best of Western literature," you say simply. "The damn thing would still be problematic, but slightly less so. The world isn't just the West."

"It is in this room," Gerald says, and you fall silent. We all do. For the first time since he stepped into this house, I feel Gerald's got a point. Here we all are, arguing about world literature like we each represent a consecutive part, but we don't, of course not. Our skin could not be

The Dinner Party

whiter, and, more importantly, we're all about as privileged as you can get. I guess you and Evan had to work hardest, the two of you with your "working-class background," as they call it here. I'm not sure what it means. But with your ginger hair, your skin is nearly translucent. And you and Evan studied in Cambridge, of all places. Do you have the right to argue for a side that isn't your own? And *can* you? Can I? I'm a foreigner here, but not nearly as much of one as many other people in the UK. And again, the money, my father's wealth, Andrew's millions. The world isn't just the West, but it is in this room.

"I suppose, on the grand scale of things, it doesn't much matter," you conclude, and a sadness settles somewhere behind my sternum. I know it matters to you. You're looking tired now, as the men go on talking and you just sit back in your chair and sip your wine. Your eyes are distant, you're watching something that isn't here. You don't move except for lifting the glass to your lips and back again. If this is you, it's a travesty, Harry. You're slipping away from me, and I sit still and don't do anything while the others pull the last scraps of flesh off the carcass and discuss the love affairs of someone called Sam, boy or girl? No idea. I don't do anything. I never do. I sit still. Don't say anything. I should be glad they're no longer talking about this canon of theirs, but I'm not glad at all. Your sudden surrender has made me realize: I surrendered a long time ago.

Andrew's chattering about something insignificant. My mouth is dry. My tongue sticks to my palate. My glass is empty. Andrew laughs so loud I startle. Evan claps him on the back and lights a fag right there in the dining room. Outside the darkness is complete. No longer can I see the edge of the pond, the outline of the trees: the night has turned opaque, and the garden is blackness. Inside a puff forms into a cloud becomes a gray mist, and the air smells of smoke and booze and cat food and liquidated — is that the word? — rabbits. Where did you leave it? What were you and Gerald discussing before you bowed out? "The West" — yes, the overextension of the term.

"'The West' doesn't exist," I say to myself, but I must have been louder than I thought because they all stop talking and stare at me. There's a buzzing in my head.

"What do you mean, darling?" Evan doesn't look skeptical for once, and the question doesn't tilt with irony. He means it, he just wants to know. What do I mean?

"It's an idea, not a territory," I try, but feel fuzzy. "Remember Yalta?"

"Don't we all, darling," Evan smiles.

"'The West' is what old men say it is."

"I've lost the thread, I'm afraid." Gerald sounds rather less oily, a bit more befuddled. He shifts his weight in his seat and groans a little. "What's this to do with anything?"

"I'm saying it's hard enough to put a label on writers themselves," I go on with renewed courage. "Who they are and where they come from. And if you look at their work, well, it's even harder. Authors usually have read so many books, watched so many movies, been to so many different places, sometimes — "

The cat skitters inside, jumps and turns in mid-air in pursuit of the toy mouse it's chasing, and the little bell attached to its plastic tail tinkles, and the cat's nails scrabble over the hardwood floor. The mouse emits a rubbery squeak as it flies through the air and is snatched again before it can land, and I scratch the skin on the inside of my wrist.

"Books are mongrels," I continue, low and slow. "All of them. And it's about time we start seeing that as a good thing."

"So instead of calling it the Canon of World Literature, we should have called it the Canon of Mongrel Literature?" Evan grins, and I can hear in his voice that he likes the idea.

The Dinner Party

"Or the Mongrel Canon," you suggest, and everyone except Andrew laughs. Feeling that this is the best I could hope for, I push my chair back and begin gathering the dishes. I start with the plates, then the bowls, stack them all up and carry the lot out of the room. My arms tremble with the weight, and the alcohol's catching up with me, sinking down into my knees, making my legs heavy. The wet patch against my lower back itches.

A bad smell clogs the air in the kitchen, much worse than I'd noticed before. I open all the windows, let in the dark air smelling of damp plants and leaves and earth sweating, birds still twittering.

Muted voices from the dining room. Soft thunks from inside the oven, cooling. A calendar on the wall, birthdays of Andrew's family, mine, his friends. Food in excess in the cellar downstairs, pineapple yogurt and organic granola with honey, posh sea-salt crisps and ten-year-old Tawny, all the kinds of food I'd never bothered to buy back in Utrecht when I was on my own. In the cupboard, fine bone china with silver filigree, silverware we've never eaten with, more glasses than we could ever use in one day, tumblers out of cut crystal, a dishwasher already half-filled. It would have made me sad with longing once, these signs of a household bigger than one person, a life that felt beyond my reach.

It all seems trite now. Has done for a while. How good it felt to come home to somebody, sit next to them on the sofa, ask them about their day. His skin flushing at my touch, moans I could pull from his mouth, the thrill of it. My nervous excitement as a guest at Andrew's parents' ruby wedding anniversary. His proposal, and inherent to it this fabled grail of "belonging." It means as little as "amazing." A fool's enterprise.

I said yes through sheer feeling. A triumphant euphoria, nerves, surprise, and sure, some social pressure. The whole room full of people, all waiting for my response. His attention not on me, not really, but on the room at large, his parents, their reaction. Not mine. My acceptance was a given.

It's an uncharitable view on things. Andrew's not a villain, and I loved him in the beginning. I know that. But right now, standing in the kitchen with my hands full of dirty dishes, I'm not feeling charitable at all. I could have said no, and perhaps I should have, if only not to have turned into what I am now: a girlfriend, housewife, wife-to-be, bingeing on booze and Netflix in an apron.

Behind me, a flutter. A breeze through the open windows sends papers flittering from the countertop toward the floor. I catch a sheet: the recipe for the chocolate cake from the Albert Heijn website. "For real chocoholics," the grocery store says in my orphan language, "velvety, sweet chocolate in *and* on the cake. You can wake us up for this." The picture is of a round cake, one slice missing, two brown, blackish slabs and brown goo spread liberally on top and in between. Bullet-point overview: 10 slices, 575 calories, 30 min. preparation, 2 hours waiting, 55 min. baking. Holy hell. Perhaps Evan will forgive me if I forgo the fucking cake tonight.

"Evan — " I begin as I step back into the dining room, but the sight of you and Gerald once again at loggerheads about how many stereotypes would go into the making of an "American" novel distracts me. I meet Evan's gaze. He rolls his eyes at me and makes to say something, but before he can his phone starts buzzing.

"Ah, pardon me," he says, gets up and steps out into the garden. I sit down in his place, next to you. Where's Andrew?

"Here." You hand me your glass, and I hum in thanks.

"It's quite entertaining, this," I say with all the false bravado I can muster. I take a swig, too large, struggle to swallow.

"What is?" You turn away from Gerald decisively, look at me.

"How much you're at odds with one another."

The Dinner Party

"Yes, well." You give Gerald a fake smile. "No hard feelings, eh."

"Of course not," Gerald agrees.

"I just don't think I'll ever come to agree with the things you've been saying this evening," you say.

"Likewise, I'm sure." Gerald smiles benevolently, as always, but his eyes are glittering, switching back and forth between you and me. "If you'll excuse me, my dears." He gets up and goes into the hallway.

I empty the glass you'd given me just now, only remember it was yours when you cock an eyebrow. "There's plenty more," I murmur, nodding at the bottles on the table.

"True." You groan as you lean forward to take one. "Oh, I'm too old to be drinking like this." You take another glass at random and fill it, fill mine as well. "And you're too young for it."

"Yes," I say, and we both swig. "I wanted to ask..."

"Yes?" you ask.

"Are you okay?"

The color rises in your cheeks. You sigh, some weight falling off you, and shrug in a way that says it's no use pretending anymore. "Not really. I mean..." You don't speak for the longest time. "There's nothing left."

I nod. I look at you and don't contradict you: this is how you feel and there's nothing I could tell you that wouldn't make it true.

"Everything that made me who I am," you go on eventually, "it's gone now."

"Can I help you?" I ask, though I've nothing real to offer you. "In any way?"

"Fran..." Your hand is on my forearm, travels to my shoulder. The pain inside your eyes frightens me.

"Brought another bottle," Andrew says, and when we both look up there he is, standing in the doorway. He takes a step forward, looking strangely timid, and puts the wine cooler on the table. He doesn't meet either of our gazes.

"Brilliant." You clear your throat. "Cheers."

Andrew hums, pushes the bottles of white in between the ice cubes. "This kind of weather, you'll be drinking glühwein in half an hour."

"Thank you," I murmur.

Andrew looks at me. "You okay?"

He's asking about before, obviously. When I ran out of the house. I don't want to talk about it when you're sitting so close, listening.

"Fine," I murmur.

"Can I get you anything, Harry?" Andrew looks at you. "Anything else to drink, maybe?"

"No, no, it's all..." You gesture at the bottles on the table. "More than enough. And the wine's lovely."

"Brilliant." He turns round again, gets ready to leave.

"Look, Andrew," you say. He stops. "I'm really sorry if it feels to you like I'm ridiculing your work, or your record. It really isn't my intention."

"Just happens, does it?"

"I'm so sorry."

"Gerald's old-fashioned."

"He's a dogmatist," you correct. Andrew's expression hardens.

"Sure," he says, and his tone matches his expression. "Yes, the man's a proper knob — "

"Andrew," I try.

" — and I'm the knob who brought him on board," he goes on, turning to me, "but Gerald got us a lot of publicity. And donors. And their money's not going into funding this canon, but it goes into research. It'll further the work of astrophysicists for years and years, and that's something me and Evan and yes, Gerald, have contributed to. And you and

The Dinner Party

Harry here can blow holes in that all evening, but tell me when you've done something like that, and we'll discuss further."

Without another word Andrew strides into the garden. We watch him go.

"D'you know," you begin, "I've got a feeling I won't be invited to your wedding."

You, a guest at my wedding — I hadn't thought that far ahead.

"Get stuck by the toilets, at best," I agree, and we both burst out laughing.

Down the hall, the toilet flushes.

" — yes darling, but I'm not the one who..." Evan's on the phone still, pacing through the garden, now and then passing the doors to the dining room. " — you left me, if you'll remember — "

"Oh dear," you whisper.

" — makes you uncommunicative, doesn't it? I would have been happy to have — "

"Jesus, Fran," you say as Evan's voice fades again, "this evening's just..."

"A disaster."

You empty your glass and lick your lips.

"Franca dear?" Gerald's in the doorway, looking rather pale and sweaty. You sigh and step out onto the patio, closing the door behind you. Gerald watches you go, then says: "I wonder if I might trouble you for a glass of water?"

"Of course." Getting up has become something of a challenge but I manage, and look up at Gerald as I pass him in the hallway. "Are you okay?"

"Just a little bit nauseous. It must be the weather. I'm not very good in this heat."

"Who is?" I hold a glass under the tap. "Here you are."

"Ah, thank you." Gerald empties the glass in one swig. "Oof."

"Here, sit." I pull out a chair for him.

"You're very kind."

"Let me refill that for you."

"Thank you."

Gerald sips. I half-heartedly put some more plates into the dishwasher. Evan passes the kitchen window, still on the phone. "Fine, I'm a brick wall, but I love you, and told you so repeatedly, and you — "

"You don't approve of me, do you?"

I turn and watch Gerald shift his weight on the chair, both hands on his belly. "You still don't get it?" I say and wipe a hand across my forehead, catch sight of the damaged skin on the inside of my wrist. It's swollen red and shiny. Sticky. I rake a fingernail over it. It throbs, and stings, so I do it again.

"'The academy and the literary world are always dominated by fools, knaves, charlatans, and bureaucrats. Any human being with a voice of his own is not going to be liked,'" Gerald quotes placidly.

"Aren't you part of that literary world, though?" I pose. "You just thrive off stoking fires. Saying controversial things, quoting controversial people. But you've no idea what you really believe." I stand on tiptoes and reach for the baking tins stacked on the top shelf. They fall out and land on the floor with an unholy clatter, worsening the throbbing in my head.

"Good books withstand the test of time," Gerald says. I scoff, cut off a sheet of parchment paper. "What?" he asks.

"Time isn't impartial," I say as I spread butter over the tin's sides. "People like you have always been the ones to set the test."

The Dinner Party

I rushed out of the restaurant. The waiters' stares, my mother's voice calling after me, the echo of my dad's. I couldn't stop moving. I walked too fast, away from my mother, away from you, my strides too long for the rest of my body, my head couldn't keep up with what was happening so suddenly, everything crumbling as soon as I touched it, certainties and the last bits of stability I'd built my life around. Only now did I see the peril I'd been in, having no one but you, you leaving for Cambridge because I couldn't love you back — that was it, wasn't it? No matter what you'd said about that job of yours, surely this is what it came down to? My mother too, leaving without warning, leaving me as well. The wall my father's death had built, bricks and mortar and I'd let it dry, had let the wall solidify, Paul hadn't been *my* family, and I'd kept my distance, had let my silent isolation show and had made my mother feel over and over and over that her capacity for love was wrong because it was so much greater than mine, and I had tested it, and tested it, and had pushed myself beyond the boundaries where her love couldn't reach, eventually, and it all was down to me, variations on a goddamn theme, the mess I'd made, the nothing I was left with, just myself and my thoughts that would never let up.

I went into the nearest liquor shop and bought six bottles of Chardonnay at 2,99 a pop, walked blindly, ran, bottles clanking, the bag cutting into my palms, and the city darkening with electric light, entirely invisible. I locked my door behind me and sank down, screwed the cap and slugged, slugged, slugged, half a bottle in half a minute, one bottle in a whole. It rolled across the grimy carpet and the bag crinkled and the second screw cap came loose in my hand and the flesh at the inside of my wrist was red and itching. I tottered toward the bed and put my headphones on, loud as they'd go, "Mad Rush" by Philip Glass and Vivaldi's "Summer" recomposed by Max Richter, a storm of sound and fury and the screw cap in my hand flaying my right arm until the blood dripped and the booze hit and I lay on the floor, stretched out, car lights traveling across the ceiling, my dad my dad Pappa what would he think of this, heart chunking out a sagging beat and my body turning thick and my thoughts oozing like treacle beneath the plinths and down the outside of the house, first floor to ground all covered in black syrup glittering like that dick who wrapped the Reichstag and a Paris bridge. My phone rang from somewhere. I let it go unanswered. I should have said this and that, clever things that would have hurt you deeply, you and my mother, whose love should have been a given.

I woke up at four the morning after, half on the sofa, half on the floor. The light outside, filtering in, was gray. Crusts ran from the corners of my eyes into my hairline. Blood dried. Dawn faded to day. Sozzled students bellowed and brayed from the street below my window. The anger had faded, and my childish self-pity had exposed itself for what it was.

I'd met you on my first day of school, and now for the first time I wondered if perhaps I'd met you too soon. Perhaps I should have made some other friends, people I wouldn't have got along with quite so well, but at least a few of whom would have stayed so that when one went away, I wouldn't have been as completely alone as I was now.

When I checked the time again, it was nine, and my mother would be on the plane to Berlin. She'd sent me an email with her new address earlier that morning, adding that she'd hoped I'd calmed down a little and that neither her relocation nor my reaction to it would alter our relationship if she were to have any say in the matter. She said to call her if I had any questions. She hadn't written anything at the end, just the automatic signature "With kind regards" in a lighter gray and her full name in the company font.

I dragged myself back to bed, pulled the covers over my head and drank the rest of the wine. My arm stung. The sheets were sticky. Kids

The Dinner Party

sang and skipped on their way to the playground, their parents telling them to slow down, cars passed, and the bikes, so many bikes, all old and making a racket. I heard the students wake and make their way down the street, laughing and shouting and singing, too, but different songs than the children's. I pondered whether you'd used me, whether this is what people meant when they said someone had hoodwinked them: laughter and joy in the beginning, confidences and something closer than friendship, and then just as suddenly the novelty wearing off, the shine fading.

The bottles were empty. I took a shower and drank from the tap. The sun went down again. I made a pot of coffee and drank it, one mug after the other, and sat staring out the window.

I didn't sleep. Didn't move for hours. Not until my arm began to throb and I got up to wipe it with disinfectant, cover the worst of it with plasters. I combed my hair in the morning and listened to the music that the girl in the room next to mine put on, her chatter with her boyfriend. The smell of bacon and burnt bread. I made another pot of coffee, drank until I couldn't stop shaking and looked at the room I'd been living in for the past two years — the unmade bed in the corner, the desk buried under books and papers and a laptop with two missing keys, the TV on a tiny table squashed in between the bed and the empty fridge — and couldn't spend another minute there.

The library was airy, white walls and large windows, and although nobody spoke a low hum of people typing, reading, making notes meant it wasn't silent. I was lucky to snatch an empty seat and as my old laptop started up I looked up at the books on shelves soaring several floors toward a square skylight and the blue sky and the squeezing feeling against my sternum that didn't let up. When I looked back down, there he was, sitting behind a laptop opposite me and flashing me a smile. It took a while before I could smile back, but the rest of it went exactly as you'd expect, and more or less as I've written it. I told him about my coursework, and he told me about his company, and then when I should have said goodbye I told him on a whim I'd be in the library the next day.

And I was.

※

"Do you think it was a sort of... precursor?" I ask Stella quietly. "That evening after Harry and my mother left? I mean the — " I break off, and rub my thumb over the inside of my wrist.

Stella understands. "What do you think?" she asks.

"With the benefit of hindsight." I shrug. Obviously.

"Had you done it before?"

"Just a few times. Superficially. Nothing major."

"And when?"

"First time when my father died," I say. "Then, every few years. Don't really know the reason. Just, whenever something went wrong. Or scared me."

"Did it make you feel better?" she asks. "For however short a while?" she amends when she catches my frown.

"No." I'd never really taken to it. Just a beginner, didn't have the guts to take it any further.

"And that final time?"

"Don't remember," I maintain. "Not until a few days afterward."

"How did you feel then?"

It's easy, this one. "A failure."

※

He was wrapped around me when I woke up. I could feel his breath on the back of my neck. The rhythm told me he was still asleep. I stretched,

The Dinner Party

wriggled my toes against his, rolled my shoulders back, made the joints crack. Pulled up the duvet. He smelled lovely. Felt lovely, too.

The light that came through the curtains was dark blue. I could hear the baby next door crying. The swoosh of a shower curtain.

Andrew had rented an entire apartment for the seven weeks he'd spend in Utrecht. I'd spent the better part of the past five weeks there with him. It was warm, clean, an amalgam of polished marble floors and gleaming countertops and all of it fucking huge, frankly. There were pictures of his family on the fridge. They were all smiling in restaurants, in parks, at graduations, shindigs in fancy bars.

I closed my eyes and thought about how he put his music on every morning while making us breakfast, how beautiful his smile was and his hair as it hung wet over his forehead after he'd taken a shower. Definitely didn't think about you, how I hadn't heard a thing since that final text you sent. Didn't think about my mother either, her new life in Berlin.

I woke up again when Andrew tightened his arms around me. "Morning," he rumbled, and I could hear the smile in his voice. "Oh, you smell good."

"So do you," I whispered.

He kissed my neck, my shoulder. "Coffee?"

"Yeah. Please."

"Hang on." He slipped out of bed, left the bedroom. The light had changed to a pale gray. Next door, the baby had stopped crying.

"Here you go." Andrew came back with two mugs. I sat up and put my pillow against the headboard, leaned back, reached for the mug. "What's that?"

I looked down. He was staring at the fresh scars on the inside of my wrist. I'd seen him notice those before. He'd never asked though.

"Nerves," I shrugged, and colored. "Sometimes when I feel anxious, I..." I mimed with my other thumb. Took the cup and sipped. Andrew got in next to me, pulled the duvet up.

"Does it hurt?" he asked.

"No. Stings and itches, sometimes. It's fine." I yawned, and rubbed my eyes. Another sip. "You make a neat cup."

"Thanks very much."

We quietly sat beside each other for a few minutes.

"Baby next door's sleeping through the night already?" Andrew asked.

"Think so. I heard her earlier, but it was already getting light by then."

"Figures," he grumbled. "Just as I'm about to leave."

I took another careful sip. "I spoke to the mother yesterday. She's really friendly."

"I know. Sorry."

I looked at him. "What for?"

"It's a dickish thing to do, complaining about a crying baby."

"It is, a little." I smiled.

"Hey." He kicked me, gently, beneath the covers.

"You're okay," I conceded. Emptied my mug. "Want another?"

"Sure."

"I'll get it."

I went into the bathroom first, peed, washed my face. I put the ground beans into the machine, pressed the button, checked my phone while I waited.

Nothing.

"What are you up to today?" Andrew asked as I slipped back into bed and handed him his coffee.

"I've got a class at noon, but I'm thinking of skipping."

"Why?"

"Didn't hand in my paper." I realized he was looking at me. "Couldn't concentrate," I explained.

"Is it to do with your mother leaving?"

"I guess. How about you? What are your plans?"

"I need to call my parents." Andrew scratched the back of his head, yawned. "They offered me the use of the house in Cambridge when I get back, but I'd rather stay in London for the moment."

"Is it nice? The flat you have there?"

"You'd like it."

I looked at him. Andrew was smiling, biting his lip. I felt a flutter that started in my belly and ended up tingling everywhere.

"Would I?"

"I'm leaving next week."

"I hadn't forgotten." The prospect had been torturing me, but I'd been determined not to let on. It wasn't cool to be this desperate, not after only a few weeks.

"You could come with."

I lowered my mug.

Andrew shrugged. "I don't want to say goodbye to you."

"No," I agreed. First you, then my mother, and now Andrew? "Neither do I."

"You could come with," Andrew said again. A delicious warmth, everywhere.

"What would I do in London?"

"You could figure something out. Perhaps get an English degree there?"

"Perhaps." I didn't feel like starting over.

"Or you could get a job somewhere. Do an internship."

"You know," I said with a smile, "we've only known each other for five weeks."

"Feels longer."

"I've never met your family," I offered, one final show of resistance.

"They'd love you."

"Really?" I couldn't help it then: I broke out in the biggest smile for him.

Andrew pulled me against his side, kissed the top of my head. "Of course. My mother's been planning a dinner party for when I come back. I'll introduce you. I haven't had a girlfriend for two years, they'll be over the moon."

I thought about my own room, the mess I'd left, the silence. I thought about you.

Too much, and much too soon. Looking back, that seems painfully obvious. But again, I try to imagine what would have happened if I'd stayed in Utrecht, in that room. Alcohol, of course, and probably much too much of that. The scratching. The isolation. Would I really have been any better off?

※

"Oof," Gerald groans.

I look round. He's put a hand on his abdomen, fingers flexing, shifts his weight on the kitchen chair.

"Are you sure you're well?" I frown.

"Oh, fine. Just a bit of a...stomachache. Sensitive bowels, you know. Runs in the family."

Realization rushes toward my cheeks. Please, tell me I didn't. Fuck. Gerald groans again.

"Can I get you anything?" I ask, as evenly as I can. Shit, shit, shit... Don't tell me I got the bowls mixed up. "Imodium or something?"

"Oh no." Gerald pats his belly. "Thank you, but I'll give it a few more hours, see if it gets any better."

The Dinner Party

I'm bright red, try to hide by scrutinizing the recipe: "Sieve the flour, cocoa powder and the salt in a bowl." I open drawers and cabinets. Here are the cups and saucers, the plates, the pasta and the rice, here are the tins of tuna and apricots and peaches and —

"I um... I need the lavatory." Gerald scrambles to his feet and hurries out of the kitchen.

The loo door closes, a pause, then a splurt and a high note.

"Oh." I scrunch up my face. A groan, then the tinkle of the toilet roll holder spinning. I tiptoe toward the kitchen door and close it. My hands on the wood for a moment longer, sliding down toward the lock, fingers touching metal. I don't want anyone here with me. The key's in between my fingertips — but I don't turn it. I press against the wood with both hands, as if to shut the door more shut than it already is. Close it closer?

Put the bowl on the scales. The flour spills. I shake the cocoa from the packet, brown clouds landing on my hands and on the countertop, sticking to the residual fat from the chicken, the chorizo, the olive oil I used for the salad and the mozzarella, and a few drops of blood, too, I guess. My blood, or the cat's? Where is the cat?

"Fran, darling." Evan strides from the garden through the back door, pocketing his phone. "Where's the key to that splendid liquor cabinet of yours?"

I put down the salt shaker. Evan's eyes are red, the collar of his shirt has turned dark with sweat. "Are you all right?" I ask him.

"Splendid."

"Was that Rosalie on the phone with you just now?"

"I don't want to talk about it," Evan says. "The key?"

"Are you sure you should?"

"No, but we all do stupid things, don't we?"

"What's happened?"

"Franca, please, just — for the love of god."

"Fine." I open the drawer, rummage through the knickknacks. Why do we even have a cabinet with a lock on it? Andrew thought it'd look cool, but it just makes you look like a knob, really. I retrieve the key and hold it out to him. "Just don't — "

"Thank you." Evan strides out of the kitchen, leaves the door open behind him. I stare after him, then follow him into the dining room, where he's already pouring a glass of something.

"Evan?"

"What'll you have?"

"No." I shake my head. "Nothing for me."

"Harry?"

I turn round. You're on your own, seated at the table. I hadn't noticed you.

"Oh, I'll join." You give me a careful look. "Bad idea, but too late now."

"Here." Evan passes a glass to you, raises his own. "To new flames."

I frown. "What's that?"

"I spoke to Rosalie just now."

"Yes, I know."

"She's found herself a new boyfriend," Evan says after swallowing. "Found him before she'd ditched me, as it turns out." He sniffs, empties the glass. "A Woolf scholar. Christ, another one of you lot."

"Sorry," you and I mutter simultaneously.

"Yeah." Evan pours himself another, drops the bottle on the table.

"Look, why don't you sit down," I try.

"It's the last one," he promises. "Hand on heart."

"Let's go outside. Sit by the pond, you can calm down."

"She's left me for some other shit!" Evan cries out, and he's not the Evan I know anymore, but someone much, much younger. "*Sitting down* won't change that!"

The Dinner Party

"I know, but — "

"She's been seeing him for two months! For Christ's sake, how is that helped in *any* way by my — "

"Sit down, mate," you say, stepping forward as I take a step back. Evan comes back to himself, turns recognizable again.

"Sorry." He takes a deep breath, rubs his face. "Sorry." He squeezes my arm and wanders through the double doors into the garden.

Another groan sounding from the hallway. The flush of the toilet.

"We're going to need more bog roll," I murmur.

I feel the warmth of your gaze on my face. "You speak differently," you say after a moment.

I turn my head as well, look at you. "Different how?"

"Your English, it's more like a...a posh person's version of colloquial. You used to speak like you'd stepped out of a nineteenth-century novel. Now you're all like..."

"Like what?"

"Like 'bog roll'."

"Oh."

We both drink. I look outside. Evan's plopped down flat on the grass, rolling the glass between his hands. Andrew walks into my line of sight, stops beside Evan, looks down on him. They talk, but I can't hear the words.

I pour a glass of whatever Evan's drinking and take it back with me into the kitchen. I unwrap two tablets of dark chocolate, put them on the chopping board, hack them into rough bits. Whatever. I might be more inclined to allow for your judgment on my life if you'd had your own affairs in order. Turn on the oven, wash my hands, take a pan and boil water, measure the sugar, butter, chocolate, open a tin of condensed milk, tip it all in. Stir, and turn the flame down to "slowly heat into a smooth mixture." I stir, and stir, and stir, and take a sip of my drink — whatever it is, it's delicious.

Gerald shuffles in. He puts a hand on the table as soon as it's within reach and shakily lowers himself down onto a chair. "I'm very sorry," he says hoarsely. "I must have caught a bug or something."

"Are you sure I can't get you anything? Or call someone, to come pick you up?"

"Oh, there's no one who'd drive out at this time of night to come and pick up my sorry arse."

I frown. "That can't be true."

"It is, I assure you." Gerald takes a handkerchief from his pocket and wipes his forehead and neck.

"But you're — "

"I'm an old man with a lot of money and the opportunity — well, the power — to present my personal opinion as gospel on TV, so I must have *everything* going for me?" Gerald blows his nose, makes a noise somewhere between a trumpet and a raspberry. "I'm just as alone as everyone else here tonight."

I stare at him. Make to say something, then stop. "I could call a cab?"

"To be frightfully honest, I don't think that would be the safest endeavor at the moment."

I go back to stirring. Is this "a smooth mixture" yet? How smooth is "smooth" exactly? I turn off the gas, tip the pan over into the bowl with the flour, slot it into the KitchenAid and turn it on to whisk.

"I'd have thought you know a lot of people," I say after a moment, watching as the clots slowly melt into the rest of the mixture.

"I do."

"But no one who'd make sure you'd get home when you're ill?" I ask. He doesn't answer. I crack two eggs and add them to the mixture in the bowl, watch as the machine carries on whisking, whisk whisk whisk. Turn it off, pour the mix into the baking tin, slip it into the oven.

The Dinner Party

There. A turd in a tin. I sit down opposite Gerald and turn the timer to fifty-five minutes. "Do you want to lie down for a bit?"

"Oh no, I'm fine."

"You've turned green," I point out.

"Have I?" Gerald inspects his reflection in the microwave. "Oh dear."

"You could lie down on the couch. Or there's a spare room upstairs."

"No, no, no." Gerald takes a couple of deep breaths. His forehead's sweaty again, shirt turning dark at the hem. "I'm — " Gerald stiffens, puts a hand on his abdomen which emits a particularly poignant set of noises. "Sorry, I'll just — " he hurries out of the kitchen. The loo door bangs shut.

"Fucking hell." I get up. Through the window, I catch a glimpse of Evan pacing the lawn, smoking a cigarette. Andrew's brooding on a deck chair, watching him.

From out of nowhere, the cat jumps onto the counter. "Where've you been then?" It meows and makes to step onto the furnace, but I quickly pick it up. "Careful. It's hot. Here." I put it down, pick up its water bowl and clean it, put fresh water in. "There. And one of your little fishy sticks..." I pull the wrapper off, hold it out. The cat starts gnawing it immediately, jumps, turns itself around in mid-air, dashes around the table, stick between its teeth, jumps onto the chair and off again, and then the other chair, and I work hard on it, seeing this for what it is, a kitten playing, nothing else, ignore the sweat trickling, know that the wetness on the small of my back is an illusion, remind myself of it, I don't want this to happen again, whatever this is, fantasy or delusion or delirium, whatever, it feels as real as anything every time it happens, and so I watch it, watch it jump on and off the chairs, on and on, circle the table —

"Think the gentlemen are starting a thirty-something midlife crisis club," you say dryly, looking outside. Andrew and Evan are both hunched up on deck chairs now, heads in their hands. "Where's Gerald?"

"Oh, I've poisoned him," I announce with false nonchalance. You'd been about to take another sip of whatever we're all drinking, but you pause.

"You what?"

I flush despite myself. "The man's been stuck inside the loo for the past half hour, hadn't you noticed?"

"What's wrong with him?"

"Diarrhea. Pretty bad, I think."

"And you think it's your food? It can't have been." You shake your head. "We've all eaten the same, and — what?" You've noticed the look on my face. "You did it on purpose?"

"Not on purpose, no."

"But you slipped something in his food?" you ask disbelievingly.

"No!" I rub the back of my neck. "The man's a shit — "

"Interesting choice of words."

" — but he doesn't deserve this. I meant to give it to Andrew, but... I must have got the bowls mixed up."

"You meant to *poison* Andrew?"

"Just to give him the shits."

"Well, you've halfway succeeded," you cry. "What the hell, Fran?"

"Oh fuck off, Harry."

"What happened with Andrew?"

"What do you mean what happened," I snap. "Nothing happened. Why would something have happened."

"Cause I'm not blind, Franca."

I roll my eyes and slap the chocolate on the chopping board.

"You flinched, Fran. Earlier this evening, right here in the kitchen. Andrew made to put his arm on your waist, and you recoiled from him."

My mouth turns dry. I try to swallow but can't. Heat spreads. Turn

The Dinner Party

my back, take a knife from the block and begin to hack the chocolate into pieces.

"I have got eyes in my head," you go on. "The way the two of you have been acting around each other..."

I put the chocolate into another bowl, take the recipe with trembling hands and try to read the next step. The letters shimmer, gray on white, never turn to words that I can decipher.

"What happened, Fran?"

"What did — " I stop myself. What did you see? How did you see? How obvious have I been, what's Andrew done to give something away? What do you think happened, what do you suspect? What would you call it, what Andrew did?

The cat's jumping up and down, trying to scale the fridge, but you ignore it. Something's changing in your expression. Something forms that I've never seen in your face before. A flash of perturbation in your eyes, a shadow of shock, something flickering.

"Nothing," I try. "It was — " My voice giving out, lungs seizing up, heart in my throat " — nothing. Just — " my shirt's clammy against my back. I can feel a drop of sweat roll down my stomach. "Just..." I can barely get the words out, "bad sex."

"Oh Jesus." There it is: realization. "Fran, what — "

"Fuck!" I shriek when the cat jumps again and latches onto my trouser leg. "Will you get it off! Get it off!"

"Calm down!" You lean down and pick up the cat by the scruff of the neck, carry it out onto the patio. I lean over the sink and turn the tap on, make the water run over my face.

"Fran?" It's Andrew. "What the fuck's going on?"

"Thumping headache." I turn the tap off, grab blindly for a towel.

"Here." Andrew holds one out. I dry my face. "I heard you scream."

I open the door to the cellar, take a deep breath in, gather myself. Andrew puts his hand on my arm.

"Don't," I warn.

"Take a breath, Franca," Andrew sneers.

I'm at the top of the stepladder, looking down into the darkness of the cellar, Andrew's sweaty grip on my arm increasing until I've lost all feeling in my fingers and I'm cold all over, turned to marble like a statue or a pillar of salt, and I can't remember what it stands for, the salt in all the stories we used to read, something essential without which life would be flavorless, perhaps, but there was more to it than that, and it's frail, the figure I make, an effigy that only needs a strong wind to crumble and spill, and Andrew's hand travels up to my elbow, fingers curling round the soft skin at the inside, and he's saying something I can't hear, though he brings his mouth very near to my ear and the sounds he makes sound wet, the scent of his breath warm and repelling, booze and cigarettes and fish, so I allow him to move in next to me at the stepladder and then I pull, a quick sharp movement, watch him tip forward in an endless curve, the momentum too big for him to stand a chance at grabbing the banister, and now his shoulders are at a level with his feet, and then his head hits the third step and his back bends in an unnatural curve and he is a tumble of hair and arms and legs and feet and movement, speed, impossible to untangle until everything stills and Andrew's at the foot of the stairs, a bundle of back and limbs sticking out at odd angles and Andrew himself no longer a man but a thing, broken, not breathing.

I don't move.

"Fran?"

I turn my head. Andrew's still beside me at the top of the stairs, looking worried and uncomfortable. He's released his grip on me.

The Dinner Party

"What do you need?" he asks, nearly a whisper. I frown at him, and he nods at the black depth of the cellar before us. "Can I get you anything?"

"I can't remember," I admit. My voice sounds like I haven't used it in years. I'm sick with relief. I need to sit down. "I — " I shake my head. "I can't."

The door to the loo opens, and Gerald shuffles out.

"Ah, apologies," he says in a feeble voice. "I'm quite indisposed." Andrew and I follow him into the kitchen, where he sits down shakily.

"You're ill?" Andrew asks. From the patio, I can hear you speaking quietly. You must be on the phone, calling a taxi, maybe. Can't wait to get away. Who could blame you? I sink down to the ground, sit with my back against the cabinet we keep the muffin tins in. Andrew's head, his neck, the pallor of his skin and his eyes empty.

"Some digestive issues," Gerald informs us all.

"Oh." Andrew's the picture of awkwardness. "I do hope it wasn't our food?"

"Oh no. The rest of you would have been in the same condition." Gerald waves a hand. "No, the food was lovely, Franca dear. As I said, sensitive bowels run in the family."

I can hear your voice, still, but not the words. Perhaps you're not calling a taxi, but a lover, telling her what a dud this evening is, that you want to leave as soon as you can? Is she prettier, smarter, more assertive? Wouldn't be a stretch.

"Andrew, mate, where've you left the bottle?" Evan appears at the window. "Oh, are we all sitting in the kitchen then?"

"Gerald's got the shits," you announce as you too step back into the kitchen.

"Oh, bad luck," Evan says. "A toast."

"Christ, not another one," you mutter under your breath. Somehow, you've crossed the room without me noticing, and now you're standing next to me.

"No, no, this one's just for us." With a sloppy little gesture, Evan raises his glass, smiles, and slurs: "So. It's been a bit of ballsed-up shambles, this evening, I think we all know that." Murmurs of assent all round. "Some rather odd behavior from some of us. Franca here's displaying a sudden and rather disturbing affinity — if not aptitude — for cookery and stuffing — oh, what's the name, flying foodstuffs?"

"Poultry," you fill in.

"Thank you. Now she's also just spent the better part of five minutes shouting at my pal Harry, who merrily shouted back — yes, we could all hear that, darling," he adds when I give him a mortified look. "Now my best friend Andrew," Evan continues, and claps Andrew on the back, making him spill his drink, "he looks like he's just been to a funeral — has done all evening." Andrew turns red. "Gerald here's been declared a prejudiced pillock — the high-speed expulsion of loose stool water his apparent punishment — and to cap it all off my darling girlfriend has been banging a colleague for weeks while she was also still banging me."

Evan pauses, and looks at each of us in turn, and we look at each other. Gerald sighs, Andrew clears his throat, and you puff up your cheeks and exhale slowly.

Andrew gets to his feet, as do I, and you adjust your position. Standing between me and Andrew, you hide him from view. Or are you hiding me?

"To Woolf scholars."

"Come on, Evan."

"To the humanities!" Evan knocks back his glass. We all drink except Gerald, who mops his head with his handkerchief.

The Dinner Party

"I hear a Coke's really good," you say to Gerald after a moment, "to clean out the stomach. Kill bacteria and stuff."

"I'm not sure that would be wise," Gerald answers in a very subdued voice, "at the moment."

I take a skewer from the drawer, open the oven and stick it into the center of the cake. It comes out glistening. Fuck. When the cake is done, the recipe says to let it cool inside the tin for thirty minutes, remove the tin and let it cool for another hour and a half. We'll have dessert by tomorrow morning at this rate.

Evan and Gerald are discussing different cures for diarrhea, Andrew's asking you about your time in Utrecht, and I am squatting in front of the oven with legs that suddenly turn soft and a lightness in my head that makes the kitchen turn several shades too pale. Gripping the handle of the oven door, I sink down onto my knees, head between my arms. Behind me, everybody keeps on talking.

"So instead of studying something similar to marketing," I hear Andrew summarize as I close my eyes, "you chose comparative literature?"

"Yeah," you begin after a moment, and there's a naked hostility in your voice that must take Andrew by surprise. "In my line of work, the way people do their jobs is based on a few assumptions they never questioned. But after a while I started to wonder."

"Wonder what?" Oh yes, Andrew's voice is colder now, too. So much for the two of you trying to get along better.

"Wonder why," you say. You sound a little condescending, to be honest. "The humanities do that. They look at how we value the things we do, see, imagine."

I grab the countertop and pull myself up. Everything recedes, for a moment, almost out of reach, but then it all sinks, much deeper than it should, into my feet, my heels.

Viola van de Sandt

"We study interpretation," you say, "not just those things that can be measured or proven," and your voice is so very distant now as the lights suddenly turn dim and outside's gone darker than I'd realized, and from where I'm cowering Andrew's neck has got a curious angle to it and there's blood on his temple, and his eyes have got a gray film on them, his lips are blue, his skin is pasty, but he is arguing with you, shaking his beautiful broken head, jaw moving like it isn't swollen black and I think all the alcohol I've drunk today has suddenly entered my bloodstream because I can't stay here, I can't, can't listen any longer, can't stay here any longer, can't be with Andrew any longer, and I shift my heavy, heavy feet — heavy like lead, or something like that — and shuffle and float and wade toward the kitchen door, out onto the patio, and just around the corner where the tap is and underneath a little square grate with holes in it that connects to the sewer and —

I throw up. It's so sour and just liquid, dark red. My throat hurts. And my wrists. And the top of my legs where —

" — so even when the simplest things are being said," your voice is faint as it reaches me through the kitchen window, and the cat meows and I turn the tap on fully, you know, you know, you *know* now, "we ask ourselves who says them."

I'm not saying anything. I throw up again, don't get to speak, and it's good, I feel better, even though it is disgusting, I am disgusting, drinking and drinking and drinking, watching *The Crown*, *Hinterland* over and over again because I can't bear the silence, stop and acknowledge that I've never earned a quid in my life, and that the man I thought I loved — what did he do to me? I'm so alone, and the kitchen's filled with people I can't talk to, not even you, and I'd love to spend an evening by the fire without booze and without other people's conversation and with only my own thoughts for company but I can't, I can't, I just can't manage to.

The Dinner Party

"And how the things we say reflect our culture and our history," you go on, and you're a hundred miles away, saying things you said in Utrecht. I retch, but nothing comes up, just a bit of bile and a hurt that's been there for years.

What the fuck is happening? It isn't just the booze, this. I've been pissed before, the hurl-all-night kind, too, but I'm going to pieces, and over something that's just... How many women must experience something similar every day, and none of them dream of killing their cats or hurting their fiancés.

Or do they?

I turn the tap. Wash my mouth, swallow, spit. Stumble toward the grass and lie down, face up, *starry starry night*.

"Do you read, Andrew?"

The question floats toward me, several seconds later, late.

"Yeah," Andrew answers from far, far, far away. "I just finished *The 7 Habits of* — "

"Any fiction? Novels, I mean?"

Am I dreaming this? Your voices take on a dreamy quality, and your sarcasm doesn't reach me, is beyond my understanding.

"Fiction's just a distraction," Andrew's voice floats in.

"A distraction from what?"

"Reality. How things really are."

How are things, really? What did Andrew do? What would he call it? What would I? And who would be right?

"Or," you begin, and pause for effect, "fiction helps us understand how we live in it. Reality, as you call it."

Who would get to decide who's right? The person who's heard, I would imagine. Who shouts a lot. Who's listened to. Not the quiet one, for sure. I roll over on my side. My head starts throbbing, drowning out your voices. I push up on my hands and knees and stand. The garden's stopped shaking, and though the pounding in my head's getting worse, my thoughts remain whole. They don't fracture like they did before. And they're mine.

I need to finish this. Finish the cake, finish this evening, end it all as quickly as I can. It's the one thing I can do, right now. I cross the lawn on steady feet and open the kitchen door. They're all still in there, talking, I don't know what about. I bend down and use a tea towel to lift the cake out of the oven. A big brown mound's formed on the top, cracked open.

"Oh fuck," Evan groans, "that smells good." He's right behind me, looking over my shoulder at the cake in its tin. I can feel his breath on the back of my neck. "Cut me a slice, darling," he says, and puts both hands on my shoulders.

"It's not ready yet," you say, stepping in. You're between me and Evan. You're making him take a step back. "Shoo," you warn. It's only half a joke, I realize.

"Just a slice."

"It needs to cool off," you say.

"Fran darling — "

What does it matter? I turn the tin upside down. The cake slides out, steaming and greasy. I turn it round again, burning my hands, take the biggest knife we have from the block and try to cut the cake into horizontal halves.

"A valiant effort," Gerald says from the kitchen table.

"Piss off," you tell him. You're staying close. Guarding me with your body, your shoulders, blind to the fact that it doesn't help, makes me as uncomfortable as Andrew touching me did.

"Poo poo," Evan snips. "I think it looks wonderful darling."

I turn to the top half, cut off the bobbly bits and put them on a plate. "There. Enjoy."

The Dinner Party

"Thank you." Evan squeezes my arm, takes the plate, sits down at the table, pops a piece in his mouth and groans. "Oh, Jesus."

"You'd think she'd put in some crack," you murmur.

"She might as well have," Evan agrees. "It's delicious. How about a fag? Darling, do you mind if I?"

I wave a hand. It doesn't matter. I don't care if the kitchen smells of cigarettes. It already smells of chicken and fat and rotting rabbits and come and sweat and cunt and Gerald's shit. Smoke would improve things. Evan takes another mouthful of cake, then lights up. Gerald scrambles to his feet, mutters an apology and hurries toward the loo.

"Drinks?" Evan holds up the bottle, and without waiting for an answer proceeds to pour a finger of Scotch into every glass on the table. Gerald comes back in, groans, draws everyone's attention. His skin has turned gray-green and his eyes are red and watery.

"Okay." Enough now. I break the surface, put one hand on Gerald's elbow, the other on his shoulder. "Come on. You should lie down. Here." I grab a bucket from under the sink and hand it to him, pick up the bag he brought, his phone on the table. "Follow me."

We climb the stairs. I step onto the landing. "Loo's in here," I say, pointing to the door, "bathroom's here — you can take a shower if you like, towels are on the rack — and you can sleep here." I stop in the doorway, allow Gerald to pass, survey the cast-iron double bed, the antique side cabinets, the old wallpaper of yellow and turquoise flowers, birds flying. A large window and green leaves pressed up against it, ticking branches.

"It's okay?" I ask.

"It's lovely, thank you."

I put Gerald's bag down by the cabinet, he puts the bucket down by the bed. "Do you need any pajamas or something?"

"Oh no, I'll be fine. I've put you to enough trouble as it is."

"No trouble." I watch as Gerald sits down gingerly on the edge of the bed. Bends down to untie his laces with one hand. "Let us know if you need anything."

"Thank you. I will." Gerald shucks off one shoe, gets started on the other. "I did have someone once, you know."

I pause. I'd been about to step out, close the door behind me. "Someone?" I ask.

"Someone who'd come and get me," Gerald explains in a quiet voice. "Make sure I got home okay, as you'd put it."

"I'm glad," I say after a moment.

"It was a long time ago." Gerald pulls off his other shoe. "We've been apart longer than we'd ever been together." He's bent forwards, hands clasped between his knees, head low. I shift my weight uncomfortably. Downstairs, Evan's cheering, Andrew's laughing.

"First time I saw him cross the street, he was wearing a white blouse, open at the collar, sleeves rolled up, collar bones and bare arms... An orchestra was playing, you know?"

I swallow. "Yeah," I say quietly.

"I wouldn't accept it." Gerald looks up. "It was a different time, sure, but that's no excuse, is it?"

I bite my lip. Gerald's purple shirt is badly wrinkled, his trousers too. The polka-dot scarf he'd neatly tucked in at the beginning of the evening has come loose, a strand of hair that's usually slicked back hangs in front of his eyes. The Rolex he wears is old, the leather band cracked and faded.

"Still," Gerald goes on in a creaky voice as he puts the watch on the bedside cabinet, "he loved me, as I was. Nowadays, many people react to me as your friend Harry does. The incredulity and outrage I've brought

The Dinner Party

on myself, of course, but with age..." He shakes his head. "Then again, this country was made for men like me."

We look at one another for a moment. Then, I close the door carefully.

Stay on the landing for another minute or two. I hear the bed creak, rustling sheets, then nothing more. I picture him, lying down in a room he's never been in before, sick as a dog and only the gathering dark for company, voices from downstairs filtering up through several closed doors. Whispers of my childhood, adults downstairs and me folded up beneath the duvet, listening, hearing everything word for word, Gerald's loneliness corresponding.

You said once I could do whatever I wanted to. It felt like a plant with glossy leaves and unfolding flowers had started growing in my chest. But I'd let it wither, sometime during the past four years, not by making any mistakes, but by doing nothing.

Spring

I SAVE THE DESK for last. I put more effort into it, visit four stores before I find one that I like. It's old and the top's worn down in places, scratched up in others, but it reminds me of the old, scratched-up floor in my new home, the lives of other people.

I buy some groceries. I turn the thermostat up high, the radiator clanks and hisses. My neighbor gives me one of his old laptops, which is still quite functional as he buys a new one every year. I put it on my new old desk and charge it, sit down. To my left-hand side, the window, children in the playground, a woman with a scarf wrapped around her head, bent over a walker. She looks up, catches my gaze and nods at me. I know her. She knows me. I take a sip of beer. I write down what I did today. What I made.

I spend the night here for the very first time. I don't dream. The silence is there, but I do not try to hide from it.

When I get back into the kitchen, you've put the cream in a pan. You've fired up the stove and are stirring slowly with a whisk, staring at the steam that's beginning to rise, clearly not listening to anything Andrew and Evan say. They're in the middle of the kind of conversation you can't catch up on if you hadn't heard the beginning. They're looking at a video on Andrew's phone together, commenting in their own shorthand, sniffing and chortling at certain points.

I join you at the stove; the two of us in our natural place, what a joke. "Got started?"

"If you don't mind?"

We both stare down at the pan. The steam's increasing. You turn the stove off, tip the chocolate into the pan. I take a spatula from the drawer and start stirring. You take a half-step toward me, standing so close now that our shoulders touch and I can smell your breath, your skin. What are you doing?

"I've got a friend," you say very, very quietly as the chocolate begins to dissolve and the cream is smeared with streaks of brown.

"Oh?" I frown when you don't go on.

"She's a doctor. A GP. Works in a practice a few miles away."

The chunks of chocolate have melted, but I'm still stirring, the cream a dark brown now, shimmering mesmerizingly. "Why are you — "

"She can be here in twenty minutes." You say it quickly, and go on even more quickly while I try to catch up with what you're actually saying: "I called her just now. She's dealt with this sort of thing before..." You look so uncomfortable as you meet my eyes, glance at Andrew, who laughs particularly boisterously right at that very moment.

"Oh," I realize, as all the blood rushes to my head, and fumble with the spatula, which drops onto the floor and splatters both our feet, the floor, the lower drawers, the table leg, "that's not — that's not how it — "

"Fran, if Andrew — " you cut off, your voice so low I have to strain to hear you, and you put your hand on mine, pressing slightly, "...you need to see a doctor."

"I thought you'd called a taxi," I whisper. The words hurt my throat.

The Dinner Party

"I'll call her again." You go to take your phone from your back pocket, but I grip your wrist and hold on tightly.

"Don't. Please." I'm speaking very quietly, but my urgency can't be mistaken. "He didn't mean — he didn't put..." I shake my head, make to finish but can't, I can't, I can't say these things to you.

"Do you think that matters? That it makes a difference, who put what where? Hell, Fran, it's — " You're reaching for your phone again, but I increase my grip on your wrist.

"Don't," I whisper. "I'm begging you. Please. Don't."

You stop moving. Your eyes connect with mine. Behind us, Evan and Andrew guffaw. They've turned up the volume on the phone. Tinny laughter fills the kitchen. I feel like I'm standing at the edge of a cliff, only you to hold on to for balance.

"Fuck, Fran," you whisper after a moment. Your eyes are glued to mine, you're not blinking, you're seeing everything, know everything, all the things I tried to hide, and now I — "Let me help you," you whisper. "I've gone through a similar thing."

Bits of the ground beneath my feet fall into the precipice. I feel my heart stutter. "You — you've what?"

"Harry!" Evan calls from the kitchen table.

"I know what it's like," you whisper.

"Harriet!"

You scowl at Evan over your shoulder. "Call me that again and I'll rip — "

"Oh shit." Evan claps his hand in front of his mouth. He's sloshed. "Shit. Sorry. I forgot." He gives you an apologetic smile, then says to Andrew out of the corner of his mouth: "She doesn't like people using her full name."

"No," you correct, "I *hate* it. So don't."

"Apologies." Evan holds both hands against his heart. "Apologies."

"Accepted." You turn back to me, wrench your hand out of my grasp and say in a rapid-fire whisper: "I'm calling a cab. It'll take at least an hour to get here, and when it does, we're both going to leave."

You stride out onto the patio before I can offer any further protest, phone already raised to your ear. I'm left alone at the edge, afraid to move, afraid to make more of the earth crumble.

"Oh, where's she going?" Evan turns to Andrew. "I was going to ask her what she thinks of... What were we watching?"

I stare at you through the window. What happened? What did you go through? How come you never talked about it? Did it happen before Utrecht, or after? Could it even have been during, and I just didn't notice? Jesus. Were you hurt? Did you see a doctor? Go to the police?

Are you all right, now?

Mechanically, I whisk the cream and chocolate "into a shining mass." Evan asks me something. The look in your eyes just now told me everything. How can this keep happening? How many people has this happened to? How can we —

You step back into the kitchen, meet my gaze and give a tiny nod. I suddenly can't swallow anymore. What is happening? I'm to go with you tonight? Step into that cab and leave Andrew here? And then what?

You take your place beside me again, look down at the chocolate cream I'm still mixing.

"Forty-five minutes," you breathe. Who hurt you? A man like Andrew, or Evan, or an older man like Gerald?

"Is it shiny?" I ask croakily.

You don't even look inside the bowl. "Yeah, I'm sure it's fine."

"Ah," Evan drawls gleefully, his feet on the table and his chair balanced on its rear legs. "Does the sudden delicious absence of that godawful racket mean that we're about to eat this wonderful cake of yours, darling?"

"It's supposed to cool for thirty minutes." The recipe says to "let it stiffen," but no chance in hell I'm using that word with Evan and Andrew in the state they're in.

"Lord almighty," Evan laments with mock exasperation.

"We can take a shortcut," you say, looking at me for agreement, but all I can think of is: you want me to come with you. It's a wonderful, terrifying idea, and I don't want to say goodbye now, when I've only just got you back. I want to spend the rest of the evening with you, no one else, tell me what has happened, who you are now, who did this thing to you — and yet, what about tomorrow? The day after? Andrew, the launch, our life together, this house? What about the cat? What about the wedding?

"Fran?" You're frowning at me, but the scrape of a chair distracts you. Evan's gotten to his feet, stepped in between the two of us and dips a finger into the chocolate mixture, groans in appreciation. "Oi," you protest.

"Oh, it's nice," Evan says, smiling. "Very dark, but not too bitter." He dips his finger in again. "How long?"

"Fran?" You turn toward me questioningly, but I've no space now for any of this shit. I've been doddering in this bloody kitchen all day, and it's all turned out rather less than average, and you're elbowing Evan out of the way until you're standing next to me again, closer than you've been all evening, keeping Evan at a distance, and now you're taking the bowl in one hand and tilting it a little to check how stiff the mixture already is. You're taking charge, you're taking care of me, and though I appreciate what you're trying to do, and why, I don't think I want this.

"Let's just pour it," I murmur, taking the bowl from you. The two halves of the cake are on the cooling rack. I tip the bowl until a thin brown stream hits the center of the bottom half and spreads, spreads, reaches the sides and droops over them onto the rack and the table underneath.

"Bit thin," you comment.

Andrew stands up as well, and there we are, all four of us, gathered round, watching. I cover the bottom half with the top one, pour the rest of the chocolate, and thin little trickles reach the edge of the kitchen table and drip down onto the floor. Four pairs of feet shuffle out of the way amid a strangely solemn silence.

For a moment, I recede. I rise and survey the kitchen, see everything exactly for what it is, the delusion of pure reality unformed by interpretation, my partisan brain making no unwarranted connections. It's an almighty mess, the cake an unholy edifice at the center spreading a shiny, sticky stain. Chocolate everywhere, a spatula on the floor, dirty dishes in the sink and on the countertop and on the table too, a dirty pan on the stove and a greasy baking tin. Fat on the chopping boards, bits of salad stuck to the tap, empty bottles leaving rings, smudgy glasses half-filled, flowers on the windowsill drooping with the heat, the cat's water bowl littered with kibble, the kibble bowl itself empty except for a few hairs on the rim, hairs on the scratching post in the corner, a mangled toy mouse, and still the smell of dead things.

I don't know how this happened. How it became such a shambles, if it was me or things I did or didn't do, if it happened this evening or really began much earlier, back when I met Andrew, or when you left me, or when I left home and came to Utrecht, when my mother turned silent, when my father died and I lost the certainty of everything.

I lie. I do know. It's not my decisions that did this, but rather the lack of them. All this isn't the result of the things I did. It's a sum of the things that happened to me. I'm floating in some non-existent space between the kitchen and the upstairs bedroom, have been floating above it all for

The Dinner Party

years and years, way before Andrew, way before you, before my mother leaving. I've been the helpless passenger of my life for as long as I can remember, ever since my father died and I stopped being good enough the way I was. Or perhaps I could only be myself with him, my dad, and I've been so busy ever since, trying to please, to feel accepted, and I've lost sight of who I was to begin with.

I descend again. Feet touching the floor, two of eight, and the blood sinking into them so that my head feels light. Here are you, and Andrew, and Evan, and here's the cake covered in goo and reminding me of that show where they put people's body parts in food and made it look appetizing. Except this cake doesn't look appetizing at all. It looks nauseating, drooping black and glistening. We all watch as you cut ten equal pieces and put four onto small plates, stick forks into the tops.

"It looks like murder on a plate," Andrew says. I look at him. You do the same. Andrew's prodding his slice with his fork. "No wonder you never bake, Fran. Should thank the lord. Allowing me to live."

"Andrew, mate, don't be a dick." Evan takes a plate out of your hand and tucks in. "It's delicious, darling," he says to me, mouth still full. "Fucking delicious. Simply scrumptious," he crows through another mouthful.

"Fran..." you begin.

"I'll check on Gerald," I say and hurry out the kitchen, up the stairs.

I can hear snoring through the door. The ventilator in the loo is on. I go into my own bedroom, our bedroom, sit down on Andrew's side. His phone charger is on his bedside cabinet, his wallet. There's an indent in the pillow where his head lay last night, the duvet thrown open sideways as it is every morning. Andrew's shoes in a row against the wall. The toes are shiny, the leather smooth. Proper Oxfords. He shines them every Sunday, in the evening, just before he goes to sleep. He doesn't like the trainers everyone in the office wears. Too American, he calls them. Evan laughs about his shined shoes every Monday.

"What are you doing?"

You stand in the doorway. I hadn't heard you come up. Your face is half-hidden by the shadows, half-lit by the lamp in the hallway downstairs. Your red hair's glowing, curls everywhere. I'm so tired.

"Sorry," I whisper. "I got confused."

"You can't stay here."

"And then what?" I wipe my nose with the back of my hand. "Say I'll come with you. And then what?"

Your eyes travel through the room, the soft blue armchair in the corner, the antique drawers, the Auping bed, the French windows opening onto the balcony, everything in pastels, and me. I make a figure. I'm aware.

"You could stay with me," you say. "For a while."

"What?"

"Look." You sigh. You sound young. You don't cross the threshold. "I know you didn't want to — " You wave a hand. "That's not the point of this. But I'm alone and at a bit of a...a dead end, right now, and I think you might be too."

"Yeah." I wipe my eyes, but not to hide. The tears don't matter. You know everything already.

"We could be — I don't know. Alone together? It's a terribly trite thing to say," you go on quickly when I make to reply, "but we could...I don't know. Try? It would be better than this fucking dinner, wouldn't it?"

"Hard not to be," I agree. "So...when did it happen?"

You look confused, but not for very long. "Oh. Years and years ago. I was your age, I think."

I try to digest, think of what to do with this. There's nothing. I open the wardrobe and take a suitcase. I fill it with jeans, shirts, I don't care which. Underwear, socks, shorts, my bathing suit: no rationale, let alone rhyme or reason. When the suitcase is full, I close it.

The Dinner Party

"Should I carry it down?" I ask.

You frown. "Perhaps get it when we leave? No use causing a scene."

Oh, there's going to be a scene in any case I think, but do not say. We go down the stairs. A boozy roar from the living room, Andrew's, Evan joining in. The clatter of the liquor cabinet. Another cheer, and cackling. Even through two closed doors, we can hear Andrew slurring his words, Evan guffawing. Then there's music, something that's all bass and no melody, thudding through the walls.

We're back in the kitchen, and I check the time. When did you call your taxi? How much time do we have left? Where will we go?

"What are you — "

A crash from the living room, muted swearing, the door opening with a bang, music swelling, and Evan striding in, nursing his hand against his chest.

"Fran, darling, you've got a towel or something? A plaster?" He speaks too loudly, and his eyes are cloudy. The front of his shirt is splattered with red, blood trickling down his wrist.

"What happened?"

"Door to the liquor cabinet swung shut, broke the glass — argh. Careful." You've taken hold of Evan's hand, held it up to the light, stretched his fingers. A gash through half his palm. "It fucking hurts."

"I'd have thought you'd hardly feel it," you murmur.

"What, with all the booze? So would I. Christ."

"It's not that deep." You look at it closely. "And I can't see any glass left in it."

"No, I took it out." Andrew's entered, a plate with shards of glass in hand. "Good for something, aren't I?"

"Sure mate. Got any bandages?"

"I'll get them." Andrew drops the glass in the bin, drops the plate in the sink with a clatter, lurches out again.

"Fuck," Evan groans. In the living room, the track changes again. The bass deepens. My head pounds in time.

"Man up, petal." You, too, have to raise your voice to make yourself heard. You wrap a clean towel around his hand, press to stem the bleeding. "We'll put a bandage on it, wrap it up, you'll be good to go."

"Bleeds like a stuck pig."

"I bleed worse than that," I murmur softly, but you hear.

"What?" You're startled. You look me up and down. "Where?"

"Every month."

Your mouth twitches. I feel mine do the same. "Ooh, I don't want to know about that," Evan complains.

"Franca."

We turn as one. Andrew's stood in the doorway. I hadn't heard him return. His eyes are wide, the skin at the hollow of his neck is wet. His eyes lock onto mine.

"What's going on?" he asks me. "What are you doing?"

"I — " I can feel you behind me.

"What is it? What's happened?" Evan asks.

"I — I'm — "

Andrew drops the suitcase I left in the bedroom. You take a step closer, another, you're a solid warmth at my side. Andrew's gaze shifts to you.

"What is this?" he asks.

Like a scene in a play, the doorbell rings.

"Who's that?"

"I — it's..." I'm sweating through my shirt, and there's a wet patch on my lower back and there's a ring on my finger. I can't swallow, can't speak.

"It's our cab," you say. You bend down and pick up your bag, sling it over your shoulder. You wait a moment, but nobody reacts. "Evan mate." You hold out your hand. "Good to see you again. Thanks for inviting me."

The Dinner Party

"Oh right." Evan tears his eyes away from me, from Andrew, makes to take your hand but remembers his injury. He kisses you on both cheeks instead. "Um. I've got your number, don't I?"

"Still the same."

"I'll give you a ring?"

"Sure."

The doorbell rings again. Again, I'm at the precipice, crumbling earth beneath my feet, a steep drop ahead, only you're no longer holding on to me.

"I'll get the door," Evan says.

"What is this?" Andrew asks as soon as he's gone. He looks at you, then at me. "Fran, what's going on?"

"I — I was thinking..."

"Yeah?"

"Cabbie's waiting," Evan says. His head's in the doorway, the rest of him still in the hall.

"Let's go." You turn to me. "Fran?"

"What are you doing?" Andrew asks. His look of betrayal and disbelief worsens every second.

"I — I want to leave," I say. I don't know if it's the truth anymore: the prospect of leaving turns my stomach, the thought of staying makes me want to cry.

"What?" Andrew turns red. "Seriously?"

"I'm — "

"Just like that?"

"I've been — "

"And we're not even going to talk about it?"

"Mate, how about you let her speak?" Your tone makes it clear that your patience with Andrew, thin as it was, has finally worn out.

"Harry, how about you just stop with the blokey thing, all right?"

"Sorry, you've got a patent?"

"This is between me and Franca, my fiancée — "

"That's not a possessive, you know. *Mate*," you add with extra emphasis.

"No, it certainly isn't," Andrew snaps, "as you've been reminding me."

"Sorry?"

"Come on. You've been making eyes at her all evening."

There's a brief pause. Everyone turns to you. You shrug. Give a small smile. "I loved her once," you say.

Oh Jesus. The kitchen swims, dizziness overtakes me. I put a hand on the counter to keep from falling. You say it like it's simple. You hold Andrew's gaze, respond to his glare with a cocked eyebrow. Evan's mouth is open. He's bleeding through the towel, doesn't notice.

You tut at Andrew, loudly. "Which is more than you can say, apparently."

"Oh, I love her," he says. He takes a step toward you, doesn't look at me. "In fact, I've lived with her for the past four years, built a home with her — "

"You bought it, mate."

" — introduced her to my parents, asked her to marry me — "

"It wasn't even the first time, was it?"

"Harry." I'm sweating even more than I was before. I touch your arm, make you stop here, but you don't look away from Andrew.

"What the hell are you talking — "

"And you don't even know what I'm talking about." You laugh, you've turned red as well, there's nothing about this that you find funny. "Are you fucking kidding me?"

"Okay." Evan steps into the kitchen. "Let's calm — "

The Dinner Party

"Either tell me what the fuck you're talking about," Andrew butts in, "or just, for just one minute in this whole fucking evening — "

"Andrew, mate — "

" — keep your mouth *shut*," he spits. I bend down, make the blood flow to my head.

"Tell 'em that often, do you?"

"Tell who?"

"The women you — "

"Harry — " I try again. Please don't.

"The women I what?"

"The women you rape."

My breath comes in short bursts, long intervals. The kitchen tiles shimmer beneath my feet.

"What?" Evan breathes. Evan thinks he knows. He thinks he knows something about me now, about what happened. Upstairs, the toilet flushes. "What are you talking about?" Evan asks. You don't respond. You're still only looking at Andrew. "Harry?"

You turn to me. "Let's go, Fran."

"I never did that." Andrew's turned pale. "I never did what you're saying. Fran." He turns to me. "What — "

"For god's sake," you scoff, "look at her."

Fuck me, they all do. And the expressions on their faces. I can't stay here. I feel the sweat collect on my upper lip. I'm hot and cold at the same time.

"I want to leave," I murmur. My mouth is dry. I can barely hear myself. I take a step toward the door, but Andrew rushes forward and puts a hand on my arm. My flesh crawls.

"Fran. What are you doing?"

"Let go of her," you say.

"What are you doing?" he asks again. He's ignoring you. His hand is still on my arm.

"I want to leave," I say quietly. I can't look at him.

"So let's go." Your hand's already on the doorknob before you pause. "Let go of her, Andrew."

"I'd never hurt you," he says to me in the urgent kind of low voice that's meant to be for the two of us, but that everyone can hear. "I never have. I never would. Why is she saying — "

"What? Let me guess. You said 'I love you' so it doesn't count?"

"Will you just *shut up*?" Andrew roars at you, and I jump with the sudden violence of his outburst. It's like a switch has been turned: his skin's turned red again, and instead of the anguish he displayed a minute ago, he's all rage now. "Will you just get into that fucking taxi and *leave*?"

"And leave her here with you?" you yell back. "Like this?"

"It's none of your business!"

"Now calm — " Evan tries.

"You think I'm just going to ignore what I saw here this evening?"

"Oh and what did you see?" Andrew rages. I step back out of his reach.

"She fucking flinched from you! You put your arm round her and she fucking flinched!"

"Franca's not afraid of me!"

"Look at her!" You point to me without taking your eyes off Andrew. You're both red in the face, standing very close to one another. "Does she look like she's comfortable?"

"You know *nothing* about her," Andrew snarls without looking. "And you know nothing about her and me, *our* relationship, which we've had for *four* years! Years! I know her better than you ever did — "

"That's not the fucking point!"

The Dinner Party

"Don't take your frustration out on me just because she wouldn't have you — yeah, Evan's told me about that! How you propositioned her when you were both at school, and she said no — "

"I told him that in confidence," you shout back with a livid glance at Evan, who's trying to get in an apology and you're not having any of it, ignoring him in favor of shouting abuse at Andrew, who's shouting back, breathing hard, the both of you, and I can't breathe at all, can't move my head and when I finally manage there are Gerald's socks at the foot of the stairs, his creased trousers, his hands wrapped around the bucket I gave him. His face is hidden, but he's standing still, turned toward the open door, he must have heard everything too, everyone knows, everyone knows now.

" — some kind of lunatic scheme to get into her pants — "

" — you fucking sick shit, that's your department, isn't it — "

" — I've had to listen to you all fucking evening and I'm — "

" — you don't know what listening *is*! You're so in love with yourself, your fucking money, your little career — "

A clock sounds in the back of my head, bang bang bangs far beyond twelve, far too loudly to be the church clock in the village.

" — you see, this is what I'm talking about. Don't talk down to people because they've got what you haven't — "

" — your little house and your little wife and everything that makes you feel successful — "

The bell tolls so loudly my ears are ringing with it.

" — because you can't even hold down a fucking marketing job, *marketing*, sitting behind a desk from nine to five selling stuff that no one needs — "

" — and you have no idea that everything about it's just pathetic. You're a small, pathetic little boy who's never created anything for himself, lived off the money of his parents, the talent of his friend — "

"Stop it," I try, but no one does. I hear the howling, yours, Andrew's. You're burning it all down now, not just Andrew's life but mine too, these are not just his but my failures you're describing. Things are being said that cannot be undone. It goes on, the two of you, shouting in each other's faces about my life, yours, Evan's and Gerald's even, all of it presented in the worst possible light, like that's the truth of us. How will we look at each other when this is over?

"Stop it, please," I repeat. "Andrew isn't a — "

But my mouth goes dry as you turn your gaze on me, burn me with disdain and disbelief. My back hits the kitchen counter. I turn round. Palms on the chopping board. Hips against the cabinet. The bruises hurt. My wrists ache.

"You'd defend him?" you ask. "After what he did?"

"You're about to leave, aren't you?" Andrew bites at you. "Well then. Cabbie's outside. What are — "

"Fran, can you make *any* decision *at all* by and for yourself?" you ask me. There's nothing left of the warmth with which you'd talked to me before: just coldness, and a level of animosity that makes me freeze.

The cat jumps onto the windowsill. It's been outside, whiskers covered in dirt, and in its mouth is a dead mouse, not a toy but a real one. It drops it onto the chopping board, next to my hand, and licks my fingers.

"Leave my house," Andrew says to you. "Now."

"Andrew — " Evan tries.

"Don't you see he doesn't even like you?" you cry, pointing your chin at Evan. "You're a pathetic hanger-on Evan can't get rid of — "

"Harry, stop this," I croak.

" — and in a minute he'll deny it, but I know what he said to me this morning, and now you do — "

"That's enough!" Evan bellows, so loudly I feel as if a vein in my

The Dinner Party

temple has just popped. "Stop it, the both you! For fuck's sake, the cabbie's probably called the police — "

Even the taxi driver knows, then, and I'm the only one who doesn't. I brush my fingers along the countertop. What happened here? What did Andrew do? The word you used, is that correct? I wipe my forehead with my palm. It comes away glistening.

"I'm leaving," you say, ignoring Andrew, who's still shouting, "Fran. Let's go." A hand on my shoulder, which I shrug off.

"You're not taking her anywhere!"

"She's not a damn toy!"

"Settle down. Both of you!"

"What's happened?" Gerald's voice is croaky, like he's got a really sore throat. "What's going on?"

"Fran." Your hand again, this time on my arm. "Come on."

"And where the fuck do you think you're taking her?" Andrew shouts. The pressure in my head worsens. I can feel them picturing it, Evan, Gerald, you, the cabbie even: the flesh and blood of it, the smells, the bruises, the sounds we made, the fluids. The voices fade in and out. These are my friends, Andrew was my family, I lived here with him, Evan was his best friend, and mine, you were the best years of my life — I've built myself around the three of you, everything you entail. It's all falling apart now. I want to leave. I don't want to be here, to watch any of this.

" — none of your business, you sanctimonious shit! D'you really think I'd — "

"I don't fucking care what you do, you can't just — "

" — just settle down! And let's talk about this like — "

"Have you been fucking listening? *Talk* about it?"

"Harry, I know this is — "

On the chopping board, the mouse twitches. One of its mauled paws, tiny nails scratching over the wood, as loud as the shouting. From the corner of my eye, I see the cat's ears prick up, its spine curl, body tense.

"I *never* did that!" Andrew roars. "I'd never touch her like that, and how you got that into your head — "

I retch, but nothing comes up, nothing comes out of my mouth.

"She's told me! She told me what you've done!"

"Fran, this isn't — "

"Don't you — stay away from her!"

"Fran, for fuck's sake — "

My silence is what I'm made of: nothing.

"I said you stay away — "

A hand on my waist. The cat's tail is a comma, its ears flatten against its head.

"Fran, just fucking say something — " Andrew's breath smells of booze and anger.

" — don't you dare — "

" — or I swear, I'll — " another hand around my jaw, clammy, squeezing too hard, turning my head forcefully. The eyes are Andrew's, but the look in them makes them seem entirely unknown to me. You're screaming. Andrew's shouting back, spittle flies, lands on my face. The cat jumps.

I take the knife from the counter.

DIGESTIF

"You told me before, in one of our first sessions, that you don't know what happened?"

Stella's wearing blue today. Dark blue slacks and a dark blue blouse with a V-neck that exposes a bit of her clavicle, bones making horizontal patterns beneath her skin. It's really hot outside, nearly forty degrees Celsius, and inside the AC's broken down. She's thrown the window open, wide as it can get, but we're both sweating. The polyester armchairs aren't helping.

"Franca? After you'd picked up the knife — "

"I know what happened," I say quietly. "You told me." Some flashes, faces mostly, doctors, officers. The crinkly sheets and the weird texture of whatever the pillow had been stuffed with, neither foam nor feathers. Waiting for the door to open.

"I know what I did," I say. "I just can't remember doing it." Can't write it down. Can't talk about it, not in my own words. I don't remember anything in between taking the knife from the counter and sitting in that white room with the door that buzzed open. Hours or days or weeks — I couldn't tell you. "It was two years ago," I add unnecessarily.

"Your recollections of the evening so far are very detailed," Stella points out.

"I know."

"But you can't access your memories of that particular moment in the kitchen, or the immediate aftermath. Do you have any idea why?"

"That's your department, isn't it?" I shrug. "Mine's Home Accessories." I shift in the chair. The covers squeak against my bare skin, stick. Stella offers me a glass of water, takes one for herself.

"People sometimes remember fragments," she goes on. "Particular moments, images, sounds, feelings. A seemingly random selection."

I swallow. Put the glass down carefully.

"I remember shouting," I admit. I do hear it, still. "Not angry shouting but, you know. Terrified."

Stella waits for a moment, then asks: "Anything else?"

I try. "Harry's eyes. She was saying things — can't remember what. I couldn't hear. She was scared, I think." Your voice, so urgent and insistent, your eyes wide, the expression on your face making it nearly unrecognizable.

Stella looks at me. I try harder.

"Warm and wet," I say slowly. "I felt it, I mean. Something warm and wet."

"The blood?"

"I'm not sure. Suppose. And hands. Not just Harry's, but — " I shift a little with the unease I feel afresh.

"Andrew's?"

"Don't know."

"You don't remember seeing him?"

The Dinner Party

"I don't — he was on the ground. We all were. Or not Gerald, I think. He was..." The echo of his voice, fast and frantic. "Did he call the ambulance?"

"He did, yes."

"He'd come downstairs, I think. Just before?"

"That's what he said, yes," Stella confirms.

I nod. Hesitate. "I've been thinking..."

"Yes?"

"Should I drop him a line? Gerald?"

"To say what?"

"Thank you." I shrug. "If it weren't for him..."

"Indeed," Stella agrees. Then: "Are you thankful, though?"

"To Gerald?"

Stella crosses her legs. "To put it bluntly, Gerald put a spanner in the works, didn't he? If he hadn't phoned for an ambulance — "

"It was the right thing," I maintain.

"What you did? Or he?"

I don't answer. I can't. Shake my head, feeling shy suddenly. Stella studies me for a few long seconds, then goes on in a refreshingly matter-of-fact voice: "All right. Tell me about your first crush."

I laugh. What a change of pace. "Julia." I can't help but smile, something close to nostalgia washing over me. "When I was eleven. She was a year older than me, a lot smarter. We both played the poor villagers in the school play. She was blond and tall and had very fair skin and I loved everything about her."

"What happened?"

"Oh, I'd asked her to come with me to a friend's slumber party after the school play. Weeks of rehearsals, standing close to her — we had to hold hands at one point," I remember, grinning. "I was *so* nervous every time I spoke to her, I made a terrible fool of myself. And I kind of knew already that she didn't like me all that much, but anyway, she said she'd go, and then just before we were about to go on stage, she told me she was going to stay over at someone else's. I remember fighting tears all the way through the performance, and after, when my mum and dad came up to me, just... a deluge."

"How did your parents react?"

"My dad was embarrassed and... angry, I think. Not a lot, just — he told me not to cry in public, it was preposterous. Why start crying when a girl had made other plans? I was a child, so was she, what was the big deal? Don't be childish, he told me."

"He didn't realize how you felt about her?"

"I didn't either. Not until years later. Can't fault him for that, not really. It never occurred to me then that I was in love."

"How did it make you feel at the time, though?"

"Embarrassed. Silly. A fool. My dad was the only one who seemed to understand me, and for him to tell me I was being an idiot..." I shake my head.

"And your mother?"

"She was silent. Just stared at me. Don't remember anything else. I'd forgotten about it, actually, until Harry kissed me, and I heard Dad's voice in my head."

Stella picks up her glass of water, takes a sip. Pulls a face.

"Oh, the water's warm. Too bloody hot in here."

"Yeah."

"Would you like to go out?"

"For a walk?" I ask doubtfully, glancing outside.

"No, no. Just to sit in the shade. There's a park just round the corner."

"I know."

"Breath of fresh — well, broiling, dusty air? Do us some good?"

The Dinner Party

I hesitate. I've never seen Stella outside this office before. To walk beside her, into the real world where I'm not just her patient and she's not just my therapist — already, she looks different. I wouldn't know how to —

"Franca?" Stella offers me a smile.

"Sure," I say. "Let's go."

※

She came to see me, back when I was still in the UK.

It's one of the first things I truly remember from afterward. A few days after the dinner, a buzz, and the door opening, creaking through the uniform impartiality of the room, my mother walking in.

She was wearing jeans, for god's sake, and a large gray cardigan I recognized from a time when my father was still alive. Her hair looked messy, not blow-dried into submission as it normally was, and she was wearing glasses instead of contact lenses. She didn't look like the woman I'd last seen in Utrecht, and as she closed the door and turned to look at me, I saw she was thinking the same about me. I hadn't seen a mirror ever since that evening, but my mother's expression told me more than I needed to know about my appearance.

She didn't say anything at first. She was red in the face, a little splotchy around the jowls. She opened her handbag, and a clear plastic bag fell out onto the floor. She rushed to pick it up, and from what I could glimpse it was filled with what looked like lipstick, a bottle of Purell, a compact. She must have flown straight from Berlin. Two-hour flight, two hours' traveling to and from the airport. Outside, the sky was darkening already, so an overnight stay, then.

"D'you have a meeting?" I croaked out, baffled despite the drugs.

"Do I have a what?"

"A meeting. Near here."

"Franca — " My mother cut herself off, sniffed, took a tissue from her pocket and wiped her nose with it. I looked on in dazed amazement. She sniffed again, fiddled with the crumpled tissue, turned it inside out.

"There's another box right there," I rasped, inclining my head.

"No, I've got my own." She sat down in the fold-out chair and rummaged in her bag. I watched as she pulled out a packet of Kleenex.

After a minute, she looked up at me.

"You look terrible, Frannie."

"Yeah." She always said it, and this time I'm sure she was right. I felt it.

"How do you feel?"

I swallowed. My mouth made a smacking noise without my permission. I rubbed my nose with the side of my thumb. My nostrils felt raw, chafed. "I'm fine."

My mother was still looking at me, into my eyes. She hadn't looked at me this long since —

"Are you in pain?" she asked.

"No." I wasn't.

"Are you on medication or something?"

"The doctor gave me something. Painkillers."

"Which ones?"

"I don't know."

"I'll ask on my way out." She put her tissues back in her bag, snapped it shut, gripping it tightly in both hands. "They told me to push the button when I want to go out." Her eyes darted round the room, quick-fire, found the small silver push-button near the handle of the door.

"You're leaving?" I surmised.

"No. No..." She noticed her hands fiddling with her bag, stilled them. "No. I'm..." She took a deep, deep breath. It looked like she hadn't taken one in a while. "I talked to Andrew." She said it like a question. I didn't respond. "He says you don't want to see him," she went on.

The Dinner Party

"I don't."

"Why?"

There was a fly caught against the window. It hit the glass. Made a little thud.

"He's okay," my mother went on. "A few stitches, that's all. He'll be fine."

"Great."

There was something at the back of my mind that kept nudging me, like a sneeze building up but never quite breaking through. It wasn't an unpleasant feeling. Rather, an unexpected frisson of joy, the promise of relief.

"What happened, Frannie? Why won't you see him?"

I didn't answer. I couldn't.

"Did he do something?"

I met my mother's eyes.

"Harm you in some way?"

"I don't want to talk about it." I was quiet, but certain. "I don't," I insisted.

She smiled nervously, so very much unlike her it just —

"They told me what you did, Franca."

"Well then, what is it?" A flare of annoyance. Here was my mother, absent for years and years and reappearing only to know better, again, to point out my mistakes, everything I'd done wrong. Things she knew nothing about.

"They say you say you can't remember."

"I can't."

"But you know what made you do it?"

"I don't want to talk about it," I said again. My mother heard the finality in my voice, and although she obviously didn't believe me, she nodded all the same. There was hurt in there, in her face and the way she tried to smile. She knew what I'd just said, that it was none of her business, not her place to ask me anything at all personal.

It wasn't anymore. Again, I swallowed noisily. My mouth was dry as tinder.

"Are you thirsty?"

"Yeah."

"I'll get you some water."

With an awkwardness I'd never known her to be capable of, my mother pushed the button. Someone opened the door to let her out. I sat on the edge of the bed. The fly flew against the glass again and dropped onto the windowsill.

She came back with a plastic cup. I had to focus not to grip it too hard, to keep the water from welling up over the brim. I sipped. The water was tepid.

"How's Paul?" I asked. My voice was a little less raspy now.

"He's good. Just got promoted again. Managing director. He's a bit nervous about it, but — "

"I'm sure he'll do very well."

My mother looked touched. "I'll tell him you said that."

It was the kind of comment that usually ended our conversations. She'd done it hundreds of times before: a welcome excuse, to pretend she was going to tell Paul right this very minute. She had a lot to do, after all, and I had nothing.

I wasn't going back, that was certain. I was never going back to the house I'd shared with Andrew. It was the only thing I knew about the future, the rest was one big question mark. So I sat on the bed like a sack of potatoes and waited, waited until I knew what to do, for my mother to reach down and grab her bag and wrap herself in her aura of busyness, two air-kisses and a whiff of perfume.

The Dinner Party

None of that, though. My mother stayed seated on the chair next to my bed. She didn't speak. I sipped my water. She watched me. Once again, I noticed that odd frisson of joy shivering to life inside my stomach.

"They lock the door at night," I murmured.

"Oh." My mother did not sound surprised. "Well, that's probably — "

"Sensible?" I met her gaze. She looked pained. "I don't want to stay," I went on. "I want to go."

"Go where?"

"I don't care. Anywhere. I just want to leave."

"I'm sure you do, Frannie. When they let you." My mother shook her head. "Oh, just look at you."

I followed her gaze, down, down, the strange clothes I couldn't remember being given, my legs dangling over the bed's edge, my hands on my lap, palms up.

My mother put her hand on top of mine. Her grip was weak and clammy.

"I'm so sorry," she whispered. "I'm so sorry this happened to you."

"Why?" I asked. "I'm not."

"Franca, you can't — "

"I don't have a fiancé. I don't have a job, or a home. I've only ever had one friend of my own and I don't know where she is at the moment, or if she still is my friend even. I don't have any money," I went on, croakily but as sincere as I'd ever been, "nowhere to go, and I am *so. fucking. relieved.*" I couldn't stop the smile from breaking through. My mother's eyes widened. "I've got *nothing*," I began to laugh, "absolutely sod all, and I get to start all over."

I couldn't stop laughing. It was deranged, the sounds I was making, how I doubled over, tears dripping onto the linoleum, laughing crying laughing and the door opening, hands on my back and voices, none of them telling me that I was free, nothing to my name and nobody to call, not even my clothes to call my own, only my body and that at the moment was a mixed blessing, but a blessing it was, oh yes, and the joy inside my chest erupted, and I shook and shook with the force of it, a blessing indeed.

※

"Do you enjoy this kind of weather?" Stella asks me as we cross the street. It's baking, the pavement so warm I can feel the heat of it through my sandals.

"I used to," I admit. "When I was a kid. We'd go on holiday and anything below forty degrees Celsius wouldn't count as summer."

"And now?"

"Too hot to breathe. Let alone *do* anything."

It's quiet in Berlin. Normally, on a Tuesday afternoon, this street would be roaring with cars and motors, the air thick with fumes. None of that today. Traffic's sedate, idling at the light, pulling up sluggishly.

We walk through the gate, pass the map on the display. Immediately, the limited noise of the traffic abates even further as the trees close in around us and the air turns just a little bit cooler. Stella turns right onto a path lined with bark chips and deep shadows.

"There's a bench just up ahead, if that's okay?"

"Sure."

I walk beside her, hands awkwardly in my pockets. The path curves, slopes upward in between the trees. Rocks have been dug into the ground at regular intervals like stairs, and for a few minutes we climb and climb and then there is indeed a bench. We sit. A stream of flowers, purples yellows blues and reds, trickling down down into a little

The Dinner Party

meadow, and off to the side a stream for real, and the water rushing over stones with such speed it must be powered, I think. There's no sound but the water, no smell but that of damp earth and the sun beating down on the leaves overhead and the warm shade. It's surreal, to sit in a place this quiet in the very center of Berlin.

"Are you well?" Stella asks. The climb, such as it was, has left me out of breath.

I nod. "Not enough exercise."

We sit in silence for a while. I can smell her perfume, I realize, a little disbelievingly. Look sideways at the face of a woman I've only ever seen from the front. She looks different like this, here, outside.

"Have you spoken to Harry recently?"

"We talk over the phone." I let my bag slip from my shoulder onto the bench. "Once a week. She calls, and then the next week I call her."

"What is she doing these days?"

"Finishing her MA. About to start her PhD."

"Oh. Very good."

I risk a peek at her face, but Stella's looking at the flowers, the creek.

"She's in London, isn't she?" she asks.

"Yeah. King's."

"Does she ever visit?"

"She's coming over next week."

"Oh, is she?" Stella smiles at me. "That's exciting."

"Yeah."

"Are you looking forward to her visit?"

"I'm a bit nervous," I admit.

"It's been a while since you've seen her, hasn't it?"

"She wanted to give me time," I remember. "Herself as well. To figure things out."

"I see."

I hesitate. "You asked me once why I turned her down."

"I did."

"At the time, I had this picture in my head," I admit. "Do you remember?"

"Yes." Stella remembers everything.

"Rolled-up shirtsleeves, broad shoulders, preppy hair and glasses..."

"That's right. You told me."

I take a breath. It's hard, admitting cowardice. "I said no because she was a woman."

As always, Stella lets it settle. "Do you know," she says after a while, "I always thought Harry was a man."

I smile. "I know."

"Only when you told me Harry had experienced something similar to yourself."

"And you... and the girl on the radio..."

"Indeed," Stella agrees.

An interlude. Just a few minutes.

"Evan's been by."

"Oh, has he?"

"Yeah. He's in town every now and then. Meetings, conferences, that kind of thing."

"Ah."

"You know they pay him to talk about it?" I pause as a jogger with earbuds in rushes by, leaves behind a whiff of some posh perfume. J'adore, I think. Andrew bought me a bottle for Christmas one year. "His involvement in the launch. The part he played in making the canon."

The Dinner Party

"Yes," Stella says. "I remember reading about it in the papers."

"The launch or the canon?"

"Both."

Another jogger follows the first. She's also wearing earbuds, going faster than her predecessor.

"I don't give a sod about the canon," I admit. It's a weight off, admitting this.

Stella turns to me and frowns. "You've talked about it a lot."

"Not a single sodding shit," I insist. "The fucking mission, the books they attached, the sculptures and paintings, the lists. I don't care," I repeat. "Men like Gerald — they ruffle feathers by operating on the assumption that books change people. Influence their behavior."

"And you don't think so?"

"No, of course I do. But there's no..." A bird lands at the edge of the stream, halfway down the meadow, begins to drink. "There's no one-to-one correlation," I go on irritably. "Playing a...a first-person shooter on a PlayStation or whatever doesn't make me go out and blow apart a café or a supermarket."

Stella turns toward me. "Because you've done more in your life than play that game. You've seen more, been more than just that violence."

"Exactly." I swallow. I didn't mean to talk about it, not right now, when we're doing something different and it all seems, feels looser, boundaries not so rigid. But Stella has a way of getting back to this, to me, and somehow I never see it coming. I am more than that violence, I agree. I've been raised by my mother. Lost my father. Went to school and talked to you, to teachers, classmates. I've been to cinemas and watched movies. I have a job and an apartment. I had and maybe have a friend who was the best friend anyone could ever have. I nearly had a husband. I had a thousand conversations, and each day my brain processes a million impressions, thoughts, feelings, words written by others.

"The only reason anyone thinks a literary canon is important," I go on after a while, "is because they believe these books are the only books most people will ever read."

"Well." Stella thinks about it for a moment. "They might be right, actually."

"So that's the real problem, isn't it."

The bird's stopped drinking. It's bathing now, wings flurrying, drops of water everywhere. Its beak burrows in between its feathers — on its back, beneath its wings.

"It's a girl, right?" I ask.

"Judging by her feathers."

I nod. Her coat is shiny. Her ritual's one of joy, I think.

"One of my teachers said that reading's like a muscle," I go on. I keep my eyes on the bird. Stella's listening. "A muscle that needs to be developed. If you're only going to read twenty-five or fifty or even a hundred books in your lifetime..." I snort.

"Yes?"

"I mean, your ability will be that of an overweight asthmatic alcoholic at the Olympics."

Stella laughs.

"You'll read a book and all you'll read is the story, a narrative," I say. "Hot air. A book just begins with the story, and only ends when it's no longer being read."

※

It took a while, but the laughing, too, ended. My entire torso hurt, lungs and midriff, stomach and intestines, and my face a smear of tears. I'd laughed so hard my face felt stiff, cheeks and lips set around a hysterical

The Dinner Party

grin. Happiness — but not really. My mother shushed me, rubbed my back, had been doing so for the past ten minutes, and I could feel the tension in the gesture, the stress in her murmuring. She handed me another cup of water. I drank it in one go.

"How did you know?" I asked her. My throat hurt, but it didn't matter. It was something I'd done to myself.

"Know what?" My mother's voice was unusually small.

"That something had happened. Who called you?"

"You did."

"What?"

"Well, technically I was the one to call you, but the way you sounded on the phone..."

"What?" I said again. "You mean when you called me during the party?"

"You sounded so unhappy, and when I asked if he was good to you, you..." My mother was blushing, for some reason, and she gripped my hand so hard it began to hurt.

"That's why you came? Because I hung up on you?"

"Look, Franca." My mother released my hand, dabbed at her nose with another tissue. "I know that in the past four years we haven't seen each other as much as I'd — "

"Don't," I interrupted, and used both hands to hide my eyes. The plastic cup dropped to the floor and rolled under the bed. "Really, Mamma. It's fine."

"I know we don't get on, particularly."

"Don't worry."

"I know you, Franca. I used to know you better than I knew myself."

"I was a child then." I looked up, straight into her eyes. "I was twelve years old when Dad died. Things happened."

"Yes, and you won't tell me about them."

"You didn't speak to me for a year."

My mother stayed silent. The bandages itched, but I resisted the urge to scratch. I'd done enough damage. I'd destroyed everything I'd built in the last decade, was right back where I'd started, where I'd never wanted to return: me and my mother drowning in a white room, drowning in silence.

"How did you find me?" I asked just for the sake of it.

"An older man came out of the house just as I arrived. Harold, I think it was."

"Gerald."

"Said he'd come to collect his belongings. Said he'd left some things in the guest room."

"He was ill."

"Yes, that's what he said. Told me where you were."

I didn't want to think about it. About the house, Gerald, Evan, that entire evening.

"Told me to give you his best," my mother added. "Seemed a very nice man."

"You *would* like him," I said under my breath.

"What was that?"

The fly collided with the glass once more. A buzz as it fell, and then it lay still.

"He said it was a country for old men," I remembered.

"What?"

"He said that's why he thrives here. Said you only had to play the part."

"That makes it rather difficult for us, then, doesn't it?" my mother scoffed.

I smiled. "That's what I said. He — " I shook my head. "He was lonely."

My mother waited a moment, clearly expecting me to say more.

The Dinner Party

When I didn't, she cleared her throat. "Well then." What she really meant was, who isn't?

"It just surprised me," I say defensively.

"What I think you need to learn, Franca, — "

"Oh, lovely, here it comes."

" — is that your feelings aren't unique, but are felt by lots of people, who do their best to hide the fact."

"That's very helpful. Thank you."

"And they do their best to *do* things, many things, nevertheless."

"Yes, thank you." I stood up, hand on the bed for support. My feet hurt. The room swam, then settled. The needle pricked. My palm on the glass of the window, the grille behind, and behind that, a courtyard, three trees, three concrete benches, a dustbin.

"Do you have anywhere to go?" my mother asked at length. "When they release you?"

"I don't know."

"You mentioned a friend?"

"She's got enough on her plate."

"Do you have a job here?"

I turned my head, watched her over my shoulder. "No."

"You'll come with me, then," my mother said. "To Berlin. When all this is over."

"I want to live on my own."

"There'll be conditions, Franca."

I fully turned toward her now, stepped away from the window. "I want to choose things. For myself."

"I'm sure you do, but you tried to — "

"I know I'm a mess. I know there's nothing left. I burned it all." I paused. My mother stared up at me with wide, red eyes. I felt my face accommodate another smile, but smaller now, not as manic, and sadder. "But I can do things differently now. Can't I? I mean," I went on quickly as my mother went to speak, "there's the space now. You can't build something new unless the old stuff's been taken down, can you?"

"'You must have chaos inside yourself to give birth to a dancing star,'" my mother murmured. She gave a small unhappy smile. "It was on his bedside table when he died."

I watched my mother for a moment. "Is that what you did?" I asked. "After he died, when you went upstairs?"

My mother sighed. Shifted a little on the edge of the bed. "You were always such a unit," she said, mostly to herself. Her gaze was on my hands and wrists. "The two of you, reading, walking, talking." She sniffed. "We had similar jobs you know." Her eyes met mine.

"You and Dad? Yeah, I know."

"We were the same age, same background, same education, even. We got the same job at similar companies, but he was thriving, fish in water, and I was..." There was an unfamiliar bitterness in my mother's face. "I was working twice the hours, trying to prove myself to... well, men... prove that I was capable, *worthy* — can you believe it? — of being there, telling these arseholes what to do."

I closed my eyes and nodded. "And there we were, Pap and I, reading to each other every Saturday. Feeling dreadfully superior, I'm sure." I sighed. "So when he died...?"

"I went upstairs and read every book he had."

※

I'd thought I'd open this letter with a "Dear Harry" or "Harriet" — but this isn't really about you anymore.

Besides, if I'd done an opening like that, I'd have had to deal with the dilemma of "Love" or "Best," "All best" or "All my best" or just an "x" with an initial.

When I began to write this thing, it was for you, Harry, but now that I'm ending it, it's for me.

"I'll have to go soon," my mother said after a while. I'd sat back down on the edge of the bed. My mother was still in her chair. We hadn't said a lot after we'd finished talking about my dad, but the silence no longer carried the weight of the past, was no longer something to fly from. The silence was benign, at least for now. It would let me speak.

"Will you be back soon?" I asked.

"Tomorrow morning."

My mother got to her feet, slung her handbag over her shoulder, exhausted movements.

"How long are you here for?" I asked.

My mother's face crumpled. For a moment, she wasn't my mother at all: nothing remained of the things that had made her who she'd been. For a moment, they'd been replaced with the opposite, turned her into the mam I'd loved and known before my father died.

It only lasted a moment, yes, but I remember.

"I'll stay until I can take you back with me," she said.

"I want my own space," I repeated, just a whisper. I felt childish, to keep saying this, insisting, considering the circumstances I was in. But still: a room of my own. Decisions.

"We'll figure it out. We can find you an apartment close by, if need be." She bent down and kissed my cheek, and then my forehead. Over her shoulder, I saw a nurse stand in the doorway, waiting, face averted for politeness. "But you can't be on your own, Franca. You need help.

Not from me," she said when she saw I was about to protest. "People who know what they're doing."

She straightened. Sniffed a little. The nurse came in. My mother took a few steps toward the door.

"Thanks for coming," I said, afraid I'd offered this too late. But my mother stopped, then turned. Her eyes had filled.

"It would have been a mistake, you know."

I nodded. I knew. I'd felt my own selfishness the moment I came to, saw the efforts strangers were making to minimize the damage I'd done. It would have been a mistake.

But not one I'd have had to live with.

※

Would it have made a difference, do you think?

If I tell you that Andrew pulled my pants down entirely, spread my legs, held me down with one hand and used the other to unzip. If I'd burned my wrist on the stove, still hot, if he'd rammed so hard my head banged against the kitchen cabinet, if flesh had been torn or I had bled. Gagged me with his hand or with a scarf or with tape wrapped around my mouth and neck.

Would the things I did that evening seem reasonable then?

Conversely, if it hadn't hurt, if I hadn't struggled, said "stop" loudly enough, bitten his hand with enough force to make the skin break, if I'd shouted or not, if the top button of my blouse hadn't come undone, if my trousers weren't quite so snug, if I hadn't criticized his work, or met Harry again, and she'd never fallen in love with me, someone who wasn't a man, if I hadn't been quite so pretty, if I hadn't been so very plain, if I hadn't begged for it or wanted it secretly or really said yes when I said no or didn't say anything, if I hadn't been Andrew's fiancée, as

The Dinner Party

good as his wife, if I'd already taken his name — would it just have been bad sex, as I once thought it was?

It would have been easier, I guess. It's nice to put a name on things. It makes us think we understand.

What's the name for what Andrew did to me that evening? Does it matter?

If I was fucked, or buggered, touched, penetrated and with what, bound or gagged or beaten up. If the bruises were dark enough. If it hurt a lot.

What matters is what I've made of it. Not what Andrew did. The influence it's had on my life, who I am, what I want and dream of.

There's no easy answer. There never is. But whatever the answer is — I listen. I read.

It must be somewhere in these pages.

The longer we sit by the stream, the more oppressive the heat's becoming. My shirt sticks to my torso. It must have stained by now, on my sternum, under my arms. I don't want to look. Rummage in my backpack instead.

"What are you looking for?" Stella asks.

"My water bottle." The heat, and the climb, and the talking... My head's swimming. "I think I've left it at home."

"Oh, and mine's at the office," she says, checking her own bag. "Are you very thirsty?"

"I'm fine."

"There's a café at the opposite end of the park."

"It's fine."

"Let's get a drink." Stella stands up. "I could do with one."

We follow the track as it slopes down alongside the brook. The air gets denser, damp. The track morphs into a gravel path, leading us through the trees and out onto a wide avenue with chestnuts on either side and an open field all round.

"How is your mother?"

"She's good." People are sitting on benches, watching their phones, watching us walk past. "Now that I'm living on my own, she drops in every other day. It's driving me insane."

Stella laughs. "There it is." She nods at the pavilion at the end of the boulevard, right in the center of an intersection of paths. Tables and chairs grouped beneath big brown parasols, people on bikes and roller skates whizzing past. We find a table beneath a tree and Stella orders a bottle of water and a cappuccino. I order water, too, and a sommerspritzer.

"Third of white wine, two thirds sparkling water," I explain when Stella looks at me questioningly. "I'm cutting back."

"That's very sensible."

We clink glasses. Drink. Watch the cyclists whizz past.

"Have you heard from Andrew?" Stella asks.

I was about to take another sip, but pause now. "He's called a few times."

"Have you answered?" Stella asks when I don't offer more.

"Yeah." I finally do take that sip. "He calls to ask how I am. Says that he misses me."

"Does he want to see you again?"

"He wants to, I think, but he knows we won't. Not for a while." I look at Stella. "And not like that."

"You don't want to get back together eventually?"

"No." I make to say that it would be ridiculous, after what I did that evening, but I know it's not the truth. A tiny little bird lands on the back of an empty chair and eyes the crumbs on our table. Crisps, I think, a little disbelievingly, feeling cold all over.

The Dinner Party

"Are you angry with him?" Stella asks at length.

"Yes." I can't believe she's asking me this. "Of course I am."

"Do you think it might be helpful, to you, I mean, if you were to tell him that?"

"He knows."

Stella hums. She waits a while before she tries from another angle. "After that night..." She raises her inflection — begins with a question. I nod to show her I understand. "Before anyone told you what had happened, was there a moment when you thought that you might have tried to hurt Andrew? Or the cat?"

"No."

Stella raises an eyebrow at the surety with which I deliver this statement.

"What, are you serious?" I can't help it, I roll my eyes at her.

"It's just a question, Franca."

"Something out of the movies," I mutter.

"What do you mean by that?"

"I mean, it's a thing, isn't it? A woman gets raped and the only way she can cope with it is not by, oh, years and years of hard effort, or trying to give it a place, grueling emotional work, trying to get back into trusting other men, relationships, or indeed by going to a therapist." I nod at Stella. "No, no, no, the only way these women ever deal with it is by *killing* the man who raped them," I spit. "I have *never* seen any other trope on my fucking screen that is so *blatantly* masculinist. It drives me up the wall."

"I can see that."

"If you look at the credits, the script's been written by a man. The director, producer, whatever — "

"All men," Stella finishes.

"'Revenge,'" I say in my most mockingly dramatic voice. "Or another doozie: a 'strong female character.' God almighty. The mere idea that killing someone counts as processing, *righting*, even, a trauma. Violence as strength." I shake my head. "And you wonder why the world's the way it is."

"All right, drink some water before you pass out." Stella opens the bottle and pours some in my glass. I drink deeply. I'd forgotten how thirsty I was.

"Look, I get that there are exceptions," I go on after a moment, "and I'd have loved to have been one because, frankly, it would have made for a better story, but ninety-nine times out of a hundred, women don't turn that kind of violence toward others." I pause again. "They hurt themselves."

"Yes," Stella says quietly. The bird hops onto our table and begins pecking at the crumbs. We watch it for a while in silence.

I remember what I'd wanted to say, a long time ago now. When I still had to get used to Stella, and she said I should never feel obliged to share my story. I hadn't been brave enough. I am now.

"What happened," I say slowly, because while I might be a little braver than I was, telling people how much they mean to you is still scary, and I meet Stella's eye to make sure she knows what I'm talking about. "You said I don't have to tell anyone."

"I remember," Stella says.

"I haven't," I say. "I've only told you."

For a moment, Stella doesn't visibly react, and I fear I've fucked it up. Then, she smiles and inclines her head, and I know she understands it's a compliment, perhaps the biggest one I've ever given.

"How's Pinot?" she asks.

"Oh, he's having a rare old time in the garden. He only ever comes inside when my mother gets the kibble out, she says."

Stella smiles. She doesn't ask anything else, though.

The Dinner Party

"Brought in a mouse the other day," I go on to fill the silence.

"Ha," Stella laughs. "Your mother must have been pleased."

"She was, actually," I grin. "They've had a few mice in the house this year, so my mother's delighted whenever one gets killed."

"Oh dear," Stella grins, but grows more serious as she watches my smile fade. "How do you — "

"It's a great failing," I answer before she can finish. Stella, again, stays silent. "Whenever I stop by for dinner," I go on, "the cat hides beneath the kitchen cupboard as soon as I step through the door." I shake my head. "Can't say I blame it — him," I correct. "I mean, that final evening... Animals are intuitive, aren't they?"

Stella nods.

We finish our drinks without saying anything else. It's not awkward, or uncomfortable. Stella out of the office turns out to be not that different from the Stella inside.

"How are you getting home?" she asks eventually.

"I came on foot."

"It's not very far from here is it, your flat?"

"No. Ten minutes. And you?"

"Oh, I'm going to head back to the office. Take the car."

"How long do you have to drive?"

"Thirty minutes. I enjoy it, actually. I like to take the time to... process the day, on my own, before I get home."

"There's someone waiting for you?"

"Yes." Stella smiles. "There has been for the past three years."

"That's lovely."

"It is." There's sadness in her smile, but there's calm, too.

We pay. I hoist my bag onto my back. We shake hands like we always do.

"I'll see you on Friday, then."

"Yeah." I smile back. Stella makes to leave, but when she sees I don't move, she pauses.

"When will Harry get here?" she asks.

"Wednesday."

"Oh great. Have you made any plans?"

I shrug. "Go for a walk. Show her the city."

"She'll like that," Stella says reassuringly.

"See you Friday then," I say, and turn.

I walk home. Orange light and baking pavements, fumes and tall buildings, Berlin in late afternoon.

Acknowledgments

The cover of this book carries my name, but its publication is very much the result of a collaborative effort, both in the US and the UK. I'm so grateful to everyone who helped bring it into being.

To my agent, Millie Hoskins, thank you so much for all your work on my behalf. This book wouldn't exist if you hadn't believed in it, and your kindness and professionalism have time and again assured me I'm in very safe hands.

To the fabulous Sally Kim, thank you for choosing *The Dinner Party* as your first acquisition at Little, Brown. I'm certain that I could not have found a better advocate for my novel. When you jumped on board, everything else followed.

Thank you to Ellie Freedman at Tinder Press for being so contagiously enthusiastic from the start, and for giving this novel such a great home. It has been such a joy working with you.

My sincere thanks to both the teams at Little, Brown and Tinder Press, in particular to Michael Noon, Sabrina Callahan, Alyssa Persons, Darcy Glastonbury, Kayleigh George, Lauren Denney, Laura Mamelok,

Acknowledgments

Alexia Thomaidis, Phoebe Kalid, and Federica Trogu. Thank you all for bringing this story to light.

A big thank you to Liesbeth Hendrix, Baiyi Sun, Mónica Santos, Stefanie Botman, Sander Hendrix, Mariska Rijk, and to Betty van der Zande, with whom I would have loved to share this. Thank you to Lisette van de Sandt and Thijs Leufkens, and of course to Finn Leufkens, light of many lives, not just mine.

To Jill Dawson, who mentored me for years and years through the Gold Dust mentoring scheme, I owe a huge debt of gratitude. I never would have continued writing without your generous advice and guidance. I have learned so much from you, and I am truly grateful to have found a friend in you.

Finally, and most importantly, I want to thank my parents, Peet and Annie van de Sandt. Thank you for standing by me, and for believing in me when I could not. I owe you both much more than words can say.

About the Author

Viola van de Sandt has degrees in journalism, comparative literature, and English literature from King's College, London. A draft of a previous novel was longlisted in the 2019 Mslexia novel competition. She lives in the Netherlands.

RAISING READERS
Books Build Bright Futures

Thank you for reading this book and for being a reader of books in general. As an author, I am so grateful to share being part of a community of readers with you, and I hope you will join me in passing our love of books on to the next generation of readers.

Did you know that reading for enjoyment is the single biggest predictor of a child's future happiness and success?

More than family circumstances, parents' educational background, or income, reading impacts a child's future academic performance, emotional well-being, communication skills, economic security, ambition, and happiness.

Studies show that kids reading for enjoyment in the US is in rapid decline:

- In 2012, 53% of 9-year-olds read almost every day. Just 10 years later, in 2022, the number had fallen to 39%.
- In 2012, 27% of 13-year-olds read for fun daily. By 2023, that number was just 14%.

Together, we can commit to Raising Readers and change this trend. How?

- Read to children in your life daily.
- Model reading as a fun activity.
- Reduce screen time.
- Start a family, school, or community book club.
- Visit bookstores and libraries regularly.
- Listen to audiobooks.
- Read the book before you see the movie.
- Encourage your child to read aloud to a pet or stuffed animal.
- Give books as gifts.
- Donate books to families and communities in need.

Books build bright futures, and **Raising Readers** is our shared responsibility.

For more information, visit **JoinRaisingReaders.com**

Sources: National Endowment for the Arts, National Assessment of Educational Progress, WorldBookDay.org, Nielsen BookData's 2023 "Understanding the Children's Book Consumer"